Phoenix and the

Blue Jay

Mark Laming

First Published in 2019 by Blossom Spring Publishing
Phoenix and the Blue Jay Copyright © 2019 Mark
Laming
ISBN 978-1-9161735-1-4
E: admin@blossomspringpublishing.com
W: www.blossomspringpublishing.com
Published in the United Kingdom. All rights reserved
under International

To all those kind-hearted people all over the world

who offer support to the homeless.

Chapter 1

It all happened so quickly, leaving no time to save the man's life. Sixty-nine floors up and standing too close to the edge, both construction workers had their minds on anything but staying safe. Phoenix, still annoyed with Cody, tripped on some welding gear and collided with his workmate who tumbled backwards and out of sight.

The blood-curdling scream that everyone in their gang must have heard, gradually lessened as Cody plummeted to the ground. The reverberation of drills and welding guns ceased as the worried men crowded around their foreman who stood close to the partially completed east wall.

Apart from the echo of hammering from the floor below, the only sounds were the rushing wind whistling through the steel and nervous chatter from the small group of men as the realisation dawned that one of them had gone over.

One of the shuttering crew, a ginger-haired man whose forehead was bathed in sweat, screamed, 'Who was it?'

Phoenix, a barrel of a man with a ponytail, clung to the steel uprights to lean over and peer down. It was too far to see anything clearly but he could make out that the traffic had stopped. His teeth were chattering and hands shaking. If only I'd been more careful, he thought, Cody would still be alive. Yes, he knew it had been an accident, but would they believe him? Phoenix regretted having left his welding gear in such a mess, which resulted in him tripping and colliding with his friend. He wondered if anyone had witnessed their heated exchange or would misinterpret him knocking into Cody.

The enormity of his actions and the consequences that would emerge began to sink in. His friend, the man from Brooklyn, a father of one, could not have survived the fall and there was the distinct possibility that the finger of suspicion was going to be pointed at him should details of their disagreement surface.

The foreman for floor sixty-nine, a wafer-thin man with dark hair and large, black glasses, frantically scanned the lists of locations and shouted out, 'Davies, Linton, Johnson, O'Sullivan, Hayes, O'Connor.'

There was a palpable feeling of unease in the air as the construction men in his team dutifully raised an arm to confirm their presence.

He paused to wipe the sweat from his brow. 'That just leaves Cody O'Brien. Has anyone seen Cody? Phoenix, did you see what happened, weren't you with him?'

For once the foghorn of a voice was silent as Phoenix, gazed towards the edge of the building. He cursed himself for not preventing the fall. Their argument had spiralled out of control and at one-point Cody threatened to end their friendship. How he wished he'd walked away or, at least, tidied up his tools that unquestionably had contributed to the accident.

A worker from D6, anxious to be heard, held up a hammer in the direction of Phoenix. 'You guys were working when I came by. Remember, you lent me this.'

With his head full of avoidable mistakes, Phoenix wished he'd been more careful on that fateful morning. He hid his eyes from his boss. 'Me... no I didn't see anything; he's probably still in the john.'

A tall, bearded man removed his hard hat and scratched his head before yelling, 'Can anyone see a body down there? Do you think it was Cody? Was he a jumper ...?'

The unfinished sentence hung heavily in the air as many of the men shook their heads. They were unable to comprehend the insensitive remarks. One of the welders turned to the man and growled, 'You airhead – why don't you sod off.'

It was at this point Phoenix felt the unmistakable sensation of nausea creeping up his throat and walked as fast as he could to the washroom where he was violently sick. His ankle was still painful from when he'd tripped and he noticed a cut on a finger that was bleeding.

All the time his mind was being bombarded with agonising questions. What if, when they found Cody, he still had his cell phone on him. The police always checked phones, didn't they? Only recently, he'd read some of his wife's messages to Cody on the smart phone she claimed she only used for her work. It was highly likely those messages still existed and he'd be implicated as the jealous husband. They would see it as a strong motive. He challenged the unfairness of it all. This man had desires on his wife, they argued, but it wasn't his fault that Cody slipped.

He deliberated on whether he hated Suzy more than Cody and chose the latter. It was only this morning he'd confronted Suzy with his evidence and she'd refused to discuss the matter. She had stormed off to work. Thoughts of her betrayal maddened him. It was only later during his shift his so-called friend Cody had denied having feelings for her and that's when things became heated. It was his lack of response to the allegation that really made him see red. The man he called his best friend had refused to comment.

7

The option of telling the truth and admitting it was an accident was quickly dismissed by Phoenix. He recalled there being many men working close by that morning, some he was aware disliked him, who may have seen them arguing or worse still might think he had done it intentionally. He'd take his chances and remain quiet. If questioned, he'd deny knowing about the fall, the texts or the affair with his wife. And, as for the quarrelling, he'd say they were simply messing about.

When Phoenix returned to the gathering of men, the foreman was finishing a call on his cell phone and was clearly shocked as he relayed the news. 'It was Cody! He must have slipped.'

There were echoes of *'not Cody'* as the welders were stunned to hear his name.

'There was nothing they could do for him. You guys need to go down to floor sixty-seven to the site office. This entire area will be closed for the investigation team to carry out their work.'

There was no rehearsal for what happened next as Phoenix burst into tears and was comforted by those standing next to him. His display of grief for his friend was a mixture of genuine emotion and an attempt to cover his back.

The foreman tried to console him but was interrupted by a number of anxious voices all competing to be heard. He put an arm in the air. 'You guys need to keep calm. Turn off all the equipment and leave it where it is; your tools will be quite safe up here. Work has finished for today; just bring your coats and bags and let's get down to my site office.'

Phoenix stood still as he went over the tragic events; as sad as it was losing Cody, he had to protect himself. He had no intention of going to prison. Cody slipped, end of.

As he turned to collect his belongings the foreman noticed he was having trouble walking and asked, 'What's wrong with your leg?'

'Not sure, must have strained it.'

'Looks like you've cut your hand as well.'

Phoenix shrugged his shoulders and continued to expand on his lies. Holding the finger in the air he made light of the small but painful wound. 'Oh yeah, no sweat, it's just a nick, it must have been on those 420 steels on zone C when I took my gloves off.'

His boss's ear pricked up on hearing this and said, 'Oh… the 420s you say, down where you were working when Cody fell.'

Phoenix shuddered as he recalled the events that led to the fall. He felt the sudden urge to pass water and the unmistakable dampness seeping through his work pants. Looking down he panicked as the wet patch grew. He turned away from his boss in an attempt to hide his embarrassment.

The foreman pulled a notebook and pen from his bag. 'I'll need to inspect the area you were both working in; let's go over there.'

The first thing that came into sight was the dead man's coat, lunchbox and Phoenix's welding rods scattered all over the concrete floor. The foreman was clearly annoyed on seeing the disorderly work area. Avoiding the tools, he walked over the area and made copious notes before turning to his employee for an explanation.

'No wonder a man lost his life with all this mess about. The safety and health guys are going to have a field day when they inspect your welding area. I've mentioned safe working practices in our meetings and just look at all the mess on this floor. Cody must have tripped and slid over the edge. What a terrible accident.'

Phoenix's loud voice had returned. 'So, you think it was an accident, do you?' He quickly added, 'That's *his* gear – I kept telling him to take more care. Mine are over there and still tidy.'

'No need to shout – I'm not drawing any conclusions and neither should you. We'll have to see what safety and health and the police think about all of this. Now Phoenix, I have to ask you some questions, as will the officers when they take your statement. You were probably the last person to see him alive so, how was he this morning? Was he worried about anything?'

'What do you mean?'

'You know upset, had a row at home.'

'I don't know.'

'You left him on his own though.'

'Yeah, only to go to the john.'

'And when you returned, he was nowhere to be seen. Didn't that strike you as a bit odd?'

'No, I didn't go straight back. I went off to talk to someone.

'Who did you go to see?'

Phoenix frowned and a lie spilled cruelly from his lips. 'Before I went back to my work, I saw the guys on the west wing, then I heard the scream. It was terrible – I knew someone had fallen.'

The next salient point referred to whether Phoenix thought Cody was working too close to the edge. Phoenix answered perhaps a little too quickly that he had been working inside the safety zone but wasn't sure of Cody's movements.

The foreman caught the look of shock on Phoenix's face when he added, 'Just refresh my mind, what time did you say you went to the washroom and which of the other guys did you go over to see?'

Phoenix kept quiet as his dislike for the foreman grew. The man was asking far too many questions for his liking.

'As I said earlier, I wasn't anywhere near Cody. I'm devastated to have lost my best friend; and for the record, I didn't actually see or speak with any of the other guys.'

The foreman shook his head forcefully. 'I warned Cody on two previous occasions to be careful when working close to the edge. It's all on his record.'

Phoenix was relieved to know there was a clear line of blame forming. Although nothing would bring Cody back, at least he wasn't going to be a suspect in connection with his death.

The silence was broken by the shrill of his cell phone ringing. He glanced at the caller details and was shocked to see it was his wife, Suzy. Now he was really panicking as he swiped the screen and turned away to take the call.

Holding the phone close to his ear he heard her say, 'Is that you Phoenix, you sound distant? I can hardly hear you.'

'What do you expect, I'm on the top of a scraper and it's windy up here.'

'Thank God you're okay. It's all over the news that someone fell from a site in East 36th Lexington. That's your one, isn't it?'

Phoenix was unsure about what he should disclose in the call and remained silent. He stared at the magnificent skyline of Manhattan with both the Chrysler

11

Building and Empire State towering over the city and wished desperately he hadn't come into work today.

'Are you still there?'

'Yeah, I'm here, just very shaken.'

'Get yourself a taxi home, but first I have to know that Cody is okay?'

Phoenix was devastated to hear his friend's name, and more importantly annoyed that his wife was so interested in him. 'I can't speak now; I've got to go.'

Suzy mentioned Cody's name again, only the line went dead as Phoenix quickly tapped the end-of-call screen

Chapter 2

With all the mayhem that accompanies an accident, it was mid-afternoon before Phoenix left his workplace and struggled to hail a cab. The police grilling had been intense and he wondered whether they believed him. There seemed to be no sign of sympathy from the officer who interviewed him, only an impatient request to complete his statement. The young man casually remarked that there had recently been a number of suicides as well as genuine workplace accidents. With an air of finality ringing in his head, Phoenix felt like his world had come crashing down leaving only regret and sadness. Today he'd seen a side of himself that he wasn't proud of. He was a desperate, conniving man who was running out of lies and would inevitably trip himself up.

When he eventually got a ride, the Asian driver, with a short beard and a well-worn sheepskin coat, insisted on talking. The inevitable question reared its head – was he a builder and where did he work?

The words fell awkwardly from Phoenix's mouth.

'Yeah… construction.'

'What do you build mister? My brother is on apartment blocks on Lower East Side. You on buildings?'

Phoenix looked out at the busy traffic that had built up on Lexington. 'Me, I'm on scrapers. Look, how long will it take to reach Christopher Street, I'm in a hurry?'

'Just need to clear this block; this traffic is mad; it's been like this for ages since that guy fell from one of the sites. Awful business – you imagine the call his wife got.'

Phoenix shuddered before closing his eyes and mouthed, 'Yes, awful.'

The taxi edged forward and he lost count of the flashing '*Walk, Don't Walk*' signs that held back the bustling crowds spilling out of shops and offices. All the time his mind was going over the arduous police interview he'd endured. It irked him that they kept repeating questions, but he was confident he'd kept to his story. He was relieved there was no actual evidence against him. The inquest would undoubtedly pinpoint the blame on Cody. The company records on the verbal warnings would count against him.

The worst thing now was, how was he going to tell Suzy the dreadful news that Cody was dead? Of course, she would be distraught, but would she confess her feelings for him?

The rest of the journey was a blur and it wasn't until he caught sight of the billboard for the new liquor store close to Washington Square that he fumbled in his pockets to extract some notes to pay the driver.

As he stepped out of the taxi, a brisk southerly wind was sending the leaves billowing and scattering across the sidewalk like confetti settling for a final time. Phoenix shuddered as he rehearsed the words he would say to his wife about the death of their friend. As if things weren't bad enough, he still had to address her flirtation with Cody.

Home was a two-bedroom apartment in West Village, Manhattan. They both had well-paid jobs and enjoyed a good standard of living. They ate regularly at local restaurants in Little Italy and Chinatown and enjoyed the social life of New York. Most Saturdays he walked into Greenwich Village to buy flowers for his wife, or took a ride to Battery Park to see the harbour. Life had seemed so perfect, but not now.

Once inside the lobby he pondered on whether to take the elevator or walk up to the seventh floor. He chose the latter, affording him extra time to think before seeing Suzy. Never having used the stairs before, he was shocked to observe small areas of plaster that were flaking away from the wall. He vowed he'd have something to say to his elusive new landlord. As he reached the third-floor landing, there was the smell of cooking coming from one of the apartments. How he hated the sickly whiff of curry that always reminded him of stale food in the trash can.

Out of breath and panting, he held onto the metal banister hauling his heavy body up each step, adding to the pain in his leg. He felt the sweat dripping down the inside of his shirt and smelt the salty odour that was seeping from his armpits. With just a few more flights to go, he stopped for a rest and leant against a wall. To his dismay he was greeted by Mrs Delgado who was putting out her trash. He observed her wrinkled, liver-spotted face, gnarled fingers and felt sorry for the old lady. However, he was apathetic listening to her hard luck story. It all seemed so insignificant in comparison to his problems. He became impatient as his mood changed, telling her rather abruptly he didn't have time to stand around talking and turned to leave.

He caught sight of himself in the hallway mirror and stared intensely at the jumbo-sized jeans with the zip at half-mast that held back an enormous stomach. The old blue coat still had traces of blood from his injured finger. Then there was his hair; perhaps in future he'd wear it shorter and forget the ponytail. He brushed back some stray grey hairs that kept falling over his face and

15

struggled to believe he was nearly fifty. Today, he thought, he looked and certainly felt much older.

Phoenix gingerly entered apartment twenty-eight having first stooped down to remove his boots. There was no point adding to the anxiety with him walking over Suzy's immaculate cream-coloured carpets. There was the distinct smell of cooking; only today he had no appetite for food.

Suzy looked like she had been crying and she gave him a brief hug. 'You look awful. I was dreading it might have been you after our row earlier.'

'I told you I was safe when you rang.' His eyes strayed to her colourful skirt and beautiful black skin and inwardly sighed.

Her next question unsettled him. 'Do you know who went over?'

There was no putting off telling her but he was intent on gauging her reaction to the news. 'I'm sorry, babe. It was Cody.'

Suzy gasped and her mouth twitched nervously at the corners. 'No... no, you must be wrong, it can't be Cody.'

She sat down firmly on the hall chair and covered her face with both hands. Her weeping upset him as he convinced himself that his friend and his wife had indeed been an item.

Aware of his powerful voice, he toned it down to a whisper. 'It was Cody. The foreman thinks he must have got too close to the edge. Apparently, they had warned him before.'

'Were you with him and did you try to save him?'

Phoenix frowned. 'Suzy, what sort of a question is that? We are talking about our friend here. I was nowhere near him so didn't see what happened. I'm as cut up about it as you.'

Her crying increased to yelps as she hysterically took in the news. He tried to console her and offered to make some coffee.

He hesitated in mid-stride and turned to stare at his pretty wife. How he loved her slim body, adorable brown eyes, smooth black skin and the hint of shiny lip gloss. Her face was so soft and the flawless complexion made her look even younger than her thirty-two years. How many times at work had he glanced at the photo he carried in his wallet? He thanked the phenomenal luck that brought her into his life. Today he felt like an old man and wondered whatever possessed her to link up with a guy like him. Whilst he badly wanted to hold her, he deliberately kept his distance. There still remained the business of her infidelity to discuss.

Up until now Suzy hadn't noticed his occasional limp but the pain was suddenly too much to endure and he stifled a groan that alerted her.

'Oh God, what's wrong, how did you hurt your leg?'

He stood rigidly still and with no sign of emotion in his voice said, 'It's an ankle strain that hurts when I put weight on it.'

'How did you do it and is that blood on your coat?'

He glanced momentarily at the dark red stain. 'Uh-huh, no sweat. That's nothing I just cut a finger on some metal. I want to talk about you and Cody. What's bugging me is I thought we were happy but you choose to go off with one of our friends.'

Suzy was startled by his remark and limply replied, 'I can't believe what you just said. What do you mean, go off? For God's sake the poor guy just lost his life and you are winding me up about having an affair. I told you this morning, there was nothing and you...'

Interrupting her, he spat out his words, 'Don't try to deny it. I saw those texts from him on your work cell phone. You know the ones that read – *don't worry, Phoenix won't get to know. Good idea you only use your work phone.*'

Suzy retorted, 'That's not fair – I can explain.'

His voice was now at booming level. 'I just wish I'd seen your texts to him but you must have wiped them out. My heart feels like it's broken. How could you do this to me? I've been thinking on the ride home, perhaps I should move out and get a room in Upper West Side. I've lost a friend today and now you.'

'No, you haven't lost me.'

'And you expect me to forgive you and move on. What sort of a guy do you think I am? I sweat my guts out to keep you and me in this place. Was it me not telling you I love you enough, or was he a better lover?'

'No, nothing like that – you have to believe me. Stop accusing me, you have it all wrong.'

Phoenix's heart sank as she produced her cell phone to show him her texts to Cody. It was then that he realised what a fool he'd been. Suzy and Cody had been arranging a fiftieth birthday party for him and there was even a message from his wife Elizabeth about the restaurant and big cake she was baking.

Unable to process the information quickly, the vacant look on his face turned to one of sheer desperation. Looking anywhere except at Suzy, he rushed his words. 'I can't believe what I've done. I thought you and he were playing away.'

'Are you out of your head! You slipped up big time.'

Phoenix was dazed as he recalled being so unfriendly to his best friend. He'd even refused to tidy up his welding equipment and rods. Irrefutably, his annoyance and lack of attention to safety must have contributed to the fall. There could be no forgiveness for his behaviour. Tears began to fall from his face like a dripping tap. Inside his head the words kept echoing away, '*You just killed a man.*'

As Suzy selected Elizabeth's number on her phone, she shook her head. 'Me and Cody, are you crazy? Wasn't it me who stood by you all those months with your illness? I never stopped telling you I loved you and you treat me like this.'

The word crazy resonated with Phoenix, as after all the time she had helped him recover from his breakdown, this is how he repaid her. He'd reached rock bottom this time and lost his friend and now feared he was about to lose his wife. He moved towards her.

Suzy waved her arm in the air in a dismissive way. 'Back off, I need to tell Elizabeth how sorry I am about her lovely husband.'

The phone was on speaker mode and Phoenix felt perturbed as he heard the distraught voice, 'Elizabeth here…'

As his wife tried to console their friend, he stared intensely at her beautiful face that today had all the signs of stress from the worry he'd brought her. He wished he'd been the one who had died. What sort of a husband had he been? How was he going to live with himself, or for that matter, Suzy?

Listening to the call, he interrupted Suzy and asked her to send his love. The look of contempt from

19

her creased face said it all. His inner voice thundered the words inside his head – *What do you expect – you have killed your mate and lied all day long to save your own skin.*

* * *

That night, Phoenix gave his teeth a slightly longer than usual brushing as he once again reflected on the horrific day. The other reason for delaying getting ready for bed was the revised sleeping arrangements – he was to stay in the spare room, something Suzy had insisted upon.

As he lay alone in the single bed, he mulled over what to do next. What hurt him most was his initial lack of reaction to losing his friend as well as the way he lied to avoid being implicated. No punishment would ever be enough for getting things so wrong. The reason they quarrelled was unfounded and the consequences would haunt him for evermore. He even contemplated making a fresh statement to the police.

He was suddenly aware of Suzy tapping on the door and anxiously jumped out of bed. Drawing his dressing gown around his naked body, he was devastated to hear her say, 'I've been thinking – did you tackle Cody on those texts?'

He stammered. 'N… n… n… no of course not!'

'Are you sure? I can't help thinking you had a go at him.'

'Stop it! I've already told you it was an accident. I was with some of the other guys at the time.'

Watching her eyes narrow with disapproval he knew exactly what she was thinking.

Chapter 3

Back in her bed, Suzy kept thinking how stupid she'd been messaging Cody instead of just ringing him and his wife to make the party arrangements. She could understand Phoenix jumping to the wrong conclusion when she discovered him checking her phone. The outcome had been that he flew into a ferocious rage that really frightened her. At the time, all she wanted to do was get as far away from him as possible.

She recalled her journey into work and struggled to comprehend, after all she'd done for him, just how he could accuse her of being unfaithful. She regretted her hasty retreat and really should have explained what she was up to. It was mid-morning before she rang him after hearing the terrible news from colleagues at work of an incident on his site.

During the previous year, hadn't she been there every inch of the way for her husband with his mental problems? Of course, she had. The many months it had taken to recover from his breakdown had been unbearable for her. For a time, he had remained confused and even self-harmed. She had wondered if he would ever get better, but she had never stopped loving him.

Due to the care and medication he had received during his stay at the Woodside Clinic, there had been a marked improvement in his wellbeing. There had been fewer incidents of mood changes and when the day had finally arrived for him to come home, she was overjoyed to get him back, but there was no denying he had changed. The man was broken and drained of any enthusiasm or drive.

At the time, the help from Phoenix's mother had been invaluable by being there at the apartment during the day, which allowed Suzy to work. But now there was no mother to help; sadly, she had died two months after Phoenix resumed his work and this had hit him badly.

It had taken five months before Phoenix was given the all clear to work and it was Cody who helped him get the new job on the construction site. To Suzy's frustration, her husband ignored her advice on declaring his illness on the application form. The first few weeks were challenging as he gradually eased himself back into the heavy manual work.

A further hurdle was his lack of self-esteem. It was Suzy who literally pushed him out of the door most mornings telling him he would cope brilliantly. Anyone who came into contact with him may have been forgiven for thinking he was a tough, no-nonsense sort of a man. On the contrary, his confidence was at its lowest point as he worried over the slightest of things. He was like the proverbial duck on water, calm on top and paddling like hell beneath the surface.

Frustrated by his stubbornness to accept help, she gave up suggesting he lose some weight. Even the doctor had warned about the strain on his heart, but he took no notice.

She was pleased his moods and irrational behaviour had become less frequent, but there was no getting away from the fact that it was all about Phoenix and it felt like her life was on hold.

Today they'd lost a dear friend and she questioned her husband's furious temper that morning. She speculated on whether he had been just as cross when he got to work. Had the two of them quarrelled and later Cody was upset, got too near the edge of the high building and fell?

In an effort to ease her troubled mind, she recalled happier times when she first met her husband at the local dance in town. The guy was gorgeous with long, dark hair tied back in a ponytail and she adored his blue eyes. He was a big man, a builder from Cleveland who spoke loudly, someone who made her laugh. Over the long hot summer of 2008, she had fallen head over heels in love. Her parents had disapproved of the older and boisterous man; a divorcee who they said would break her heart and today it felt like he'd done just that.

On the day he had proposed, she had waited patiently for him to arrive. Sat in the quiet seclusion of the veranda, rocking in grandma's old chair, she relaxed as she waited for him to show. She stared across the fields as the birds swooped over the banks of the Ohio River and listened to the hum of the cars on the Old Blossom Road that had once been a track. It was in this much-loved garden that Suzy had always enjoyed watching the blue jays with their beautiful plumage. She often joked that in her next life she would come back as a bird.

There followed nine years of blissful marriage spent living in New York. Yes, she was sad they couldn't have children, but Phoenix brought her so much happiness that was enough for her. Then unexpectedly their lives were to change forever when Phoenix suffered a breakdown. And now with losing Cody, she wondered if she could take any more heartbreak.

Her reveries were abruptly interrupted as she heard Phoenix crashing about in the next room. A moment of panic swept through her mind – *had he taken his tablets?*

She leapt from the bed and quickly made her way to the spare room. The light was on and she was shocked to see him standing naked on the small balcony. The net curtains were drawn and blowing in the breeze. Even at this ungodly hour the traffic below was still thundering past their apartment block. She cautiously moved over to the doors. His body was swaying as if he was deciding which direction to go next. She could smell his sweat and sense his desperation. Calling out his name, he turned swiftly to face her with a vacant expression. The long, dark hair was no longer tied back and hung loosely over his shoulders. She noticed his rings, watch and Saint Christopher chain lay abandoned on the floor.

So as not to startle him, she calmly said, 'Come away from the wall darling, its cold out there.'

He was mumbling something about Cody being the best friend a man could ask for and it should have been him. She reached out to guide him back into the safety of the room. Her worst nightmare was back – Phoenix had flipped again. Going back to work hadn't been a good idea and now losing their friend was the final straw.

She settled him on the bedside chair, first having persuaded him to put on the much-crumpled dressing gown that had become wedged between the bed and the wall. The room was in complete disarray with the doors of both closets open and clothes strewn all over the floor. The bed looked like he'd been fighting with the duvet and pillows. She asked him if he'd be alright while she made him a drink – there was no response.

Suzy yanked the heavy balcony doors shut and after securing them took the key with her. She also decided to lock the living room balcony doors, just in case!

She glanced back at Phoenix who was slumped in the chair with his hands covering his eyes; he looked in a terrible state.

'Okay if I leave you for a minute?'

She was disturbed to hear him say he hated himself and wished himself dead.

As she walked slowly to the kitchen, her arm trailed along the wall as she tried desperately not to cry. What a mess they were in and what was she going to do? Once again, his mind had tripped across the thin line that divided sanity from madness. The one thing she was sure about was her husband was in deep shock and whilst there may have been an argument with his friend, he wasn't responsible for his death. The trauma had catapulted him into a state of utter turmoil and he needed help.

How could she turn her back on him now? An option could be to make a new start, leave the city to return to Ohio and live in the countryside. They'd rent a small place and start over again. She knew it was a big ask, but her parents would help them settle back into their old town.

The next morning she'd take him to the doctor and then the loneliness would really set in for her as she knew there was the distinct possibility he'd be sectioned immediately for his own safety. First, she had to get through the rest of the night. There was a lot to do getting him showered and back into their bed. They were both exhausted. She kissed his damp forehead and fell asleep gripping the hand of the man she loved with all her heart.

They slept until eight o'clock and he awoke with a start. To her utter surprise Phoenix was very talkative and in a cheery mood. It was like he'd forgotten the last twenty-four hours.

He drew back the curtains and the bright light flooded into the bedroom. 'Hey, we are really late for work, best get a move on.'

'No work today, Phoenix.'

'What do you mean? It's a busy day for me out in the truck making deliveries; also remind me to ring my Mum tonight.'

She didn't have the heart to remind him that in his previous job he'd been a driver but now worked as a welder. His Mum had died some months back; surely, he would have remembered her passing? He'd forgotten the terrifying events of the previous day and night. He really was ill.

As she threw her nightie onto the bed, she turned away from him to dress. He was soon behind her. She trembled as his naked body enveloped her and his rough hands cupped both breasts. His pummelling of her skin hurt and she pulled away sharply.

'Not so rough, that really hurts.'

Phoenix immediately muttered, 'Sorry, I got carried away, babe.'

Again, he moved over to hold her. This time he kissed her on the lips and she responded. She could feel his excitement as he held her tight. His hands dropped to her waist, then thighs. Uncomfortable with the idea of making love, she tried to encourage him to stop.

Phoenix was persistent and stroked her arm. 'Come here, you know you want me. There's still time before work. Let's go back to bed.'

Suzy quickly moved over to the closet to pull out a blouse and held it in front of her body. She lied when she said, 'We only made love the day before yesterday and you need to get breakfast before your check up with the doctor.'

'Are you sure it's today, only those guys in transport will be wondering where I got to.'

'Yes, Phoenix, I'm the one who keeps the diary.'

'Not sure I need to go to see the doc. I tell you I feel so much better these days. I feel like a million dollars – it must be those tablets she gives me.'

As Suzy buttoned up her blouse she started to panic. What if there was a problem in getting a doctor to see him at such short notice? She would insist they needed an emergency appointment.

She turned to Phoenix, who was struggling to tie back his hair, and said, 'Here, let me do it.'

'Thanks. I'm always having problems with this ruddy clasp. I've been thinking about cutting my hair.'

'Keep still and don't talk nonsense, you know I love your hair the way it is.'

'There's something I want to ask you – isn't it about time we got Elizabeth and Cody over for a meal? And hey, let's not forget Cameron.'

Suzy swallowed hard – she was shocked to hear him mention Cody's name. She was also cross with herself as she thought back to the call she'd made to Elizabeth. She'd forgotten to enquire after their son Cameron who was in his final year of college. The poor boy had just lost his father.

Her attention switched to Phoenix who was now anxiously holding up the new suit he'd worn at a friend's wedding. 'What do you think – shall I wear this for work?'

And that's how the rest of the morning panned out with Phoenix getting more perplexed as the hours passed until they saw Dr Creedy.

* * *

After an early lunch they walked the six blocks to the surgery. All the time Suzy hung firmly onto Phoenix's hand, just in case he did anything foolish. She booked him in at reception ignoring the young girl's comments on whether they were taking a vacation this year.

The doctor was running late and Suzy deliberately chose to sit in the far corner of the room for fear of her husband upsetting the other patients. Phoenix, who was calmer than at breakfast, had picked up a magazine on cameras and was thumbing through the contents. He looked relaxed, glancing up every so often to smile at other patients.

'Anything good in there?'

'Actually yes, this new SLR is definitely something I'm interested in. The improved shutter speed and stabiliser are awesome.'

His next statement clearly shocked her. 'There's something I gotta to tell you about yesterday.'

'Oh yes…'

'I know why we are here to see the doc as I've been confused and done some crazy things. Walking here this afternoon it was like a switch had suddenly activated. I can now remember everything and it's frightened the shit out of me. I know Cody's gone and nothing will bring him back and I've put you through hell.'

Relieved to learn his rational thoughts had kicked in, she replied, 'You've been under a lot of strain and, with our loss, it was all too much for you.'

It was feasible that Phoenix hadn't even heard his wife speak as he hurriedly told her, 'I think it was the questions those officers asked that really got under my skin; they kept going on and on… It was doing my head in. You do believe me when I say I didn't have anything to do with the fall?'

Suzy grabbed his hand in an effort to reassure him. She must have wondered how anyone could display severe mental issues one moment and the next act so calmly, appearing to be in control.

'We still need to talk to the doctor to check you out. If she says you need a few days in the Woodside, then let's just go with it. I don't want you putting up a fight saying you are better and not agreeing to accept help. You may need to rest for a day or two.'

He shook his head. 'I was suffering from shock and now I'm...'

She lowered her voice for fear of other people listening in. 'Of course, you are okay, but you were saying some crazy things. Do you remember anything about last night – you know, being on the bedroom balcony?'

'Yep... it's all come back to me and I'm stunned to even think I'd sunk so low. There's no way I would have done anything. Me jump, for God's sake Suzy, I get dizzy just standing on the first floor of the Empire State.'

'But you work on the tops of buildings.'

He smiled and for a moment she saw the old fun-loving Phoenix always ready to crack a joke. Then his tone became conciliatory. 'You gotta believe me, I'm fine. Thank you, babe, for being here for me. I know I've caused you so much pain.'

A smile lit up his face, 'I know it's probably not the right time to be fooling about, but I can now see the funny side of me asking you if I should wear my best suit to work. Also, thinking I was still driving trucks, as that was my last job, wasn't it? And, as for my Mum, I don't even want to go there, as I know she passed some time ago. You see I am okay. I can recall everything that happened and there's no-one sorrier than me.'

Suzy sighed and then looked up sharply, her brow furrowed. 'But Phoenix, how can I be sure you won't have more setbacks? I don't think I can cope with any more of this. You really frightened me.'

Before he had a chance to reply they were joined by an elderly man dressed in black jeans and sweater who slumped onto a seat next to them. His explosive sneezing and waving of tissues continued until, to their relief, the receptionist called them in to see the doctor.

They were shown into the cramped office that housed large floor-to-ceiling brown wooden cabinets and a bed with a curtain partially drawn around it. The room needed decorating with cracks to the plaster on the window wall. There was the distinct smell of air freshener, overpowering lavender, and the tin on the floor next to the desk had its lid missing. Suzy's eyes were drawn to Dr Creedy's tired face and her shoulder length, silver grey hair.

'Hello Phoenix and Suzy, what can I do for you today?'

Phoenix spoke first relaying the sad news about Cody and how he'd buckled under the strain. He emphasized the fact that he'd experienced dark thoughts about ending his life. He stressed that for a while he'd shut out the events of the previous day. He reached for Suzy's hand. In a confident voice he announced he was now back in control and embarrassed by his actions.

Dr Creedy swept aside some documents from the untidy desk and positioned her hands in a pinnacle shape. 'That's good, very good, that you have things in perspective. Just one thing – you have been taking your medication – no slip ups?'

'No probs there, we have a chart. Suzy does the ticking of boxes and I swallow them with a beer.' He quickly added, 'That was a joke.'

There was no reaction from the doctor who angled her screen away from them to study her patient's history. As she re-acquainted herself with the details of his previous breakdown, she kept nodding her head. She read the lengthy text on his stay in the clinic then inputted the current disturbing events. She must have been questioning whether Phoenix was putting on a performance in an effort to avoid being referred back to the psychiatrist. She checked his blood pressure and confirmed the level was slightly higher than last time and screwed up her eyes. 'You mentioned those suicidal thoughts; how are you feeling now?'

Phoenix remained quiet and Suzy let go of his hand to gently touch him on the shoulder. He flinched and shook his head. 'I already told you that was a one off; I'm fine now. I'd just lost a friend and my mind was in a mess. For a short while nothing mattered. I was a real airhead. I think I must have been in denial.'

Dr Creedy frowned as she read his notes that stated *'high risk level eight – self-harmed earlier in the year.'*

Her bony fingers rolled a pen backward and forwards on top of some files and she sympathetically replied, 'That's the fighting spirit I like to hear. With what you've been through I think anyone would feel poorly. To be on the safe side we can't ignore those irrational thoughts and how upset you became. I'm not saying you will have to undergo respite again, but how about I schedule an appointment with those guys at the Woodside?'

Phoenix's expression turned to one of sadness. He put a thumb in the air. 'Okay, how soon do I get that appointment?'

***

As they waited for the appointment day to arrive, a calmer Phoenix was making an enormous effort to rein in his depression to avoid being sectioned again under the Mental Health Act. It was imperative that Suzy was spared further anxiety in having to support him through the nightmare of nightmares that was still torturing his mind. Convincing the guys at the Woodside that he was in no danger wasn't going to be plain sailing. His earlier experience of their methods for establishing the extent of his illness worried him. This time he would need to be on his guard to convince them otherwise. A plan was already forming in his head.

The day before the appointment, Phoenix surprised Suzy with an early birthday present. It was something he'd bought a few weeks back and couldn't wait to show her. He took pleasure in insisting she tried the garment on.

His eyes lit up at the sight of Suzy in the new short, red, tartan skirt. Her slim, long legs encased in white tights left him feeling aroused and anxious to carry her off to bed.

Suzy, smoothed the fabric of the garment and tutted, 'Thanks, but it's too short; not something I would have chosen. I could never go out in it, let alone sit down.'

Moving his glance higher, his desire to undress her grew. He stared at her white work blouse and played with the idea of slowly unbuttoning it. He was aware she

32

was already late leaving for the office. Suzy pulled on the elasticated waist of the skirt and frowned.

The quiver in his voice grew as he tried to play down the cheap and ridiculously short hemline of the garment. 'I think you look great in it and I'm not suggesting you wear it to your fancy advertising agency job, am I?'

Moving forward he placed both arms around her shoulders. The warmth of her body thrilled him as he kissed the side of her neck. Suzy's whole body tightened as she said, 'Hold on there, this doesn't seem right with us still grieving for Cody.'

For the hundredth time, Cody's fall and agonising scream thundered away in Phoenix's head. Had they not been arguing; the outcome could have played out so differently and Cody would still be alive.

He pulled away sharply. 'I'm done with crying. Nothing is going to bring him back. What we need is a moment of happiness. Don't you want me?'

'Of course, I do, but I gotta get off to work.' In an unconvincing voice she added, 'Maybe later.'

'No, I want you now. Can't you text that boss of yours and say you are held up.'

Once again, he drew her to his side. He lowered a hand to her waist and gently squeezed her slender body. Her reaction was to kiss him and push one of her legs hard against him. The skirt rose higher on her thigh as his hands worked the material. To his delight Suzy pulled away and started to remove the blouse. With every button she unfastened, she momentarily closed her eyes. Through tight lips she moaned with pleasure. He was aware of the amazing fragrance of her favourite perfume that reminded him of the roses he often bought her at the weekend. Phoenix ran a hand over Suzie's wonderfully soft skin and whispered, 'I love you.'

As he guided her through the kitchen, she glanced at the clock on the wall that was running ten minutes slow and sighed.

Once in the bedroom they both undressed and their frantic lovemaking became the most important thing in the world. A short while later, lying in bed with the duvet pulled up high to their chins, Phoenix kept kissing Suzy's forehead.

'You are like a woodpecker with your kisses – it's ruining my makeup.'

'That's because I love you and I've never been happier in my life. You and I really have something special.'

Suzy grasped his hand firmly. 'Yeah, and I love you too.'

She then reached down to the floor to pick up the bedside clock that had been knocked over during their hectic tumble. She mentioned just how late it was, glanced at her work bag on the chair and said, 'Damn, I forgot to charge my cell phone.'

***

Arriving so late at the office was bound to upset her boss. Logan Mansen, a nasty vindictive man, had recently shown his true colours making her life unpleasant. She couldn't afford to risk losing the well-paid advertising agency job so she scooped up her clothes from the floor and hurriedly started to dress.

With eyes focusing on the buttoning of her shirt she muttered, 'God, I'm really late for work.'

'You must love that job of yours.'

There was no reply as numbness edged through Suzy's body. She stood perfectly still. For a moment her thoughts centred on Logan Mansen, the man she hated with all her heart. Then her mind switched to her husband and all the worries about his mental health. Balancing her work commitments by taking holiday time off or arranging for friends to stay in with Phoenix during the day was proving tricky. Today it was imperative she attended a major client meeting and then get back home to his side. The idea of not being with him during the morning worried her, but fortunately an old friend was on hand to help. How much longer could she keep taking holiday leave or begging favours from people? A further concern was whether Phoenix would have to stay at the Woodside Clinic, just like the last time.

As she closed the front door to leave, she nervously said, 'You will be okay until your friend arrives?'

'Behave, won't you. I'm not going to come to any harm or try and kill myself, am I?'

Disturbed by his remark, she dropped the work bag on the wooden floor and put her warm hand in his and said, 'Just remember I love you.'

Chapter 4

Sitting in the car after dropping Phoenix off at the clinic, Suzy was silent listening to the slow swoosh of the windshield wipers. Her eyes were weary and her skin sallow without a trace of makeup. Her curly black hair was damp as was the new blue dress she'd worn for the first time today.

Grasping the car keys, her thoughts returned to the string of problems that had disrupted their lives. She was disturbed that Phoenix insisted he attend his appointment today without her. He ignored the secretary in the bookings office who advised he bring in an overnight bag in case of a stay-over. The meeting was scheduled to last two hours and involved seeing a psychiatrist. Phoenix had made his mind up he wasn't going to stay there again and his instruction for her was to return at exactly eleven twenty to bring him home.

As the noisy motor of their old red Chevrolet roared into life, she rubbed her hand over the misted-up windshield and engaged drive. The car shuddered as it moved forward and the driver's door rattled. Guiding the heavy vehicle around the circular gravel drive, she brought it to a sudden halt as something caught her eye. She lowered the window and the rain started to penetrate the interior of the car. Phoenix was standing there waving madly and she called out to him, 'You are going to go in, aren't you?'

'Get outta here! Of course, I'm going in.'

It was obvious he was in no hurry to enter and she was concerned he'd miss his appointment. She watched him mount the steps and breathed a sigh of relief as he entered the reception. The car window was raised and she drove through enormous puddles and out of the gates heading in the direction of the freeway.

She decided against going home and chose to have a coffee at a diner she'd noticed on the way in. Her plan was to ring Elizabeth again to offer help, only this time she would definitely enquire after her son, Cameron. Of course, it was too early to know the date for the funeral. She wondered how Phoenix was going to cope if he came along, that was if his mental state was deemed good enough to attend.

The journey back to pick up Phoenix was far from straightforward as there was a diversion due to an accident. Persistent rain hammered on the glass obscuring her vision and the wipers battled to clear the water. Anxious not to be late, she kept checking the clock on the dashboard and panicked as she remembered it was always running ten minutes slow. How many times had she asked her husband to make the adjustment and he always forgot?

As for the car, well it was clapped out and needed replacing. To her annoyance Phoenix had recently wasted over a hundred dollars to fix the hood that flopped up and down when the car was moving. It needed repairing again. This vehicle reminded Phoenix of his first old red Ford that he claimed never let him down. He ignored the fact that their twenty-year-old rust bucket regularly required attention. Replacing the Chevrolet was bottom of his list of things to do. It was Suzy who mainly drove it and was constantly calling out the tow truck.

Arriving fifteen minutes late, she was shocked to spot Phoenix sheltering under a tree on the edge of the drive. His coat was unbuttoned and he was holding an umbrella at an angle away from his body. It was obvious he was wet through. Climbing into the car, he disregarded her apology for not being there sooner and abruptly said, 'Where have you been? I've been freezing my butt off out there and I'm soaked. Look at the state of these new pants.'

They continued in silence as Suzy manoeuvred the car back onto the highway. She was terrified of him becoming angry and sparking off a fight.

She plucked up the courage to ask him how it went and to her surprise he was affable and over-apologetic for snapping at her. She was infuriated by his sudden change of manner and strained her ears to listen to his news.

'Yeah, I sailed through their tests. They say I need to go next month to see that Creedy lady. So, I was right, no need to stay at the Woodside again. I thought they were going to insist I upped my medication, but they didn't.'

Knowing how ill he'd become over the last few days, she was worried by his revelation but chose to say nothing.

'They say I'm not to work for six weeks and need the doc's letter before I go back. I'm not sure my site will want me on their payroll should they get wind of my problems though. It's probably best not to tell them I got stressed out.'

Suzy eased off the gas, the decrease in noise from the powerful motor made it easier to hear him. She still shouted. 'It's awesome that they think you are not too unwell. Now you have to take things easy; promise you will listen to me when I try to help you.' She made no comment on his ridiculous statement about not declaring his medical condition to the firm.

She chanced what she said next. 'I've been doing some thinking and this is just an idea. Don't go worrying about your job as when you are feeling better again, perhaps we could leave the city and start over again. You could go back to having your own business. You were a great builder.'

'Move, are you mad? Why and where would we move to?'

'Ohio. My parents will fix us up.'

He raised his voice and she knew he was displeased. 'You haven't told them about me, have you?'

As she concentrated on her driving she nervously replied, 'They are worried about you and send their love. It doesn't have to be Ohio... we could go wherever you choose. Look, I shouldn't have mentioned moving. We don't have to start over.'

Phoenix tapped his forehead and sarcastically remarked, 'Oh well, now you've brought it up, let's just live over the other side of the pond in London town. Is that far enough away for you?'

Suzy mused over his remark and couldn't help saying, 'Well there is that old uncle of yours who rang us on Thanksgiving last year. What was his name?'

'Behave! I'm not leaving New York at a time when Elizabeth and Cameron need our support.'

She knew he was right; there was no turning their backs on their friend and her son.

* * *

Suzy pulled into a gas station and Phoenix insisted on filling up the tank. On returning to the car he sat patiently waiting for her to start the motor.

He anxiously said, 'I really don't want to go back to the Woodside Clinic again.'

'Yes, I know it must have been hard. I was just

thinking – are you going to be alright coming to Cody's funeral?'

'I need to be there.'

Back on the highway Suzy was about to miss the turn off for the city. The car swerved as she changed lanes and she bit her lip as she apologised.

'Bloody hell Suzy; watch your driving!'

He quickly changed the subject. 'It strikes me you haven't thought through the Ohio idea, have you? Weren't you listening – I just told you I can't work for another six weeks? How are we going to manage to pay our bills if I don't go back soon?'

'Calm down – we still have all that money my granddaddy left us and my father may help out.'

'Please don't mention your father. What about that time I did your parents a favour replacing those two short lengths of clapboard on their house and he gave us all that money?'

Suzy sighed, 'Well, that was kind of him.'

'Yeah, five hundred dollars! I told him we weren't a charity case.'

'Please don't go over all that again.'

Phoenix switched the conversation to the funeral asking if she knew the date. She told him the inquest was still ongoing and Cody's body had only just been released for burial. Elizabeth was hoping for Thursday week depending on the arrangements.

Above the roar of the motor his sigh was just audible and judging by how quiet he went he was clearly upset. She hoped the nightmare wasn't once again pounding away in his head.

* * *

The rest of the ride home was uneventful until Phoenix commented on buying a new car in the near future – not that they could afford it. He broached the subject of decorating the hallway in the apartment and asked if they could they make a stop for some paint from a hardware store.

Suzy sighed. 'You really want to buy some paint? It's been a long morning, let's just go home.'

'No, it won't take a moment. I need a project to take my mind off Cody. Now, take a right here up Union and the store is a few blocks up on the left. There's also that deli I keep telling you about. I'm starving.'

There was no point in arguing with him as his mind was set on keeping busy. If decorating was his release from the trauma, then bring on the tubs of paint.

His idea of a few blocks was at least two miles and when they eventually arrived Suzy had problems squeezing the large car into the last space outside 'Big Joes.' Phoenix frowned as she slammed the driver's door shut.

'Bloody hell girl, not so hard. I bet you haven't locked it.'

'What's the point, nobody is going to steal our car.'

He laughed and led the way to the deli on the corner of the next block.

'Aren't you forgetting the paint? Didn't we come to buy paint?'

'Oh, that can wait; I'm not into decorating any longer. I've no energy for all of that. But I could do with something to eat. You just have to taste the salt beef at Arnie's – it's gotta be the best in New York.'

41

With all the mood swings and changes of plan, it brought home Phoenix's indecisiveness. She questioned just what the guys at the Woodside were thinking of not insisting on a programme of treatment.

Suzy increased her pace and they entered the store. The incredible smell of cooked meats made her feel hungry. Judging by the immense choice of food and beers on sale, it made sense to take their lunch home.

As they waited for their turn to be served, an elderly man struggled to extract a note from his wallet and then dropped his stick on the floor. All the time Suzy sensed Phoenix's impatience as he tutted and kept shuffling his feet, not for one moment attempting to assist the man.

The younger of the two men behind the counter asked for their order. Phoenix whispered to Suzy, 'The big guy over there is his father and he's more generous with the meats than his son.'

Phoenix gave his order. 'Give me one of those heroes with extra boloney and go easy on the radish.'

'No probs, mister. You taking a beer out?'

Before Phoenix had a chance to reply, the young man with the short hair and red shirt asked, 'Where's your mate, the small guy you sometimes come in with?'

Phoenix had to steady himself on the counter and Suzy was unsure how to help him.

His voice stammered, 'Co… Co… Cody.'

'You okay mister, need a seat?'

Phoenix instantly recovered from his shock. 'Did I mention extra boloney?'

Suzy was anxious to get Phoenix home quickly and chose the salami capicola with cheese topping. When he was handed their lunch, Phoenix thanked the man and, to Suzy's amazement, he turned to leave.

'Excuse me, sir, that's eight dollars twenty.'

Phoenix swivelled around to face him. 'I've already paid you. Come on Suzy, let's get outta here.'

He marched out of the store in the direction of the car but Suzy remained to sort things out. By now the older man joined his son and was making his way to the door. He looked angry and snarled, 'Hey Larry, has that guy left without paying?'

Suzy put a hand in the air as she hurriedly took out a twenty-dollar bill and handed it to the young man.

'Look I'm really sorry. My husband got confused, he's in a bad way, he recently lost his friend.'

Both men were saddened to hear this and even more so when she filled them in with the news, 'The friend, well he was the guy who fell off the building in Lexington.'

When she reached Phoenix, he was standing next to the car staring into one of the open sandwich boxes. 'Smells great, let's get home.'

Back in the car she went to start the motor and he said, 'Hang on a moment, I'm sorry for earlier, all that business about buying the paint. My head's all over the place, one minute I am thinking something and the next... I'm not even sure if I paid those guys back there for the lunch.'

'Don't worry I settled the bill. It's going to take a while to come to terms with what's happened. Only don't get any more ideas on home improvements and leave the shopping to me.'

They both laughed.

The rest of the journey went smoothly and they were soon home. She let him out just before the ramp that led down to the parking lot. He made his way to the

43

stairs. As she was about to climb out of the car, she burst into tears. She must have only been crying for a few moments when she was startled by a tap on the window and Phoenix's loud voice. 'I don't have my keys.'

She opened the door and leant forward and he noticed how distressed she looked.

'Hey, you just let it all out. This is me causing you all this stress. You do know I love you, honey?'

He held her hand all the way back to the apartment. He was talkative but kept coming out with the wrong words, which made him cross. Then he mentioned he might not have taken his medication.

Suzy took a deep breath and went for it. 'Look darling, I think we ought to make another appointment with the doctor.'

He snapped, 'You mean I need to see the shrink again.'

'No, just our doctor.'

* * *

Two days later they were sitting in front of the doctor again and Phoenix mentioned he'd slipped up on taking his tablets. The doctor's eyes narrowed. The seriousness of missing out on medication would definitely have consequences.

Suzy stared down at the floor and nervously fidgeted with the straps on her bag.

The doctor raised her head. 'Now let's go over your visit to the Woodside.'

Staring at the screen she read out the relevant information. 'The general opinion was you were still in a state of shock and suffering from depression. I have the request for a monthly visit to see me. It appears you were deemed well enough to carry on without admission. The only stipulation was no work for a while and a medication update in two months. They gave you a prescription for Citalopram – how is that going?'

Suzy swung her body around to face Phoenix. 'When I picked you up from the clinic you definitely said they hadn't altered your medication.'

'Did I? Well no sweat there. Right now, I'm just trying to get my head around this nightmare without you having a go at me.'

Doctor Creedy restored some calm back into their discussion. 'The flipside of all this is we need to concentrate on you getting better, so let's diary in those dates for you to see me. Here is your prescription to collect from the drugstore. Can I suggest your wife takes control of your tablets?'

Suzy scribbled the appointment details down in her diary and they got up to leave.

'Oh, Phoenix, just one final thing, remember my door is always open. If anything changes in your health, come back to see me.'

* * *

Back in the apartment Suzy nervously brought up the subject of her needing to return to work. A week had shot by and her boss had been applying pressure by e-mailing and calling her. Whilst the HR department had been sympathetic and told her to take time off work, her boss had other plans. Her role as account executive for the advertising agency was at times demanding but well paid. With a business trip to Pittsburgh scheduled for a week's time, leaving Phoenix alone would not be ideal.

Her plan was to take up her mother's offer to fly in from Ohio to help with Phoenix. In an earlier phone call, she'd managed to discuss his current mental health, indecisiveness and mood swings. There was also the matter of overseeing his daily medication log and checking he kept up his visits to the doctor. When Phoenix heard that Marlene was coming, she knew only too well he'd throw a wobbly, saying he was fine and that he just needed space. In the past he'd made no secret of his dislike for her family.

At first, he remained silent, then surprisingly warmed to seeing his mother-in law. He told Suzy that he understood that with her being the main breadwinner, her work came first.

Suzy suggested he contact the insurance company to chase up his sickness cover. He sheepishly informed her he'd fallen behind with the payments. Instead of rebuking him she reminded him they still had her monthly pay check and her savings.

* * *

Later in the week, unbeknown to Suzy, Phoenix contacted his foreman and made light of the severity of his illness. He also informed his company he wouldn't be returning.

He was certain that going back to the Lexington site was going to be too hard to endure. Applying for a transfer to a new office development off Madison seemed the only alternative. Commencement for construction was two months off, affording him ample time to secure the role and make a good recovery.

The thought of going up in the cage elevator to the top of any building terrified him. What if he froze and was unable to work and they had to ring Suzy to collect him? Or, if he imagined Cody also worked there. A new scenario saw him reach out in time to pull him to safety. The two men would undoubtedly laugh off Phoenix's misunderstanding after he learnt the truth behind the texts on his wife's cell phone. They would chat about Phoenix's birthday and the surprise party they'd been planning.

There was no getting away from the fact that Cody, the man from Cleveland with the nervous stutter and infectious laugh, who first met Phoenix fifteen years ago, had been a great friend. He was the man at their wedding who made that heartfelt speech and gave him the wonderful watch. How many times had he stared at the engraving on the back plate that read: *Happiness is only a moment away*?

Since losing Cody, Phoenix still failed to comprehend his delayed reaction to the loss of someone so special. Why didn't he come clean at the time explaining it had been an accident? Possibly because he made no effort to reach out to save Cody from falling. Instead, those few precious seconds were frozen in time as his friend tumbled to his death. He had indeed cheated him of his life. Worse still, Elizabeth and Cameron were now on their own.

For Phoenix, there still remained the nagging thought of what had happened to Cody's phone when they found the body. So far, he'd heard nothing, so imagined and hoped that this was the end of the matter.

He pondered on Suzy's suggestion that he return to his former work as a private builder and make a fresh start. It would mean using her inheritance to get up and running. But, Ohio? Well, he wasn't that keen with his ex-wife Barbara living there or Suzy's parents being so close.

Another negative would be missing visits from his thirty-year-old son Dale, who came up to the city on business from Orlando and often stayed with him and Suzy. There wasn't a day that went by that Phoenix didn't think of his son, but he wouldn't be seeing him just yet. He begged Suzy not to tell him about his illness or what happened to Cody. For the meantime, he'd have to be content with just chatting on Facetime.

* * *

When Suzy took the call from Elizabeth, Phoenix's heart missed more than a beat on hearing her discuss the funeral. It was to be on Friday, in just four days' time. When she ended the call, she told him the days ahead were going to be testing. He tried to reassure her he would cope. She wasn't so sure.

Getting her mother over to New York was paramount. As she made the arrangements, Phoenix heard her say. 'That's great you can come next week as I plan to go back to the office. Mail me with your flight details. Thanks Mom – love to Dad.'

Chapter 5

On the day of the funeral in the Mount Olivetti Cemetery, the sun was pleasantly warm with a slight breeze rattling the immaculately manicured bushes. A large group of mourners stood beside the hearse that brought Cody from the funeral home. There were so many wreaths that it took three people to unload them from the hearse. It was only then that the small brown casket with silver handles came into sight.

Phoenix was holding back his tears as he remembered his friend and gripped Suzy's hand tightly. He averted his eyes as the procession moved inside for the service. Only when he felt composed enough did they enter the church. Seated next to some of Cody's family, they watched the upsetting scene as Elizabeth and her son consoled each other in the front row of the church. She was crying and the echo was a sound that Phoenix knew would haunt him for the rest of his life.

He stared at the sea of faces, family members and friends and heard their sad voices discussing the wonderful man who had died so young. Shuffling along the benches to allow more people to sit, Phoenix sat next to the foreman of his site. He made no attempt to greet him and sat perfectly still ignoring Suzy's request to pass him a service sheet.

There followed some wonderful tributes and Cody's favourite music tracks. Prayers were short and everyone watched in silence as Elizabeth rose from her chair to touch the casket. It seemed an age before she moved away and Cody was carried out to his final resting place.

Much to everyone's surprise, outside the weather had changed with heavy drizzle wetting the shiny wooden casket that was being lowered into the grave. Phoenix put a hand to his mouth as the smell of the damp soil filled his nostrils. Refusing to shelter under Suzy's umbrella, he held his head down low privately saying a prayer for Cody. When it came to throwing the earth down into the grave, he felt sick and yanked on Suzy's arm to leave. The thudding sound of the mud coming into contact with the wood reminded him of knocking into Cody on that fateful morning.

Elizabeth had chosen not to have a reception and after the funeral there were many people waiting to talk to the family to say goodbye. When it was their turn to pay their respects, there was much hugging and tears as they conveyed how sorry they were for their loss.

Cameron's tear-stained face brought home the agony he must have been feeling on losing his father. Phoenix shook his hand and to Suzy's amazement, and probably anyone-else listening, muttered, 'He was my best friend and somehow I feel responsible for all this. I'm going to make all of this up to you.'

Elizabeth's face creased on hearing her husband's name. 'Thank you, Phoenix. Cody thought the world of you and we are proud to have you and Suzy as our friends.'

Both Suzy and Phoenix felt very humble and nodded their heads in unison.

Cody's silver cased watch was brought out from Phoenix's coat pocket and turned over to reveal the inscription.

'Well young man, your dad gave me this wonderful watch and I figure it's about time it went to you. He was always positive about life and kept telling me off whenever I messed up. See here on the back the inscription your dad had done for me.'

Before walking his mother to the limousine, Cameron smiled and thanked them for coming and then hugged Phoenix. There was empathy between the two men and both Elizabeth and Suzy closed their eyes as they heard their sobs of despair.

On the way back to their car Phoenix calmly said, 'Wasn't it sad coming up here and leaving Cody behind. And that boy, I mean young man; he's just like his father.'

'No, Cameron is really tall and looks nothing like Cody.'

'Suppose so, but I detected something that reminded me of him. You know the way he turns up the edges of his mouth and those freckles.'

'Obviously, you're more observant than me. Let's get out of this rain, come on.'

Just before they reached the car, they were aware of someone calling Phoenix's name. It was the site foreman. 'Awful business, so young and a family. Now Phoenix, how are you? Your mates miss you and send their best wishes.'

'The doc wants me to take it easy for a few weeks.'

'It's more like a few months,' snapped Suzy.

* * *

As they reached the Chevrolet, Phoenix insisted on driving home and produced his own car key. Suzy protested saying the insurance wouldn't cover him whilst he was ill. He pulled a frightening face at her and was soon in the driving seat, turning over the motor and demanding she got in.

'Stop worrying, I need to drive to take my mind off this morning. I don't want to fall out with you, so just give me a break.'

Reluctantly, Suzy climbed into the passenger seat, fastened her belt and snapped, 'And you too, put yours on.'

For a split second he couldn't remember the procedure for selecting reverse drive. The gearbox emitted a crunching sound. He nervously laughed it off.

'It's not funny; I don't think you should be doing this. Let's change over.'

'Behave won't you. I've been driving for the last thirty odd years and that's as long as you've been alive. I'm up for driving, so lay back in the seat and lower that window as I need air.'

He steered the car out of the cemetery gates and Suzy waited for him to complete the right turn before saying, 'Back there, what was that you said about somehow you were going to make all of this up to them? I'm wondering just what you meant.'

A desperate voice inside Phoenix's head screamed, *Oh Jesus, she knows – she's guessed. What am I going to do? If I tell her, she'll hate me forever, and if I stay quiet the nightmare will keep on rolling.*

Any decision about what to reply was short-lived as Suzy shouted above the roar of the car engine, 'I just realised what you meant. That was a lovely thing to say. You would have done everything possible to save him if you'd been there. And, giving Cameron the watch; I know it meant the world to you.'

'Sure thing, honey, friendships don't come cheap in my book. Making it up to them is my way of signifying the love and help we give.'

She touched his hand briefly. 'That's awesome. I'm totally with you on looking out for them, only we mustn't crowd them. These things take time.'

He stared at the road ahead feeling wretched with what he'd said back there in the cemetery. He questioned just how in God's name was he going to make it up to Cody's family?

'Still okay to drive Phoenix?' You've gone all quiet on me.'

There was no reply and she screamed as she realised he'd shot a red light and they were hurtling into the path of an enormous truck. Somehow Phoenix managed to steer the car to safety and braked hard.

Suzy yelled at him, 'Jesus, you nearly killed us! What were you thinking?'

'I'm sorry, I messed up.'

'You shouldn't have been driving it's too soon. I just knew something would happen. I could see the guy in the truck was shaken up. We're lucky the police weren't about. Let me drive now.'

'Oh yeah, tell it like it is. It's me the crazy man driving who accidentally, for the first time in his life, jumps the light. There's no harm been done, so stop hitting on me.'

'Keep your voice down, there's no need to shout. I figure you need a break, so take a right and pull over.'

'Listen to yourself Suzy — breaks are for guys visiting Coney Island. It's me at the wheel and you're quite safe.'

She gritted her teeth.

'Didn't the doctor say you really shouldn't drive?'

'No.'

The ride was frightening as Suzy sat glued to the seat wringing her hands in fear. She must have been praying he'd have to stop at a red light sometime soon. The speed increased and, judging by the sound of the noisy motor, he was pumping the gas at an alarming rate. She gripped the torn leather edge of the seat and drove her foot down hard on an imaginary brake.

The speed he was driving over the bumpy road felt like they were peas bubbling to the boil. He needed to slow down.

'Please go slower, we're not on the freeway. Pull over and let me drive. It's not good for your blood pressure getting this cross.'

Like many times before he changed swiftly from his mad and irrational world to the kind and considerate man she loved. There was a noticeable change in his driving but this time the car was going along at crawling pace.

'You can go a little faster.'

'Now hold on there lady, I wanna get you back in one piece. If there's one thing I can't stand, it's a bad driver. Now help me with this left. Is it the next block or am I getting confused? These blocks all look the same to me.'

She was cautious with her reply. 'Quicker to take a right.'

'And a right it will be.'

Chapter 6

Early one weekday morning, the city was taking a bashing with torrential rain flooding the sidewalks and the traffic had ground to a halt. Penetratingly cold air whistled around the streets as pedestrians raised their collars to keep out the chill. Many of the subways were closed due to the treacherous weather and the stop lights swung crazily overhead as the wind raced between the buildings. There was talk of this being the worst storm that had ever hit the city.

Enduring the awful journey into work, Suzy pressed on but her mind was on greater things. Three long months had passed since Cody had died and Phoenix was now well enough to start thinking about returning to work. There had been no instant cure for mending broken heads and hearts but surely, day-by-day, he had improved sufficiently to be taken off Doctor Creedy's watch list. But getting there hadn't been easy. He could be so maddening to live with when he vented his frustration on her. On one occasion he even hinted they should split saying he was a bad man and didn't deserve her. She never raised the issue again of moving back to Ohio believing stability was crucial for his return to a normal life.

If it hadn't been for Suzy's mother helping out, she wouldn't have been able to work. Her father came up just the once to stay. Any fears of Phoenix throwing his toys out of the pram were short-lived as he began to warm to Donald. It appeared he no longer mistrusted his father-in-law. He was, however, unaware of Donald and Marlene's intervention in paying the bills or the discussions with their daughter about the option of moving back to Ohio.

Now her parents had gone home and they were on their own again. All went well for a while but there were a few scary days when she was at work. Disturbingly, one evening she was unable to enter the apartment as he'd put the bolt on the door. It took a while to get his attention as she frantically rang the bell and called his cell phone. When he finally let her in, he kept saying it was to keep out bad people who may harm him. This was of course nonsense as Phoenix was more than capable of looking after himself. He was a large man with a fist that could end any fight in seconds.

* * *

Due to the appalling weather conditions, Suzy was already over an hour late for her client meeting. The signal on her cell phone was poor and she was unable to get through to her boss. She dreaded the repercussions from Logan who had recently been giving her a hard time. She was resolute that the day was fast approaching when she'd tell him where to stick his job.

If the worst were to happen, they would manage on her inheritance until she secured alternative employment. She was pleased that Phoenix had found work on a new site but felt uneasy when he told her the floor build was eventually to be seventy-nine. There were still a few days until his start date.

When she finally reached Madison Avenue and entered the plush advertising agency offices, she felt dishevelled, her clothes were soaked through. Waiting at the front desk was Logan Mansen who greeted her like a long-lost friend.

'Suzy, oh my God you are so wet; let me take your coat. I've been so worried about you in all this weather. The meeting is off. The client rang me at seven this morning. His wife has been taken ill.'

'Oh, for God's sake, give me strength. I've had the commute from hell and I'm wiped out. Why didn't you call me before I left home?'

'I did, I left a message with your husband.'

She felt his eyes scanning her body as he said, 'I hope you don't catch a cold; as I said, I was worried about you.'

Suzy stood staring at her boss – here was the forty-something Accounts Director in his immaculate, smart, pinstripe suit and polished brown shoes, while she was soaked through and dripping on the lobby's green carpet. The question that was bugging her was why he was so concerned for her. Normally communication from this man was limited to grunts; something was definitely up. Was he going to fire her? Despite her earlier thoughts on resigning, the realisation dawned on her that they needed the money. She wasn't going to walk away from her mid-term bonus. She flinched when he put his arm around her and guided her towards his office.

He hung her wet coat over a chair before ushering her into his room. To her annoyance, to prevent her wetness dampening the material of the pastel blue sofa, he first placed an opened magazine before allowing her to sit. She stared at his tidy desk with the carefully stacked documents and shiny, red laptop with the lid closed. Her boss sat down and removed his glasses to wipe away a smear on the lenses then stared at Suzy without saying a word.

While they waited for coffee to be sent up, he asked if Phoenix was back at work and what had been wrong with him? Irked by his sudden interest in her husband, she walked over to the window to look out at the rain that was still pounding the city.

Logan's deep voice always annoyed her. 'Suzy, I've been doing some thinking; possibly I was a bit harsh on you yesterday. I'm not saying losing the pizza account to Morgan Brown wasn't a blow for our agency. We must do some moving and shaking to get extra pitches and increase the spend by our existing clients. Now, that's what I want to talk to you about. Your new cosmetics account has potential for big billings. You need to beef up their budget if we are going to hit our target.'

Suzy moved away from the window. 'Mmm, hold on there, I have already told you, Logan, they are dipping their toes before committing to big bucks.'

'Tell them their main competitor is increasing their advertising spend in the market and so should they.'

'Are you saying I should lie to the client?'

'Man up Suzy… your job is to push for more.'

Suzy, annoyed with his remark, shook her head. 'Don't speak to me like that! We secured a fair slice of Party Six Mascara and I can't go back before mid-term contract to ask for more.'

'Of course, you can. I knew you'd understand – good girl.'

The conversation was interrupted by the arrival of the coffee. Suzy was close to boiling point. How dare he refer to her as a good girl!

She watched him lean back on his chair and sip his drink. He frowned, 'Mine's cold, how about yours?'

Suzy enjoyed her lie. 'Actually, mine's piping hot.' Patting her damp skirt, she added, 'Is that everything; can I go now to get cleaned up?'

'Just one last thing, I want you to come on a road trip with me next week. I'm already booked to see Bluetons in Pittsburgh, Hank at Lorna Davis Foods and still waiting on Bell Sounds in Los Angeles. We'll be away for four days max.'

'Four days! No, I'm too busy to leave at short notice.'

The truth be known, there was no way she could leave Phoenix alone for his first week back at work. Also, she wasn't keen on spending so much time with Logan.

'Oh, come on Suzy, I'm saying we go. I don't want to force the issue.'

Suzy was panicking. Was now the time to quit her work with the agency? Then an idea came to her. 'Look I'd love to help you out on those meetings, only there's something I need to tell you.'

'Oh yes…'

'Next week I have a hospital appointment and you must remember there is also the presentation for Dormer Sental.'

'Oh yeah, I got you, it must have slipped my mind. That's one company our agency would love to get into bed with. You do your best on that one and I'll do the trip on my own. But, hey, are you alright, what's wrong?'

In a low voice she said the first thing that came into her mind. 'Oh, just women's problems, nothing major.'

She cringed as he leant over and momentarily held her hand. 'Poor old you. Anything I can help with?'

She felt uncomfortable as she vividly recalled the past Washington business trip. They'd both had too much to drink. She still fretted over having let him into her room. Despite Suzy's plea for him to stop, Logan had tried to undress her and slid a hand up her thigh. He kept repeating that she should relax. His breathing got heavier as he moved in on her again and attempted to raise her skirt that little bit higher. It was only when she managed to shout for help, that he came to his senses.

Reminding him that she was a married woman and that he'd got her drunk, she threatened to report him to the police as well as their chairman. This brought Logan down to earth and he apologised, blaming it on the liquor. Still feeling tipsy, Suzy started to feel sick and insisted he leave her bedroom. He'd made her feel dirty and keeping the secret from Phoenix was going to be hard. After Logan had returned to his room she showered and knew that no amount of soap or scrubbing would ever erase the memory of that terrible night.

Over the weeks that followed, there had been no more incidents involving Logan. Suzy remained at the agency and her boss never crossed that line again, but she never forgave him for taking advantage of her. Somehow, she'd move on and for the immediate future she wasn't going to walk away from her large salary and mid-term bonus.

She promised herself that if Logan ever came on heavy again, that would be it; she'd resign from her post.

Only today he was acting like a real airhead. Still feeling uncomfortable in her damp clothes, she panicked when she realised he was staring at her top. One of the buttons had come undone exposing her rose pink bra. She struggled to fasten it up and to her disgust he smiled and winked a number of times.

'Don't mind me. Take your time with that button.'

'Don't be so disgusting. I'm warning you this has to stop.'

He wasn't giving up. 'I figure you and I make a great team. How about after work we go for a bite at that new Italian restaurant off Madison? Some of the guys in production say it's awesome.'

She quickly turned away from him and knew what she had to do.

'You know, I think I've had enough – I quit.'

'QUIT! Are you out of your mind? I need your support with all the business we have here. Your contribution is valued and you could soon be on fast track to greater things. Is it extra salary you want?'

'No, and it's certainly not you.'

She took pleasure in studying his smug face and mouth that twisted in a humourless smile as his voice rose to shouting. 'Well, what in hell do you want?'

With a grin on her face that felt good she replied, 'You know what Logan, I just want out. I've been doing some thinking… advertising stinks, almost as much as you.'

* * *

'You did what?'

'Yes Phoenix, I told him to stick his job. I'd had enough and there was too much travelling coming up. My boss is a pig and I'm leaving the farmyard.'

Phoenix snorted loudly and they both fell about laughing before opening a further bottle of Malbec to celebrate.

Feeling tipsy, she shouted, 'Hey, I just said goodbye to my great salary and that pretentious boss of mine. That's me finished with advertising.'

Phoenix nodded his head. 'No sweat there. My new job back on the scraper will pay well. I'm sure you'll soon find work.'

'Bless you darling. I have an appointment with the guys in HR tomorrow; no doubt they will try to change my mind about going. I'm tied into a contract and that means seeing my time out with Logan.'

Phoenix's face looked angry on hearing this. 'A clean break would be better. If that guy steps over the line, I'll break more than his neck.'

Suzy smiled and turned the conversation to his work. 'You must be looking forward to going back to your welding?

'Yeah, but I know I'll be thinking of Cody.'

'You'll be fine.'

'Thanks babe, but I want you to level with me please. That guy, your boss Logan, he wasn't unreasonable, was he?'

Suzy nervously stroked the edge of her glass. 'No, he's just a pompous little shit doing his job and expecting too much from me. The targets were unreal with so much pressure on to make endless presentations. I decided I'd had enough.'

'Are you sure about that? If I thought for one minute he was giving you a hard time, I'd rip his head off.'

Suzy laughed, not because she needed to laugh, more out of nervousness as she feared Phoenix would intervene in something she'd already sorted. She wished her notice period was shorter and there wasn't the clause in the small print that stopped her working for a competitor for six months. Not that she wanted to return to advertising, but it did limit her opportunities particularly as this had been her career for many years.

There were deadlines and pitches to be finalised before she could leave and she prayed that Logan would show less interest in her.

* * *

The morning after Suzy's showdown with Logan, he scheduled a breakfast meeting in a diner off Union Square. She sat awkwardly at the cramped table and stared at her boss's long chin and the hairs he'd missed whilst shaving. He looked a mess this morning, like he'd got a hangover. His stale breath wafted into her face and she kept turning away to breathe. He really was the most unpleasant person to be with and she was glad she'd not worn a skirt as she didn't want him staring at her legs.

The diner was busy and she was nervous that others would overhear their conversation. She glanced down at the now cold cheese omelette that she hadn't touched. She turned her nose up at the smell of the extra cheese that had been loaded onto her meal. It was apparent that other diners were enjoying their breakfast. Judging by the smell of the bacon and pancakes it was appetising food, only today she wasn't hungry. She wished she were anywhere but with Logan.

Conversation centred on whether she'd changed her mind. There was the offer of a hike in salary if she stayed, but she was resolute about leaving.

'But why throw away your job? Is it me – have I upset you?'

A look of exasperation crossed her face on hearing this. 'You know you have! You just won't leave me alone.'

'Now hold on there, that's some accusation.'

He kept trying to break her down and she was beginning to get bored.

'Suzy, you know I always look out for you. There's the new cosmetics pitch we're just starting on and I want you on the team. You can be my deputy. How does that sound?'

Deep down, even putting his flirting to one side, she knew they couldn't work together.

Logan then switched to his nasty mode reminding her she still had to work her notice. Her six-thousand-dollar performance bonus was dependent on a satisfactory termination. If she decided not to leave, the even better mid-term payment, close to fourteen, was hers for the taking.

'No, I already told you, I've had enough.'

Annoyed by her insistence on leaving the agency, he handed her a spreadsheet of the many client visits and overnight stays she would be expected to make within her notice period. She frowned when he reminisced about the hotel they'd stayed at in San Francisco last fall. This was the place he spotted their business colleagues getting the bedroom doors mixed up. He referred to it as Lover's Alley as he gently punched Suzy on the arm.

It was obvious he was never going to give up. Irrefutably, Logan was a jerk and intent on chasing anything in a skirt. The man was a bully and determined to get his way with her. She had also heard he'd recently left his wife and wondered if he'd been hitting on the other girls in the office. Knowing Phoenix's temper, if he got a sniff of Logan messing with her, he'd do more than just tear his head off.

The breakfast meeting saw Suzy say goodbye to her job as she insisted on leaving the agency with immediate effect. She handed over the company iPad, laptop, cell phone and expenses card. Logan threatened to sue for breach of contract and as she stood up to leave, he told her to go back to her loser of a husband.

* * *

Walking back home she had no regrets; things were going to be tight but she was doing the right thing leaving. She recalled the years she'd slogged away hanging onto clients, also the late nights with the stay overs. All that mattered now was returning home to Phoenix, the person she loved more than anything in the world.

She'd coped well with Phoenix's problems and her staying power was unbelievable. Over the last few years she kept getting knocked down only to rise up that bit stronger. And who wouldn't go through all that worry when the man in question had done so much for her.

Casting her mind back to her late teens and living in Ohio, it was Phoenix who had rescued her on that hot summer's evening all those years ago. It was their first meeting and he risked his life as he leant across the iron beams and calmly talked her down from the railroad bridge. Suzy, standing erect, had been determined to jump but was persuaded to climb back to safety with him.

It was witnessing her father in an intimate situation with another man that had been too much for her to shoulder. It was no wonder Phoenix, after hearing her revelation, felt uncomfortable in Donald's company. Six months later he placed a small thin golden band on her finger as a token of his love for her, something she treasured. Phoenix was her life.

* * *

When Suzy arrived at the apartment block, Mrs Delgado collared her and wanted to know how they both were. They went through the pleasantries of daily life, before she calmly informed Suzy she had cancer. Saddened to hear this, she asked if her neighbour had family close by. She was shocked to learn her daughter rarely kept in touch. It appeared the poor woman only had a year to live. It brought back the frailty of life and the importance of living every day to the fullest. She made up her mind they would have to keep an eye on this lady.

When Suzy finally let herself into the apartment, she heard music coming from the lounge and there was the distinct smell of paint. Phoenix appeared wearing a pair of shorts and tee shirt. He had paint on his cheeks and was holding a heavily loaded brush of bright blue.

He turned down the radio. 'Hi, you are home early. I took a ride out to buy the paint. What do you think?'

'Well it's blue – bright blue.'

He led the way through and his handiwork came into view. All the walls were painted the same colour. She observed his carelessness in not covering up the furniture. He hadn't even moved her clock that was still on the mantelpiece. The edges of the beige carpet had not escaped the splodges of paint either. His attempt to wash out the blue had made it worse.

Suzy forced a smile. 'Looks great, but how about I help you cover up the sofa?'

'No need, I've got a steady hand when it comes to painting.'

Her eyes were drawn to the lounge curtains he'd failed to take down before decorating. Miraculously, they had escaped the fury of the decorator. At times, his idiosyncratic behaviour could be so infuriating.

Trying to encourage him, Suzy touched him on his shoulder. 'You've done a great job, but do be careful of the furniture and carpet.'

Returning to the hall she smelt cooking coming from the kitchen.

'Is something on the stove?'

'It's tomato soup. I was getting myself some lunch.'

When they reached the cooker, she quickly turned off the power. The pan of bright orange soup had already started to boil over and a pool was forming on the worktop.

'Look what you've done. I keep telling you to take care when cooking.'

Phoenix pulled a face. 'There's nothing wrong with my cooking. It's the stove; the heat varies. We need a new stove.'

Suzy stared at the relatively new cooker. 'Well I don't have problems when I use it. I don't want you burning the place down.'

* * *

Later on, Suzy discussed Mrs Delgado and how poorly she was. Phoenix was concerned and agreed they should look out for her. This was the old Phoenix she knew and loved, always caring for others.

Later that evening Suzy told him she'd finished for good with the agency. A feeling of happiness calmed her mind. They were finally back on track with all loose ends neatly clipped, or so she thought.

* * *

Over the next few days Suzy was contacted by the CEO of the advertising agency, who offered to meet with her to resolve their differences. She made it perfectly clear that her mind was set and she wasn't coming back. It was at this juncture, the main shareholder of Riva Goldberg Advertising, advised her they were suing for breach of contract.

Choosing her moment, she told Phoenix about the legal implications of her leaving, and that she'd been to see a lawyer already. He was not to worry as these things often fizzled out. She related a story of one of their account executives who was fired for using her company credit card for clothes. The firm threatened her with litigation for theft, but nothing came of it.

'There's more to it than that,' Phoenix stressed.

'You are right, they didn't sue, but they did pile the pressure on her.'

Phoenix was deep in thought and biting his fingernails. 'Why not just serve out your time and then leave.'

'You have to understand they are only worried about me going to another agency and exchanging details on accounts. The problem with advertising is you get so immersed in securing business and they push you constantly. My lawyer is preparing a formal letter of complaint. It will lay out the mental pressure Logan put me through and all the...'

Phoenix looked puzzled. 'Mental pressure you say, are you sure it wasn't more than that? I keep thinking all this seems strange you leaving the job you liked and that creep Logan. I need to get a measure of the guy.'

Suzy frowned. 'Forget him, he's a control freak. He'll slip up big time one day.'

She took a deep breath. Today she had to tell him about Logan only she would definitely hold back on the detail.

'Now Phoenix, I don't want you reading anything into this. Nothing happened, I promise. I'm sure it was the liquor talking when he came onto me. I stopped him in his tracks and I'm sure he regrets it. You know what advertising is like with entertaining clients and people doing crazy things. Now promise me you won't go putting two and two together and making five.'

Phoenix's face had turned to a bright red and he thumped the dishwasher so hard that she was sure something would be broken. His voice roared, 'Just what do you mean? Either the guy came on to you, or he didn't. He sounds like a skirt chaser to me.'

'Stop it! I said nothing happened.'

'When and where did this happen and did he touch you? I wanna know, so no holding back.'

'It was on the Washington trip and it was just the once. You do believe me, don't you?'

He raised a reassuring hand and was thankfully calm which surprised her. 'It's a good job I'm thinking straight nowadays or I'd tear the balls off that sonofabitch. What hurts is this guy hits on my wife and you hide it from me. You should have told me at the time. We shouldn't have any secrets.'

In tears Suzy offered, 'You were having problems and something like this may have added to your stress.'

He gestured for her to join him. 'Come here, babe, and stop that crying. Of course, I believe you; all this advertising nonsense is soon going in the garbage. I'm a hundred percent behind you. And as for that creep, I believe you totally and we'll put it behind us.'

Suzy was relieved to hear him speaking like this and the fact he was so in control of his feelings reassured her. She'd been upfront with him and now he was there for her. She brushed away her tears and kissed him on the cheek.

'I say we get on with our lives and hope that boss of yours drops off the planet sometime soon. Being honest with me was the right thing to do as couples shouldn't hold back on anything.'

* * *

Alone in their bedroom Suzy was confident Phoenix was out of earshot and mumbled, *you bastard Logan, but this time I told him about you.*

Recalling the CEO's call and how he threatened they'd file a writ against her, she deliberated on how this would leave them financially, but there was no turning back.

Chapter 7

The following morning Suzy walked with Phoenix to his new work place. The weather had improved significantly but the wind was strong as it caught Suzy's long, black hair buffeting it about her head. She could sense he was uneasy about entering the site and squeezed his hand for reassurance. He kept checking his watch, then asking the time.

'You'll be fine. You have your lunch and security pass, so you are ready to go.'

There was a moment of panic as he frantically searched his coat pockets.

'Just kidding, here it is.'

He flashed the plastic swipe card with the unflattering picture that made him look older. His hair, tied back in a ponytail, was now much longer than before he stopped working.

When it came to saying goodbye, he mentioned he'd ring her during the morning break. He quickly added, 'If they contact you, you will come and get me, won't you?'

'Come on, Phoenix, the site at the moment is only at ground level; even you won't be scared at that height. You'll be fine. I ought to go now as I need to ring my lawyer and the agency.'

'Good luck with that, but keep your cell phone on in case I ring.'

'Yes, now off you go.'

She watched as he showed his card to the guard and momentarily turned back to see if she was still there. Of course, she was there. She was in for the full ride.

* * *

Inside the compound, the full extent of the enormous skyscraper base became evident with the grey iron skeleton already taking shape. The bright red cranes were moving over the Manhattan skyline. There was much activity on the site as the steel uprights and beams were being lowered into position.

Phoenix went through a security process that included being searched, then scrutiny of his ID. He was shown to an office and introduced to a man in a suit, who was not particularly responsive, and a young woman dressed in smart navy-blue jeans and a three-quarter length, black coat. Both shared the role of foreman and wore white hard hats. The woman was frantically swiping the screen of her company iPad.

Seated in the damp iron shipping container that served as an office, Phoenix was shown a video on workplace safety and health. Timekeeping was addressed along with guidance for using the swipe card that recorded attendance times. He listened intently to the procedures for storing tools and equipment. It was all so different from the last site and definitely more professional with its approach to new recruits.

The woman, who introduced herself as Amy Morgan, was an attractive redhead who kept tapping her pen on the desk. It was clear it wasn't going to take rocket science to guess where her line of questioning was heading.

'You worked for just under a year at the Clancy site and left suddenly.'

Phoenix, on the defence, replied, 'Yes, that's right. I was one of the crew who were on site when we lost a man. He was my friend and I suffered shock that resulted in having time off. I'm okay now.'

'That must have been very stressful and we are sorry for your loss. Your references were all in line and I see you have a medical certificate with a clean bill of health. You are married, fifty years old and live in Manhattan.' She looked up from her iPad. 'I've always wanted to live in Manhattan.'

'Yeah, it's cool in the village.'

'Welcome to our company; we have a great bunch of guys out there. For the first week you will shadow Ethan Jacobs. The two of you should get on fine. He'll show you where to store your tools and welding helmet.'

Phoenix smiled, 'Yeah, I'm looking forward to getting back to my welding.'

She leaned forward to stare down at Phoenix's footwear, 'Great, I can see you have new work boots.'

His boots were indeed new and had cost over a hundred dollars. Safety was vital, especially as within a short time the building was going up to the next level, then up really high.

A hard hat was placed on his head that felt uncomfortable over his ponytail. He repositioned the hat, much to Amy's amusement.

'Just a quick question – how long until we leave ground level and start up higher?'

Amy checked a document on her untidy desk and casually informed him, 'Four days, dependent on the weather.'

Plenty of time for Phoenix to acquaint himself with the workings and people on the site. His face suddenly went blank as he started to think about Suzy and whether the agency was going to carry out their threat.'

'Are you all right Phoenix, you've gone a funny colour? Would you like some water?'

Forced away from his thoughts, he managed to smile. 'No thanks, I'm fine it's just so hot in here with that blower on my face, but I suppose it is winter.'

'And a very cold winter it is,' replied the man who until this moment had not uttered a single word.

Amy stood still. He noticed how slim and attractive she was. 'Well, that's about all for now. My door is always open; any further questions?'

He shook his head but was still wondering about Suzy and that creep Logan with whom he would eventually wipe the floor.

The induction over, he was taken for a brief site visit before meeting Ethan who was to become his mentor. The noise was overpowering with so many people all busy readying the skyscraper for its big climb into the sky.

Meeting Ethan put Phoenix at ease as the two men found they had much in common having both previously been independent builders. Ethan was almost Phoenix's height but carried less weight and walked with a stoop. The weathered face and scars suggested he'd worked in heavy construction for some time. His finely cut hairstyle was a contrast to Phoenix's long locks that were held back in a red clasp. He made a crack that his new friend could easily be mistaken for a woman. Phoenix was irked by the remark and replied, 'Just as long as you don't call me Amy.'

Due to the noise Ethan raised his voice. 'You'll have to shout I can hardly hear you. It sounds like you met our supervisor at your induction. She's one hell of a girl, our Amy, with the big tits. One of the shuttering guys reckoned he had a chance with her; she soon put him right.'

Phoenix made light of what he said, 'Oh yeah, suppose so, I wasn't taking that much notice of her. How about you show me my tools and acetylene? Also, where do I get the gloves?'

'Okay, follow me, only first I'll introduce you to the guys on our shift. Are you permanently on the 7am?'

'Yep,'

'That's good, so am I. So, where do you live?'

'Oh, not far off, West Village.'

'Jesus, you must be rolling in bucks. I'm over in South Bronx.'

Phoenix's overtly stifled yawn hinted that he no longer wanted to continue with the conversation. He said the first thing that came into his mind. 'What time is lunch?'

Meeting the other workers went well and they seemed happy in their work. Remembering their names was going to be another matter. There were four groups of welders and Phoenix was in a small team of three reporting to Amy Morgan. Ethan kept making references about Amy's curvaceous figure and it was starting to annoy him.

The morning soon shot by and he rang Suzy who sounded pleased he was settling in well. He deliberately hung back from asking her how the call with the lawyer went.

Working on this site should prove to be a treat as most of the equipment was new. Ethan's eye for detail impressed Phoenix and he was happy to receive help on his first day. He was pleasantly surprised by the friendliness of his workmates; so different from the last place. People appeared to be taking pride in their work and commenting on how spectacular the building would look when completed. A few of the men enquired where he had previously worked and, having told them, he quickly changed the subject.

* * *

At the close of work, Suzy was waiting just a few blocks down from the site. He noticed she was dressed in her work clothes. As they waited to cross Madison Avenue, she had trouble getting a word in edgeways as he excitedly unloaded his news.

Eventually she managed to tell him she'd been into work to meet with the CEO and now everything was sorted. An agreement had been reached for waiving the notice period and the icing on the cake was that the bonus would be paid. A clause in her contract still prevented her from joining a competitor advertising agency for the specified period.

Phoenix was ecstatic; it really had been a good day with his work and now this. He bent down to kiss his beautiful wife full on the lips.

'What was that for?'

'I can't get over your news and how brilliant you are. We'll have to celebrate tonight.'

'I told you I'd sort things. I even got to tell Logan where to get off.'

'Tell me Suzy, did you tell the CEO about Logan's womanising and how he tried it on with you?'

They were aware of other people listening to their conversation. 'Shush… keep your voice down; there's no need to shout. Yes, he knows everything, so now you have the full picture. Logan won't be bothering us again – please believe me.'

Phoenix nodded.

'Tell me more about your day. Do you like your boss, what's his name?'

'It's Amy – the foreman is a lady.'

'A lady! Well I never.'

Phoenix, as loud as ever, rushed his words. 'There's also a guy called Ethan who's showing me the ropes, but never stops talking. My news is nowhere as good as yours. Now, where shall we dine tonight? Do you fancy that new pizza place or the Italian off West 9th?'

* * *

As they entered the subway Suzy cast her mind back to her meeting in the advertising agency. She had decided not to relate any of it back to Phoenix because the risk of upsetting him was too high. During the discussion with the CEO, she had held nothing back. She relayed in detail the sexual harassment and unreasonable work pressure his employee Logan had placed on her. The head of the company, obviously not wanting the matter to escalate, agreed to release her from her contractual obligations.

She left his office in a triumphant mood and headed for her desk to retrieve her personal belongings. It was lunchtime and there was only one other person there and he was on the phone. He put a hand up and continued with his call. Then she spotted Logan hotfooting it through the production department. Judging by the smile on his face, it was apparent he was unaware of her meeting with the head of their company.

On reaching her, he shrugged his shoulders before stretching out a hand for her to shake.

She stared intensely at his neatly combed hair that today was parted in the middle, and shook her head.

His annoyance was apparent as he raised his voice. 'Not changed your mind then. Make sure you don't take anything that doesn't belong to you. I'll wait to see you off the premises.'

'The sooner the better, I can't wait to go.'

Logan was a real jerk and she was suddenly aware of him staring at her blouse.

'Just make sure you keep a hold of those buttons on your shirt. You don't want the guys in your new work place getting bad thoughts.'

'You disgust me; now get out of my way.'

As she gathered up the last of her things he laughed. It was a cruel laugh that went on for some time before he spat out his warning. 'You do realise you'll never work in advertising again if I have anything to with it. News travels quickly and no agency will have you. If it wasn't for me making those pitches, you'd have gone long ago.'

'That's not how it was and you know it. I sweated buckets to bring in that business.'

'Face it you're a loser; you'll be better off out of advertising. How about you work in a care home looking after sick guys like your husband?'

'Get stuffed, Logan. I'll soon be out of your way and I'm sure the CEO, with whom I just had coffee, will shortly be calling you in for a chat. He knows everything and I mean everything.'

His face was a picture as she pushed past him and made her way to the elevator.

Off course she wasn't under any illusion that Logan was going to be sacked or even reprimanded. He was too useful to the agency, but his card had definitely been marked.

* * *

As Phoenix and Suzy got closer to the street where they lived, she kept squeezing his hand. With only one thing on their minds, they increased their pace and reached the apartment in record time. They both pressed the elevator call button a number of times as their impatience grew. Once inside the cramped enclosure they were aware of the security camera. They resisted the temptation to kiss and stood apart. On reaching the landing, Phoenix longed to make love to his beautiful young wife and struggled with the lock on the apartment door, blaming the key.

They never made it to their bedroom. The guest room that served as an office for Suzy, was covered in documents waiting to be returned to her old company. Suzy grabbed the bedspread off the single bed and shook it fiercely sending papers high into the air that pirouetted down like broken helicopters. Phoenix stood back and enjoyed watching Suzy peel off her blouse and discard it on the floor along with the long, pencil skirt.

As she removed her underwear she moaned, 'Hurry up – I need you.'

Taking off the dusty jeans and heavy work coat, he was aware of his body odour that was far from pleasant, but the passion to join her on the bed was overwhelming. Moving over to her, he noticed her eyes were closed and a smile was radiating from her beautiful face. He stared at the new lingerie he had recently bought her and longed to complete her undressing.

Phoenix was thrilled by Suzy taking control of their lovemaking. She was like a woman on fire as their craving grew to the point of no control. Minutes later, lying in the cramped bed both were satisfied and exchanged kisses. Contentment was riding high for this happy couple. They were so much in love and nothing would ever part them.

* * *

The weeks shot past and Phoenix was enjoying his work and new friends. Each morning, before setting off, he'd wish Suzy luck with her search for work. It concerned him that she was finding it harder than she initially thought. Companies were asking tricky questions on her decision to leave one of the top advertising agencies in the city. The stumbling block was why she was prepared to take a lower paid post.

Phoenix's commute to work took thirty minutes and he tried to arrive early to catch up with his workmates before making their way to the tool compound. The site was always noisy with the heavy crane shifting the steels as work progressed on the tower. With the floor beams now in place, Phoenix transferred his gear to the next level using the cage elevator. He knew it wouldn't be long before he'd be up really high again. He was determined it would not become an issue.

Ethan, despite Phoenix's earlier reservations, turned out to be a great mate. He was a real joker. On one occasion he brought him lunch – a chicken burger meal in a box. Phoenix, unaware that his workmate was struggling to hold the flimsy container, looked forward to his meal. He was shocked to discover the box contained heavy bolts. The two men fell about in laughter making crazy chicken noises. Foreman Amy, standing close by, failed to see the funny side and her glance brought the fooling about to a close. She reminded them of their target for the day. Not that they needed reminding as both men were fanatical about ensuring their work remained at the highest standard and on time.

* * *

One evening Suzy was fretting as she waited for Phoenix to return home. He was over an hour later than his normal time, which was unusual for him. She knew he wouldn't be out drinking as he'd mentioned he wanted to be home in time to watch the Yankees' ball game. The oven was turned down low and she told herself that the transport links must be the reason for his delay. For the third time that evening, she raided the cookie jar and vowed in future she would stop having so many snacks. Her waistline was suffering and Phoenix had mentioned she was putting on weight.

She was startled by the shrill of her cell phone.

'It's me. I'm sorry I didn't ring you.'

Phoenix sounded terrible and was rushing his words.

'Are you okay, where are you?'

'Don't go worrying, but I'm at the hospital – Saint Vincent's Hospital.'

'In hospital, oh my God. Are you hurt?'

'I'm fine, it's Mrs Delgado, she's had a heart attack. When I got home tonight, I found her in the lobby and she looked real bad. There was so much happening and I know I should have banged on our door, but I couldn't leave her. I took the ride with her to the hospital.'

Breathing a sigh of relief that Phoenix was safe, she was now concerned for their neighbour. Phoenix hurriedly informed Suzy that Mrs Delgado had died. He said he held her hand up to the end and she kept thanking him. She then lost consciousness as the ambulance guy tried to save her.

'They found a number for her daughter, Ella, who will be here shortly. I bet she didn't even know her mother was dying from cancer as they rarely spoke. And now the poor woman has died of a heart attack.'

Suzy was devastated to hear the news. 'I can't imagine how the girl will feel when she gets there. I'll get the car out to fetch you.'

'Thanks babe, but you need to leave it for at least another hour as I'm waiting for Ella to arrive. At a time like this she doesn't need to be alone. Whatever her differences with her mother, it's going to be a shock learning the news. The doc will tell her, but I said I would be present.'

'Give me a bell when you want me to come and get you.'

Waiting for his call Suzy turned on the radio and sat anxiously by the phone. They were playing one of her favourite songs. She felt overcome with sadness on hearing the relevant verses that seemed to sum up their last few years. There was, however, the satisfying line that echoed there was always hope.

Three hours later Suzy set off and, driving through Greenwich Village, all she could think about was her wonderful husband. This was so characteristic of him being kind and helping others. Unquestionably, Phoenix would give his last cent to help someone in trouble. Taking into account the ups and downs of living with him, he was still the kindest person in the world. She knew he loved her with all his heart. If ever there was a person with redeeming qualities, it had to be her Phoenix.

* * *

82

It took Phoenix almost eight months to let go of the nightmare that had haunted him for so long. Now his life had a purpose and he looked forward to each day. The job on the construction site suited him and working high up was not an issue.

Suzy found work in the marketing department of a cosmetics company with offices in New York and London. The down side was this company used her old advertising agency and, to her annoyance, Logan visited for meetings. She kept reminding herself that this time she was the client and Logan was sure to be on his best behaviour.

Yes, her career was demanding, but she managed to find a balance. Life was pleasant once again and they were planning a vacation to San Francisco to visit friends. There was also a new addition to the family as their old car had been replaced with a smaller, but more up to date, Ford two-door coupé.

They met up with Elizabeth at least once a month. Understandably, she was finding it hard after losing Cody, but had managed to return to work. She was so kind to Phoenix and Suzy, often saying she didn't know what she'd do without their support and friendship. A couple of months back they'd all gone to Coney Island where Phoenix and Cameron rode the Wonder Wheel. It was a wonderfully warm day with everyone enjoying the fairground. They dined on hotdogs and possibly for the first time in ages did not dwell on the past. In reality, everyone knew life would never be the same again, but the four friends did have each other.

Chapter 8

Up on level fourteen, Phoenix sighed as he took a call from Amy asking him to come down to her office. He was apprehensive wondering what she had in store for him and prayed he wasn't going to be laid off.

It took a while for the elevator to arrive and he glanced up at the dirty black clouds wishing he were somewhere warmer. He'd promised Suzy he'd help with some shopping after work but, to be honest, he wasn't up to trailing around stores. All he wanted to do was get home, have dinner and snuggle up to his pretty wife.

When he reached the steel hut that was Amy's office, he commented on how cold it was and accepted a coffee. He grasped the hot cardboard cup in an effort to warm his hands. Amy couldn't help notice the look of worry on his face.

'Relax, there's not a problem.'

She pulled on her red scarf for warmth and took a sip of her steaming hot chocolate drink.

'The weather is bad out there Phoenix, it's hard to believe it at this time of year. I normally take my holiday about now. It must be this climate warming they keep talking about.'

Phoenix shrugged his shoulders. 'It's the newspaper guys who report on all that fake news.'

He glanced at the untidy office where many documents had found a home on the metal floor and said, 'Now, what was it you wanted?'

'There are going to be changes to the rota this week and I need your help.'

'Oh yeah.'

'You'll be on the east wing of level twelve. It's your turn to be a mentor to a new guy.'

'No sweat there then.'

'You have a choice of a lady or a guy; both are welders.'

'I'll stick with the guy.'

'Just see him through his first full day and then you'll be back to your normal job. I'll bring him round to meet you in about an hour's time. Any questions?'

'Well, actually yes, what's his name?'

Amy reached for her smart phone and scanned the lists of names. 'Wakeman... Gray Wakeman.'

'Okay, I got that. See you later then.'

* * *

Well into the morning shift, Phoenix was busy completing a section of steel that was almost ready for lifting into place. The sparks were flying in all directions and through the tinted glass of his hood he could see Amy waiting for him with the new man.

Cocooned in the heavy welding helmet, he glanced out past his supervisor to a large man in a green coat. It took him a few moments to finish his work, disconnect the gun and pull off the uncomfortable headgear. To his horror, there stood one of the workers who'd been on his last site. He'd never known his name, but was aware the man had disliked him. The obese black man with the curly, short hair was even larger than he was. His rugged and mostly toothless face, with a tattoo of an evil looking crow on his neck, unsettled Phoenix.

Amy made the introductions and, from the look on her face, she was concerned the two men were uneasy with each other.

'Am I reading this right, do you guys already know each other?'

85

Gray's growling voice worried Phoenix, 'I already know you from Clancy's. You were the guy who shouts all the time and a mate of Cody. You do remember poor old Cody who ended up as strawberry jam on Lexington?'

Struggling to control his temper, Phoenix would definitely have started a fight if Amy hadn't been present.

'What did you say? Say that again and I'll wipe the floor with you. Come on man, where's your respect for a guy who lost his life.'

Gray moved a step forward. 'Kiss my ass.'

Amy thrust an arm in the air and shouted, 'Just calm it guys. Losing a man is tragic and I agree with Phoenix it's not respectful to talk like that.'

Gray shook his head, 'The guy really winds me up.'

Phoenix, still furious with him, steered the conversation back to work. 'I'll be showing you the ropes for a while.'

'Oh, so you're going to show me how to weld. That should be fun.'

Concerned that Amy didn't read too much into the two men's history, Phoenix laughed nervously as he patted Gray on the arm. 'Really Amy, we'll be fine.'

It was clear that she was both puzzled and annoyed. 'Look, I won't stand for any trouble on my site. Step up, or you'll both get your cards. Do I make myself clear?'

On leaving them, she pulled out her cell phone and it was obvious she was reporting the incident.

The next forty minutes were testing as they set to work. When the noisy popping sound of the guns quietened down, the welders took their break and, to Phoenix's alarm, the larger man edged him into a corner.

'Get away from me.'

'So, you thought you'd seen the last of me, did you?'

'I never got it why you had it in for me – we never fell out or anything. How about we wipe the slate and get on with working together?'

'That's a great plan, but I don't like working with a murderer.'

Steadying himself against a pile of wooden pallets, Phoenix felt giddy. Suddenly his whole world was crashing around him again. Surely this guy hadn't seen anything, but why was he calling him a murderer?

'What... what did you call me? I lost my friend back there.'

Gray positioned his large, unshaven face right up against Phoenix's cheek and waved a fist as he spoke. 'Just look at you – you pathetic lump of shit? The welder from West Village, no less. Your secret is out.'

'Secret, there is no secret. I still can't believe that remark of yours about Cody.'

'Oh, the jam on the sidewalk, well it's how he ended up.'

Goading Phoenix into throwing the first punch, Gray screamed, 'You want to hit me – go on then, hit me. You want to know why I don't like you, I'll tell you. You showed off too many times about where you lived and how much dough you had. You think you are better than us, well you're not.'

'That doesn't make me a murderer. Look, I'm sorry if I caused offence.'

'I saw you two arguing when you arrived for work and then later, up high, just before he fell. Or, perhaps he didn't fall, you pushed him.'

Phoenix's inner voice flatly echoed: *He knows, God he knows and he's going to tell someone. Maybe he'll file a statement and the police will come looking for me.*

'Of course, I didn't push him.'

'More like shove than a push, was it?'

'Look, I don't know what you think you saw or heard but you are wrong jumping to a conclusion like that. We were mucking about, like you do as mates and that was all there was to it. I had nothing to do with his fall. I wasn't even there at the time. Besides, the police accepted my account.'

'I know what I saw. You two guys were going daggers at each other.'

'No, you are wrong, it was an accident.'

Gray spat hard on the ground. 'Oh yeah, whatever. You just stay out of my way.'

He moved over to where Phoenix's welding helmet lay and kicked it with all his might. It spun around and shot past Amy who, unbeknown to the two men, had returned. Clutching her cell phone, she called for assistance.

She quickly crossed over and shouted, 'Gray, you leave my site now. As for you Phoenix, report to my office immediately.'

A crowd gathered close to where they were standing.

Dropping his helmet and glasses at Amy's feet, Gray menacingly waved a fist in the air then yelled, 'Suits me lady.'

Amy looked frightened and Phoenix swiftly intervened placing himself between her and the madman. Gray's heavy punch to Phoenix's head sent him crashing into a pile of empty wooden pallets and then onto the floor.

Two men in suits and hard hats, who could only be management, arrived in time to escort Gray to the elevator. He kept shouting out Phoenix's name and making threats about getting even. Even from where Amy stood, she could see him thumping the call button as he waited for the ride down. One of the men attempting to calm him down was calling for security to alert the police.

Amy leant down to help Phoenix and was joined by a number of concerned workers. One of the supervisors was already calling for the first aider.

Crouching down next to Phoenix on the cold concrete, Amy shouted, 'Are you okay? Hold on there, help is on its way.'

Phoenix remained silent. It was obvious he was in pain with a head wound and needed help to get to his feet. Bright red blood ran down his face. He became unsteady leaving no time for anyone to prevent him from collapsing back onto the floor.

Amy screamed, 'Everyone stand back.'

Shaking her head in disbelief she realised Phoenix was now unconscious and was having trouble breathing. With the help of one of the welders, they rolled Phoenix onto his side to ensure his airway wasn't blocked. She then tried to stem the flow of blood from the wound with her scarf. Level fourteen became silent as everyone stopped working and came over to see if they could help.

Amy's blood-stained fingers punched the keys on her phone as she called the emergency services. 'We need an ambulance urgently to Horter Toby Construction, Madison East 40th.'

All the time she answered their questions, she became more concerned as she stared down at Phoenix's motionless body on the floor.

The company first-aider ran the last few yards and had to push through the crowd to attend to the injured man. 'They said it was a blow to the head and his name is Phoenix. How long has he been like this?'

Amy, who was showing signs of severe panic, struggled to get her words out, 'I don't know, three or four minutes. He hasn't moved for a while and his breathing doesn't look right.'

'How many times was he punched and did he hit his head on falling?'

'Not sure, it happened so quickly, I think it was one punch. Is he going to be okay?'

Amy whipped her coat off and went to cover Phoenix to keep him warm. The first-aider abruptly barked back at her. 'Jesus, don't cover him, I need to examine him. If you want to help me – stand back.'

He quickly established the pulse was there, but low. There was little colour in Phoenix's face and his complexion was a pasty grey. His breathing was shallow and, alarmingly, the pool of dark red blood was growing. The medic applied a dressing that instantly became soaked.

Someone shouted, 'God, is he still alive, he's not moving?'

Amy caught the look of concern on her colleague's face as he kept talking to Phoenix. 'Can you hear me, Phoenix? Don't go to sleep on me.' He raised his voice, 'Can you squeeze my hand? Hello Phoenix.'

One of the onlookers, who was kneeling on the concrete and had splashes of Phoenix's blood on his hands, looked up to Amy. 'Where's that ambulance got to? Do you have his details of next of kin? Is he married?'

'Yes, I've got it all in the office. I'll go and make the call. No, no I had better wait here until we get some help.'

It seemed an age before the paramedics arrived and they immediately set to work checking Phoenix's vitals, his airway and inserting a line in his arm. An oxygen mask was placed on his face while monitoring of his pulse and heart continued.

They struggled to lift Phoenix's two hundred and twenty pounds onto the blue padded stretcher. All the time they were talking to him repeating the same question, 'Can you hear me Phoenix?'

It was at this point Ethan, who'd been on his break, appeared on the scene. He rushed over to the stretcher and looked shocked as he saw his colleague's face. Amy informed him that an agency guy had attacked him.

'You'll have to ring his wife, Suzy. I've only got their home number, but she'll be at work. She works for Marcello Bay Cosmetics on West 34th.'

* * *

With the siren screaming, the ambulance sped across Manhattan squeezing past heavy traffic on its way to the hospital. The paramedic shouted into his handset, advising the five-minute ETA and reported on the worsening condition of their patient.

* * *

Back on the site there was much commotion as the anxious workers returned to their duties. Ethan was really upset with Amy for not allowing him to ride in the ambulance and kept asking if there was any news.

Meanwhile, Amy was on ground level in the main office and struggling to get hold of Suzy. With the phone glued to her ear, her works director was demanding to know what had occurred between the two men. As she waited to be connected, she related details of the incident. Her boss shook his head in disbelief on hearing one of their employees had been accused of murder. Amy explained that Phoenix had been totally open with them when he joined the company; there had been no issues. The allegation that Phoenix was responsible for his friend's death was preposterous.

Her boss said sternly, 'Well, we'll see what the police have to say about all of this. This is bad news for us. Why didn't you take control of the situation sooner?'

She put a hand in the air. 'Hold on, James, her office is putting me through.'

She took a deep breath and spoke calmly, 'Hello, is that Mrs Harrison? My name is Amy Morgan and I'm your husband's foreman. Yes, hello to you too. I'm calling you from his workplace. I don't want to alarm you but...'

Chapter 9

After what seemed the longest wait in Suzy's life, a medic entered the family waiting area. He stretched out his hand to welcome her and she immediately asked how her husband was.

He drew breath before speaking, having first removed his glasses to polish the smeared lenses on the fabric of his green, short-sleeved shirt.

'Well Mrs Harris, these things are never easy and…'

'Actually, it's Harrison. Can I see my husband?'

'I'm afraid not yet. He suffered a heavy blow to the head and is still unconscious. He's in a coma. When and if he wakes, and subject to the severity of the injury, we will be able to tell you more.'

Suzy shrieked, 'You just said, if he wakes.'

'I assure you Mrs Harrison we are doing everything in our power to help your husband. It's early days and you have to understand with this sort of injury we have to run the scans to decide on the best line of treatment. At present his body has gone into lockdown and the machines are taking over. He's in the critical care unit and, I have to be frank with you, at the moment it's not looking good.'

'But when will he wake up?'

'It can take hours or longer,'

'Define longer, are we talking days?'

Suzy's heart sank. The medic's emotionless face said all she needed to know that Phoenix was in a bad way.

He asked if she would like to ring a friend or family. There was no reply as she grasped her cell phone wondering who to ring first.

She chose Phoenix's son, Dale, who was devastated to hear her news. He told her he would be catching the first plane out from Orlando. Next, she rang her parents. She heard her father gasp, 'Oh no, not Phoenix.'

* * *

The following days were harrowing as Suzy and Dale kept vigil at Phoenix's bedside. It was disturbing seeing him lying so still with all the intravenous lines and equipment continually buzzing and bleeping. A ventilator was assisting his breathing and Suzy watched his ribcage rise and fall as the machine kept him alive. All the time she held his hand never wanting to let go. They were told that Phoenix's medical rating was at level one and referred to no eye, verbal or voluntary movement. Dale and Suzy weren't giving up and kept talking to him. They were convinced he heard every word.

Phoenix had lost his father at an early age, and now his mother had passed not long ago. Suzy was not aware of any other relatives. There were friends who she was attempting to contact, but for the meantime, the only visitors were the immediate family.

* * *

Dale, unlike his father, was super thin and a smart dresser. He wore an earring and his immaculately combed long hair was parted in the middle. His handsome, tanned face and high cheekbones reminded Suzy of her husband. Dale's work in the paper business, supplying reels of newsprint, saw him constantly travelling around America with little time for settling down and consequently he had never married.

Some time ago there had been a woman in his life but it didn't work out. For the last couple of years he had freewheeled with no intention of letting anyone back into his heart. That was until more recently when he met Tara. They fell in love in Rome and she soon moved into his home in Johnson Village, Orlando.

Just like Suzy, Dale kept talking to his father hoping he'd respond. He told him stories about Tara, saying how much he loved her. He was scared seeing him lying so still in the critical care department. He made it clear he was going to wait as long as it took for him to wake from the coma. A week had already passed and there had been no signs of improvement.

***

Evenings in the West Village apartment were long as the conversation invariably switched to Phoenix. There were numerous phone calls from friends and workplace colleagues who were genuinely concerned about him. Suzy spoke frequently with Elizabeth and Cameron who were devastated knowing how poorly their friend was.

Suzy deliberated on how exactly the fight had started. Had Phoenix upset this guy? All the girl from his site had said was that he'd been attacked and an enquiry was ongoing.

* * *

One evening, after returning from hospital, two detectives paid Suzy a visit. She was happy to answer their questions if it meant the culprit, the man who'd hurt her husband, was to be convicted.

Both men were seated on her sofa and she hoped they didn't notice the carpet that needed hoovering. Dale had promised to help with the housework but, after the tiring visits to the hospital, there were more important things to worry about. As she sat waiting for them to speak, she could hear her stepson in the kitchen talking on his phone to Tara.

Both men handed over their ID cards, putting Suzy at ease. She settled back into her chair and stared at the younger man in the dark suit who extracted a file from his bag.

'Once again, Mrs Harrison, we are sorry to hear about your husband. Has there been any better news this week and have you plenty of family around to support you?'

'Yes, my parents will soon be here and Phoenix's son is in the kitchen. And no, there is no change.'

'Well let's keep our fingers crossed. Now are you happy to help with our enquiries.'

Suzy nodded.

'Turning to the horrendous attack on your husband, I can confirm the man in question has been charged with assault. We were hoping you could throw light on the argument that led to the incident.'

'Well, not really as I hadn't even heard of him before the police told me his name. Does that maniac even know what he's done to my husband? Tell me, has he previous form?'

The detective rubbed the stubble on his face. He was either trying to grow a beard or had missed his morning shave. He shook his head and feebly said, 'I'm unable to comment.'

The other man kept looking around the room as if weighing up items for an inventory. When he did speak, he spoke quietly, 'I'm sure you appreciate that when your husband recovers and is ready, we will require a statement from him.' He paused for a moment as the clock on the mantelpiece noisily chimed eight o'clock. 'Now for the record, are you saying you never met Gray Wakeman?'

'I've already told you I never even heard of the guy.'

'He was from his old site.'

'Oh, I see.'

The next few questions upset Suzy. With Phoenix's recent illness, was he still suffering from stress and had he been seeing a psychiatrist? Was he on medication?

'Now hold on there, what has all this got to do with some maniac landing my husband in hospital? Yes, Phoenix suffered stress after losing a friend.'

'These questions are important and we understand it will be distressing for you. Your husband's attacker made a statement in which he alleges Phoenix was arguing with Cody O'Brien prior to the fall.'

Suzy was stunned to hear this and tried to choose her words carefully to avoid saying the wrong thing. 'Jesus, the guy is off his head. Did he say he actually saw my husband arguing? The suggestion is preposterous as the two men were close friends. Perhaps someone should tell him that the incident was classed as an accident, as I am sure you already know.'

'Yes, Mrs Harrison. This is a new line of information we have to follow up.'

'How dare this man say Phoenix had anything to do with Cody's death.'

'Returning to the attack, it would appear Phoenix and Wakeman were disagreeing on something. A Miss Amy Morgan, of Horter Toby Construction, has made a statement. She claims to have overheard their quarrel and the allegation of murder. Would you say your husband argues with many people Mrs Harrison?'

Suzy burst into tears and Dale entered the room.

Dale, now at Suzy's side, was furious to see his stepmother so upset. 'What in God's name is happening here?'

'And you are, sir?'

As Dale comforted Suzy, he confirmed his name and status.

Suzy held onto his arm really tightly. 'I can't believe what he just said, Dale. He said Phoenix killed Cody?'

'With respect, that is not what I said or implied. We are simply reporting back on statements received.'

'Are you mad? My dad wouldn't hurt a fly.'

The detective shuffled his large body on the sofa and tapped his pen on the file. 'I repeat I never said Mr Harrison killed anyone. We have to establish the facts.'

Dale was determined to bring the meeting to a close. 'I think if you have any further questions Mrs Harrison's lawyer should be present. You've obviously upset my stepmother, now please leave.'

Both men were apologetic stating they were only doing their job.

As Dale opened the apartment door for them to leave, he quietly said, 'Was all that necessary? You do know my dad's in a bad way and might even die.'

* * *

Once they had gone, Dale hugged Suzy telling her the man who attacked his father was clearly out of his mind. She wasn't listening as her mind played over the scene when Phoenix returned to the apartment on the day of Cody's death. His confusion over the text messages on her phone and the strange things he said still worried her. At the time, she questioned Phoenix's side of the story, but never believed he was covering up vital evidence. She would keep her thoughts to herself and focus on him waking up without any brain damage.

* * *

A month passed and every day in the hospital was depressingly the same. Spending their time between the family room and Phoenix's bed, they stared at the clock on the wall, willing a medic to enter their cramped space with better news.

Dale's company insisted that he take his holiday allowance, but even that was running out. His place was with his father, but soon the day would come when he would have to return to Orlando.

Every day they visited the hospital the routine was much the same as they stared at Phoenix's long dark hair that lay lank on the white sheet. His head was tilted to one side with the tubes and lines helping to keep him alive.

One morning they were asked to return to the lounge to meet with a consultant, a lady who was assigned to Phoenix's case. The middle-aged woman, in a skirt that was obviously unsuitably short for a hospital doctor, sat with her legs crossed on one of the red plastic chairs. Dale and Suzy hung on her every word.

'I know it must be a very upsetting time for you. The scan shows a small bleed to the brain that hopefully should correct itself. On the scale of one to fifteen the severity of the injury is around the eleven marker which is serious, but does not necessarily suggest brain damage.'

'Well, that is the first bit of good news,' stammered Suzy before adding that they would prefer the doctor to be upfront and not hold anything back.

The consultant continued, 'Phoenix remains in the coma and there have been no voluntary movements. We had hoped for signs of the odd jerk or reflex. Sometimes patients in this state move a hand but nothing at the moment. I have a theory that people in a coma do hear what we're saying, so I can't emphasise enough the importance of talking to him. My experience is they almost imperceptibly react when we speak to them.'

Dale gripped the side of his chair. 'We won't stop talking. My dad's a fighter. How long do you think it's going to be before he opens his eyes and wakes?'

The consultant frowned and Suzy instinctively knew there was more coming.

'Normally people wake within a few hours, some take a week or two, but we have passed that stage now. At week five your husband remains locked in the coma and medically, and I don't want you to be alarmed, we have to classify him at this point as being in a prolonged vegetative state.'

The consultant observed the look of horror on their faces and it was obvious she wished she'd phrased the news differently.

Dale grasped Suzy's hand and mouthed quietly, 'Vegetative! We're not giving up on my dad. He can't possibly be that far along the line.'

'You asked me to be upfront and I can only report on our findings. If it helps, I can tell you we have had patients with longer coma periods who finally woke and went on to lead perfectly normal lives. Others, sadly, suffer reduced memory and body functions. Most went on to undergo physiotherapy and occupational therapy.'

Suzy pushed her back hard into the chair and in an emotional voice said, 'If he comes out of this, what are his chances?'

Tight-lipped, the consultant spoke softly, 'I honestly don't know.'

Dale craned his neck to face Suzy and said, 'He's going to die, isn't he?'

* * *

Ethan, from the construction site, rang Suzy a number of times and, whilst she told him there was no news, he kept asking if he could visit the hospital. Her initial reaction was to say no as she didn't want anyone from his work visiting. All his problems evolved from working on those buildings, but this man wouldn't take the hint to back off. Although he was a friend of Phoenix, she'd never actually met him and just wished he'd go away and stop bothering her.

* * *

One Saturday morning Suzy was entering the hospital when a man stopped her. Momentarily she was taken aback as she stared at the scars on his cheeks and hands and wondered just what he wanted of her. She then observed his finely combed hair, smart black winter coat and scarf and immediately warmed to the gentle voice.

'I am sorry to disturb you – I'm Ethan, Phoenix's friend.'

'Oh… hello Ethan. We spoke on the phone, but how did you know what I looked like?'

'Oh, no great mystery, your husband showed me your photo often enough. I had a lot of time for him.'

'What do you mean had? He's not dead. Now if you don't mind, I'm late as it is.'

'Oh, I'm sorry I used the wrong word. I just want to see him. How's he doing this week?'

'Please leave us alone. Isn't it bad enough one of your mates did this to him?'

'He wasn't one of my mates; I never even met the guy. Give me a break; I'm genuinely concerned. I meant no harm coming here.'

Suzy barged past him and in a harsh voice said, 'You're not welcome, or anyone from that bloody site.'

She instantly regretted her outburst and struggled to understand how insensitive she'd been. The man was worrying about his friend and she was being over-protective blaming him just because he worked on the site. She had to make amends.

Ethan was clearly shocked and turned to leave. Suzy watched him heading down the steps and called out his name. He stopped to turn. She apologised and put out a hand of friendship.

'I'm sorry; I don't know what came over me. You must come up and see him, only prepare yourself as he doesn't look well.'

'Don't you go worrying lady; he's going to come through all of this. He's a fighter that one. We work at crazy heights in all sorts of weather. Phoenix must have told you I'm the joker, but I have to tell you that's just my way of coping. I also get scared.'

It was a vivid picture Ethan painted as she imagined how the men worked. Even if her husband recovered sufficiently, she vowed there was no way he was going back to that line of business.

They took the elevator and he chatted about his wife, Grace, who liked Phoenix when he had visited them. He related how he sent them a card to pass to their daughter who lost a baby in childbirth. Suzy's heart went out to Ethan. It just showed you had to look deeper than the scars on a face to detect a kind person.

As they entered the ward, Ethan pulled from his coat pocket a small box of candy and handed it to Suzy. 'This is from Grace and me.'

On entering the busy critical care unit, they walked past cubicles of desperately ill people being kept alive by machines. They had to wait for a moment as a medic and nurses rushed past them.

Ethan stopped in his tracks at the sight of Phoenix. Suzy watched him move to the bedside and lean over to hold his friend's limp hand.

When he moved away, he sighed, 'Oh, my God, I had no idea it was this bad. I can't get over how much weight he's lost. Can he hear me?'

Dale, who had just arrived, went over to introduce himself and put out his hand, 'I'm Phoenix's son, Dale, and you are?'

'I'm Ethan, a friend from work. Pleased to meet you. I'm sorry about your dad. I won't stay long.'

'Pleased to meet you and yes, he can hear you.'

Suzy explained that Dale was returning to Orlando that afternoon.

Ethan moved back to the bed and was talking quietly to Phoenix who was lying so still on the sterile white sheet. He glanced up at the monitors and then to the tubes and wires. With every bleep or noise from the machines he looked unsettled. It was obviously a disturbing experience for this man.

Dale urged Suzy to step outside the cubicle to chat. 'Shall I get rid of him? I'm not sure I like the look of him. Did you see the scars on his face?'

'No, leave him alone. He's a really kind-hearted man who has been good to your father. He just needs a little time, that's all.'

'Okay, as long as you are sure. Now, this afternoon when Elizabeth and Cameron come for the first time, do you think you will be able to cope with them being upset? I just wish I didn't have to go home today.'

'Yep, I'll be fine. You need to get back to Tara and that job of yours. You do know your Dad is very proud of you.'

'Do you really think he knows we are even here?'

She playfully punched him on his arm. 'Of course, he does. He's going to wake soon and you will be the first person I call. I'm going to give him all your love.'

They were interrupted by Ethan, 'I'll be off now. Best I leave it a while before contacting you again. Do you mind if I give you my e-mail address?'

Suzy pulled out her cell phone, swiped the front screen and up came her favourite picture of her husband. It was an image of him smiling, the one she'd taken on their tenth wedding anniversary. She tapped Ethan's details into her contacts list and then said goodbye to him.

Dale clung to Suzy saying he was unsure about leaving her. She pulled away and said, 'You have four hours until your flight and need to get going. How about

I leave you alone with your dad and I'll go over to the washroom.'

* * *

Later that afternoon, Elizabeth and Cameron arrived at the hospital and Suzy showed them in. As expected, they were shocked to see their friend so dangerously ill.

Suzy cradled Phoenix's hand and spoke softly, 'Elizabeth and Cameron are here to see you, darling. They say it's a lovely day outside and they've been to Macey's to do some shopping.'

Cameron leant over to talk to Phoenix and pulled up his sweater sleeve to reveal his father's watch. 'I feel, for the meantime, you should have this back. It will bring you luck. I'm going to leave it with Suzy.'

Suzy nodded and turned her attention to Phoenix. Gripping his hand, she studied his eyes for any sign of movement only to be disappointed. 'Squeeze my hand if you heard what Cameron said. He wants us to look after the watch.'

She then encouraged Elizabeth to sit down to talk to Phoenix.

'Hi Phoenix, I have to tell you things have been busy with that new job of mine. You know I'm working for the library services; well I'm not enjoying it. They have some strange guys running distribution and the place is a mess and I'm thinking...'

She was interrupted by Suzy who raised her voice. 'He blinked. I definitely saw him move his eye. Quick Cameron, press that buzzer, we need a medic.'

The young man grabbed the lead and was about to push the large red button when one of the male nurses came in to check the monitors and print off data.

Suzy was relieved to see him and excitedly explained there was movement in the patient's left eye.

'Was it just the once or were there any other voluntary movements you noticed?'

'Not sure, but something was definitely happening with his eye. I saw the lashes move, then he blinked. Is he about to wake up?'

The nurse shook his head and his vague response worried Suzy.'

'Why don't you believe me? Look, I want to see someone more senior.'

The disgruntled nurse frowned and it took a few minutes until an examination of Phoenix's head and hands took place. The young doctor explained that sometimes there was the odd jerk or eyelids appearing to crease. In this case he was not convinced it was a sign of the patient waking.

'Well, I think you are wrong. Why don't you believe me? He definitely moved his eyelid What more can I say?'

The medic nodded his head. 'I assure you we will observe your husband continually and no-one will be more pleased than me to give you better news. I'm sorry, but I have to go.'

When Elizabeth and Cameron decided to leave, Suzy studied Phoenix's face for a long period, not daring to glance away for fear of missing another sign that he was on the mend.

At the end of her stay she kissed his cold cheek and went on to brush his hair away from his face. Her parting words were, 'I know you're trying to talk to me and I'm listening. And don't worry about Cody's watch as it's safe with me. When you are better you can give it back to Cameron. I'll be off now; I'll see you tomorrow. Lots of love darling.'

Chapter 10

On the day that Suzy's company was selecting a new advertising agency, she kept checking her cell phone for messages from the hospital. They had promised to contact her if there was any change in Phoenix's condition.

Seated in the boardroom, Suzy reluctantly switched her phone to silent. Four major New York agencies had been selected to pitch for their account. One of the companies involved was her old employer who was anxious to retain the business. The brief was to demonstrate a unique plan for boosting product awareness and sales. Two new ranges of mascaras were scheduled to be marketed in the UK for the first time.

Suzy was pleased that her boss, Diana Sorrows, head of marketing, was determined not to award the three-year contract to her old company who would be the last to pitch. Diana's doubts on their suitability were down to their recent air of complacency. There was also a long-standing issue on spiralling production costs and low rebates.

With this bit of information swimming around Suzy's head, she told herself that there was the distinct possibility her old boss, Logan, would finally be history. Whilst he acted professionally when he visited her company, she continued to hate the man who treated her so badly.

Suzy was responsible for branding, but not for the ultimate decision on awarding the contract and she hoped Logan's team fell short in their presentation pitch. The icing on the cake would be if he made a mess of delivering his precious thirty minutes of show time. She knew his strengths and weaknesses and hoped there would be tricky questions for him to address. Logan was known for winging presentations. Casting her mind back to her old job and the number of large clients she'd won, wasn't it him who always stole the limelight? It was payback time for the little shit.

When the presentation started, she was surprised not to see Logan there. There were some old faces she recognised from his company and she enquired after him. The reply that came back was that he wasn't available. In his place was Debbie Cohen who was a real go-getter. Suzy panicked as her presentation skills may well impress the board members with their suitability to hang onto the account.

Suzy could sense they were warming to this woman as she delivered her powerful message that included storyboards and mock TV advertisements. They planned on attracting the younger generation with web messaging teasers. Suzy feared the meeting was going too well.

* * *

With all the presentations completed, there was a directors' meeting and a decision would be reached before the end of the day. Suzy returned to her office to check for any messages from the hospital. Still no news.

Her afternoon was spent working on the weekly sales stats and a meeting with the packaging team. A new company logo was being planned and Suzy knew she would be expected to work with the new advertising agency. This would involve many meetings. She prayed it wouldn't be with Logan.

She glanced at her watch and was surprised to see how late it was and wondered where the time had gone.

As she left for the hospital, she remembered she'd missed lunch and felt hungry. She decided to stop at a gas station to grab a coffee and a candy bar. On the way down to the car lot, her cell phone rang.

Flustered, and in a hurry to get going, she made an effort to speak calmly, 'Hi Dale, yes I'm fine, how are you? I'm just off there now. Can I give you a call later?'

She drove up the ramp onto the busy road. The traffic edged forward slowly and she turned on the radio for company. It took twenty minutes before she reached the gas station.

Once she'd filled up the tank and paid, she set off again. She searched for a place to park up. With the dim overhead light on, she munched on her candy bar and sipped the scorching hot coffee from the cardboard cup. The jarring sound of her cell phone made her jump and she struggled to place the drink in the dashboard cup holder. It was her boss, Diana.

'Hi Suzy, I'm sorry to disturb you. Are you at the hospital?'

'No, not yet, I'm having a bite first. What's up?'

Diana's excited voice left Suzy wondering what she wanted.

'I've just come out of the meeting with our CEO and thought you'd like to know which agency we've picked. Well, it's Steven Mayors Associates. They were steps ahead of your old company. How about that for good news?'

Suzy was elated. At last Logan was off the scene and it sounded like the best deal had been secured.

'Wow, that's great. Now I'd better set off or I'll be late for visiting. I really must go, Diana.'

'Hold on there, just a moment. I saved the best bit for last. Logan Mansen is the man who will be heading up the team at the new agency we've picked; isn't that awesome?'

Suzy was devastated to hear the mention of his name. 'Sorry, did you say Logan Mansen – do I read you right? Doesn't Logan still work for my old place? He wasn't at the meeting today so couldn't make the pitch.'

In a triumphant voice Diana went on. 'That's right; he doesn't work for them anymore. It turns out he left two months ago and has been on garden leave. He must have had a short-term contract with his employer as it's normally six months.'

Suzy sighed loudly.

Her colleague continued. 'It seems Steven Mayors has hired him. It means we have a top guy batting for us. Logan is a gentleman and for a man of his age, he's a right looker.'

Suzy couldn't believe what she was hearing. Good looking and gentleman, definitely not!

Diana added, 'I just talked with him on the phone. He spoke highly of you Suzy. You two will be seeing a lot more of each other. You must be pleased.'

Suzy was silently fuming and thumped the dashboard with her hand.

'What was that noise, are you still there?'

Choking on her words, she managed to reply, possibly too abruptly, 'Y… y… yes, I'm here. I really must go now.'

She swore loudly as she emptied the coffee down the sidewalk gutter. Was there no end to the anguish Logan brought to her life? But now she had to get a grip of things and remain calm. Counting backwards from ten she relaxed her taught fingers before taking a deep breath.

Combing her hair in the poor overhead light, she applied perfume, then put on the seat belt and started the engine to make the short journey to the hospital.

It was an easy drive and her thoughts were on seeing Phoenix. She allowed herself a moment to acknowledge how ridiculously she had reacted to Diana's news. Logan had jumped ship to work in a rival agency and they'd won the business – end of. Putting it all into perspective, work was work, and she had more important matters to attend to. Looking forward to her husband recovering was all that mattered.

When she arrived at the hospital and told Phoenix her news, she would have to watch he didn't detect worry in her voice. He may still be trapped in his coma, but he could hear her every word. He always knew when something was worrying her. Well, not this time.

Chapter 11

There was only one person present on the day Phoenix started to wake from the coma, and that was Dale. And he was likely to be the only visitor for a while. Suzy's parents had returned home, but he was sure they would be coming back to the hospital when he called them with his news.

Tears streamed down his face as he held his father's hand encouraging him to open his eyes again. The ventilator had been removed, the tube had gone and Phoenix was breathing by himself. The process of waking up seemed glacial as the hours passed before further movements of the eyes and face were detected.

Dale was relieved that at long last something was happening, but he was also hurting so desperately inside. Burying his stepmother last week had been soul destroying. He'd lost a wonderful friend and his father had yet to learn that his wife, Suzy, had died.

He cursed God for taking Suzy.

On the evening her company selected the new advertising agency, Suzy drove to the hospital and was only a few blocks away when a trucker shot a red light and collided with her car. She had died at the scene. There was nothing the paramedics could do to save her life as the fire services cut her from the tangled wreck.

The police had found Dale's number on Suzy's cell phone and contacted him. He jumped on the first plane back to New York. The following day her parents arrived and it was agonising sharing their grief. It was hard to take in that they wouldn't be seeing Suzy again. The world had indeed tumbled again for this family. How many more shocks could they take? Everyone at the hospital who looked after Phoenix was stunned to hear about Suzy.

* * *

The previous week on a bitterly cold winter morning, the funeral was held at the Mt Olivetti Cemetery. There were so many mourners at the graveside as they lowered Suzy's white casket into the ground. It was the saddest of days with so many well-wishers and meaningful tributes being paid. Suzy was a much loved and popular person. Her parents were beside themselves at losing their daughter. Marlene broke down and wept loudly on her husband's shoulder.

During the service Dale stood up at the front to address the packed church. As he began to speak his eyes strayed to the slim, white wooden casket with the photograph of Suzy balanced on top. Memories flooded back of happier times when the three of them took holidays in Florida and the UK. During his college days his stepmother had always been there for him and she'd been so proud on his graduation day. She was thrilled when he met Tara. In Dale's mind, Suzy was the mother he never had, and now he'd lost her.

The saddest thing was his father was not at the funeral. He was still lying with his head to one side and the nurses keeping watch on his progress. Hopefully, the frequency of his eyes blinking was increasing and the waking up process would speed up.

Was he dreaming of Suzy or had he heard their whispers and already knew of the tragedy? There was no-one today to keep him company and this saddened Dale. It scared him to think that the day would soon come when his father would wake and be asking for her. How would he answer him?

After the service Dale tried to comfort Elizabeth and handed back Cody's watch to her son. Earlier that morning he'd read the inscription on the back plate *'Happiness is just a moment away.'* At this particular moment there was no happiness, just sadness.

It must have been a heart-breaking visit for Elizabeth and Cameron coming back to the graveyard, as it was here that they brought Cody to his final resting place. His white marble stone was visible from where they were burying Suzy. Later they crossed over to lay a single rose on the grave and Dale heard Elizabeth's sobbing.

Standing in the freezing cold wind there were many people from Suzy's workplace who said kind things to the family. They were aware that the next funeral was about to take place and it was time to leave. There would be no reception to attend as Dale and Suzy's parents were anxious to get back to the hospital.

As the mourners started to thin out, a man in a smart, long, black, winter coat and scarf spoke with Dale. He held a black hat in both hands and spoke kindly, 'I just wanted to pay my respects and say sorry for your loss.'

Dale was unsure who this stranger was. 'Did Suzy work with you in advertising?'

'Yes, that's right, it was a while ago; I had a lot of time for her. She was on fast track to the big time and I admired her tenacity in getting things done. She was a natural and I only regret not telling her how good she was. I hadn't seen her for a while and heard the awful news through the grapevine. I also learnt from an old colleague about your father. Is there any news?'

'No, I'm afraid not, but I really must see the parents into the cars. It was a pleasure meeting you.'

'The same to you. Here is my card, please keep me informed on Phoenix. If there is anything I can do to help, please don't hesitate to give me a bell.'

Dale warmed to the kind man and made a mental note to drop him an e-mail to update him on his father.

As Dale turned to walk over to Marlene and Donald, he flipped the card over and read the name: Logan Mansen. He was puzzled – who was Logan? Then he recalled Suzy once confiding in him about a crazy man, with the same name, who made her life hell and how she hated him. He bent the card in half and cursed the beast of a man who dared to attend her funeral.

As Dale got closer to the cars, unbeknown to Donald and Marlene, he overheard them talking. Donald was venting his anger. 'I can't come to terms with having our princess snatched away from us. Why didn't Phoenix die from his injuries and not Suzy? If he hadn't got into a fight none of this would have happened. He wouldn't have been in hospital and she wouldn't have been in the wrong place at the wrong time.'

Donald helped Marlene into the funeral home car and encouraged Dale to join them. Dale said he needed time on his own and wandered off through the graveyard to stand by his stepmother's grave where the process of filling in the hole had started. It was too distressing to watch so he said a short prayer and hurried away to return to the hospital.

Chapter 12

Dale's company was showing signs of impatience with the amount of time he'd had off. His plan was to return to Orlando directly after going to see his father in hospital. He was of the opinion that if push came to shove, he'd resign from his post. He'd contact the real estate manager and give them notice on the house. Then he'd speak with Tara about joining him to live in New York. They would rent an apartment whilst he searched for work.

Marlene and Donald vowed to stay as long as it took for Phoenix to recover and live in the apartment. They were having a hard time coping with losing their daughter and now this added responsibility of caring for her husband was testing. They couldn't get used to the idea that Suzy was gone. They talked over the nightmare scenario of Phoenix waking and being incapacitated then needing all round care. Would he even recall who Suzy was?

Only time would tell and the stress levels for them would be challenging. The one certain thing was that Phoenix was going to need a lot of care with the lion's share falling on his son's shoulders.

Telling Phoenix his wife had died would inevitably be hard, that's if he fully understood. Without Suzy, how would he get on and who would nurse him through his convalescence? The other worrying factor was how they were they going to pay for all the hospital treatment or anything else that followed? Suzy's parents wished there were relatives of Phoenix to call on, but there weren't.

* * *

November tripped into December as Phoenix still remained in the coma. There had been signs of waking but these were put down to false alarms. Marlene and Donald still continued with their support. They made it clear to Dale that they needed to spend time back home in Ohio. They had already effectively cancelled Christmas at home to spend the break supporting Dale and his father.

One rainy afternoon they arrived at the hospital and took the elevator to level six. As they sanitised their hands before going in, one of the medics they'd grown to like and trust, had some promising news for them. Excited, they had hoped to see Phoenix propped up in bed and asking where was he. On the contrary, he was in his usual position lying completely still. The nurses were taking his vitals and monitoring stats. Apparently, there had been infrequent wrist jolts as well as slight eye movements. Donald knew he should have called Dale but hung back. He first wanted to check if there was sufficient progress before making the call to Orlando.

As the day drew to a close, Marlene noticed a shuddering from Phoenix's shoulder and alerted Donald. She spoke softly to Phoenix. 'Are you waking up? This is Marlene here – squeeze my hand if you can hear me.'

To her delight there was the gentlest touch to her fingers and a sudden flick of his wrist but then nothing. One of the nurses, a young woman with a blue tattoo of a butterfly on her hand, examined Phoenix and shone a light in his eyes. She smiled and nodded back to them. She left to fetch a medic and suddenly there was a lot of activity around the bedside as checks were made on their patient.

Still he remained motionless and the medical team looked concerned as they gazed at the monitors checking for any change in heartbeat and respiration. They were talking quietly and this worried Donald and Marlene.

'Is there something wrong?' asked Donald in a nervous voice.

One of the medics touched him on the shoulder. 'No, I think we are okay, it's often like this as they wake. Don't be frightened. Why don't you and your wife wait in the lounge while we check Phoenix out? We'll call you back in as soon as we've finished.'

'What's wrong?'

'Please don't be alarmed, everything is under control; just give us a moment to sort out a few things.'

Donald noticed him shaking his head as he gave instructions to his team. He knew there were problems and shuddered with the thought that this may be the end for Phoenix.

They were encouraged to leave with a nurse called Piper and walked along the sterile white corridor with the green strip half way up the wall. Donald squeezed his wife's hand while she talked to the nurse. She was close to tears. 'I don't know how much more of this we can take. We lost our daughter recently.'

'Yes, I know and I am so sorry. I can't begin to imagine your grief. Let me make some coffee and we can talk.'

Donald pulled out his cell phone and had trouble getting a signal.

'Oh, no, not again. Why is it every time I need to make a call, I get a problem here? Hold on – now I have four bars, no three ...'

He swiped the speed dial number for Dale and it took a while for him to pick up.

'Hi Dale. No, I'm not out of breath, I'm fine. We are going to need you here as your father is waking. Get your flight booked. Love to Tara.'

* * *

It was early evening before there was any news. Phoenix's slow heartbeat had been an issue and was now resolved. Arm and facial movements had been more frequent and he was finally breathing on his own without the aid of the machine. He was even starting to react to commands. Donald and Marlene were still not allowed to see him before one of the team chatted to them.

It was a senior medic, someone they'd never met before, a tall Indian man with smart, short hair accompanied by protruding cheekbones. He spoke softly with a New York accent and listened to their concerns.

'Thank you for waiting so long, which I know must have been upsetting for you. The good news is that Phoenix is out of danger. There were concerns over his heart but he is doing without the ventilator and I...'

Marlene interrupted. 'And his heart.'

'Yes, that is all normal now. He is quite stable.'

'Can we see him?'

'First let's chat more about the process of waking. We will have to monitor him for brain damage that might affect memory recall and full use of his limbs. Let's hope none of these things are relevant, but there is something else that concerns me.'

'Surely there can't be more.'

'Phoenix will inevitably at first be confused and unable to focus properly. He'll be very tired and you guys will only be able to stay a while.'

'Please, can we see him now?'

120

'Be prepared for him to ask where his late wife is. You may have to ignore his questions or just go for it. Either way, we have to limit the strain on him. Would you like to speak with our Father Larry Johnson before you go in? He's a great guy who is used to this sort of thing.'

Donald sucked in breath. 'Sure, he's going to ask where Suzy is. However, his son is on the way and it's down to him to make that call. Thanks for the offer to talk to someone, we would appreciate that.'

* * *

Twenty minutes passed before they finally met up with the hospital priest who was just about to go home. As they began to speak, Donald took a call from Dale.

'Any news on that flight? It's a pivotal moment for your dad. That's great, we'll see you tomorrow.'

The advice the priest gave was to be honest with the patient, but to choose the right moment. He said a small prayer for Phoenix and one for Marlene and Donald. He offered to see them again when he was next on duty.

When they were finally shown in to see Phoenix there was a marked change in him. He was wriggling the fingers on his left hand and there was much fluttering of eyelashes. They tried to talk to him but it was evident he was not fully awake. Suzy's parents felt worn out and after saying goodnight to Phoenix, made their way out of the building to take the subway back to the apartment. They chatted on the way about eventually easing off with the visits, but not until Dale was ready to take over.

* * *

Sunday turned to Monday and they were back again at the hospital. This time they were in for a surprise as Phoenix had his eyes partly open and was staring at the ceiling. He was trying to form words only the croaky sound was difficult to understand. There was considerable movement in his hands as the fingers bent and straightened as if trying to grasp something. His body appeared to shake and then he remained as still as when he'd been in the coma.

'Hello Phoenix, it's Donald and Marlene here. How are you feeling?'

Phoenix's face screwed up as if he was in pain and his mouth emitted a strange growling sound that went on for at least five seconds. He was dribbling and Donald patted the wet lips with a wipe. Phoenix's head jerked away with the horrible sound returning for a few moments.

'Come and sit here,' pleaded Marlene.

Donald joined his wife lowering his heavy body onto the plastic chair.

'It's roasting in here; I need some air.'

* * *

Marlene moved over to the bed and spoke slowly to Phoenix, 'Talk to me and squeeze my hand to let me know you are okay.'

She jumped away from him when he spoke in a gravelly voice that was just about audible.

'Who are you? I can't see you properly.'

'I'm Marlene, your mother-in-law. Donald is my husband, only he's just stepped out.'

122

There was a pause before Phoenix spoke again. He was frantically rubbing his eyes in an effort to focus and waved a hand in front of Marlene's face which frightened her.

'I don't know you.'

She remained silent and moved away from the bed.

A medic, a large black woman with short, curly hair, was now on the scene and instructing Phoenix to lay his head back and take gentle breaths.

She spoke quietly to Marlene. 'I think we may need to ask you to let him rest as he is very weak. It will all take time.'

Marlene joined her husband who stood in the doorway. He was surprised and frightened to see Phoenix thrashing around on the bed. Two nurses desperately tried to settle him to avoid him pulling out the tubes. They checked the bedside guards were secured.

'I can't see; everything is blurred. Tell that awful woman to go. Where am I? Please tell me, where am I?'

The doctor urged the couple to leave and suggested they come back later in the day. He leant over the bed and gently spoke, 'There's no need to be frightened. You are in hospital and I'm just going to make you more comfortable.'

'What's happening to me?'

'You suffered a blow to the head and have been in a coma. Soon you will be able to see properly. It will take a while for your eyes to adjust to the light – now please try to relax. It's harder to breathe when you are upset. We are going to give you something to make you sleep. Keep that arm down please.'

In a sleepy voice Phoenix said, 'Me in hospital –
what happened…?'

A few seconds later he was fast asleep. The nurses
made sure he was safe and that a regular watch was kept
on him.

He would soon learn Suzy wouldn't be coming in
to see him, and if he fully understood what he'd been
told, his heart would be broken.

* * *

When Donald and Marlene met Dale at the airport, he
was pleased to hear his father was at long last awake. He
acknowledged there would be teething problems with
eyesight and memory. He was disturbed to hear them say
his father had a memory block and saw them only as
strangers. Would he even remember Suzy? It was agreed
he would eventually have that important son to father
chat.

Driving rain thundered down on the taxi and Dale
mentioned, in his haste to leave, he had forgotten his
winter coat and would have to buy a new one the next
day. Donald lent him his scarf.

When Dale arrived at the hospital, Phoenix had
been moved to a recovery room and was propped up in
bed shielding his eyes with a hand. There were less tubes
and much of the equipment had been removed. His voice
had vastly improved and one of the nurses had tied back
his hair. Dale was amazed to see the improvement in his
father.

He prayed he'd know it was him. 'Dad it's me.
Can you see me?'

The reply was slow in coming and croaky in its delivery. 'My eyes are better than yesterday but still blurry. I should be out of here soon. Who did you say you were?'

Dale tried again. 'It's your son, Dale. Dad it's me.'

Phoenix had a few attempts to speak while he cleared his throat. 'Is it really you Dale? I've been so frightened and think I'm going out of my mind. I can't understand what's happened to me.'

'I'm here now and going to look after you.'

He squeezed his father's arm. 'You've had a blow to the head and been unconscious for ages, that's why you are in hospital.'

'How long have I been here?'

'You were in a coma for nearly four months. I've been so worried about you and have been waiting for you to wake. Marlene and Donald have been incredible helping out; I don't know what I'd have done without them. They were here when you came out of the coma.'

'The lady yesterday you mean. No, I don't know her.'

'Dad, you are still a bit confused. Marlene is Suzy's mother.'

Dale ground his teeth as he realised he'd mentioned Suzy's name and there was every chance the subject would now switch to where she was.

'Now son, you say I was in some sort of an accident. Was it a car accident?'

'No, someone thumped you at work. Do you remember anything about an argument?'

'Not sure, I can't think about things without getting mixed up. I don't even know what sort of work I do. You'll have to help me with that one. And why would anyone hit me? I can't have lost my memory because I remember you.'

'The doctor says you are doing well and memory problems are often for just a short while. They will do more scans and, with luck, a few days from now you'll be back home. You won't be returning to work for some time though.'

He lightened the conversation saying how much weight he'd lost being in hospital.

'I suppose so, but tell me son, what was my job?'

'You worked on the scrapers, welding up high.'

'See, I can't remember that, but I do know I have a lovely wife. I'm sure Suzy has had a rough time with me being in here for so long. I can't wait to see her. I know she's busy with that new job of hers. She will be coming in soon, won't she? She does know I'm out of the coma?'

Dale's eyes welled up and he acknowledged it was time. 'Give me your hand, Dad. I want you to be strong as there is something I need to tell you.'

'You two haven't split, have you? Tara sounded a great girl.'

Dale was amazed he'd remembered his girlfriend's name.

'No, it's not about Tara and me. It's your wife, Suzy.'

Phoenix lowered his head onto the pillow and pulled on his son's hand.

'Suzy's been in a terrible car accident and…'

'Oh my God, is she in this hospital? I have to see her. Help me up son. Do you know where she is?'

Tears were streaming down Dale's face as he forced the words out. 'Dad, she died. I am so sorry.'

'No, it can't be true! Please tell me I'm back in that coma. Not Suzy.'

The screams that followed were so loud that a number of medical staff rushed in and Dale put an arm in the air. 'Give us a few moments.'

Phoenix kept crying and wouldn't be drawn into conversation. Dale waited patiently for his father to speak and when he did it was a jumble of words and a return to his weeping.

Dale tried to console him and was surprised when he finally said, 'You'll have to get me out of here for her funeral.'

'Dad, that was some time ago. You were still in the coma.'

'You are telling me I wasn't even there to say goodbye to my wife. Leave me now as I need to be alone. I just lost the most beautiful lady and my heart feels like it's broken in two. There's no point in my life without her. Did they find the other driver? You say it was a car accident. Why did God take her from me? She was so young, so pretty, my Suzy.'

Dale stood outside in the corridor. He leant his head against a wall and tried desperately to hide his crying. As he walked to the lounge, he took a call from Tara. From the tone of his voice when he greeted her it was clear that he'd had a bad time telling his father the news.

* * *

For two days Phoenix went into mourning, refusing to see anyone. He kept saying how wonderful Suzy was and wished he could have just one day with her to say how sorry he was.

He had been moved to a private room on the east wing of the hospital and was able to use the bathroom on his own. His vision had improved and he was in better shape. He even surprised Dale saying he knew who Donald and Marlene were. This information came as some relief to Dale as they had kindly offered to help out when Phoenix left the hospital.

* * *

The countdown for going home was not far off. Although there had been a small bleed in the brain, the latest scans were encouraging. Phoenix was still confused and lacked confidence. The hospital wanted assurance that there would be someone with him twenty-four seven for the first two weeks. He would also be referred to the memory clinic. Dale used all of his savings to pay the hospital bill. Phoenix never enquired about how this had been settled.

Dale's plan was to spend the first week with his father and he was eternally grateful to Donald and Marlene who would stay with him for a while longer. However, they did make it clear they had to get back to their life in Ohio. They were finding it hard to cope looking after a grown man who was acting strangely most of the time. They had lowered their finances by flying over so many times and Dale was thankful for all their support. It was only fair they called a halt as Phoenix was not even their child; in fact, he was only five years younger than themselves.

Ethan rang the apartment and was pleased Phoenix was now on the mend. Dale didn't have the heart to tell his father his friend had called as he probably wouldn't remember him.

Just before Phoenix was to be discharged from hospital, Elizabeth and Cameron visited but they became upset as he clearly didn't know who they were.

'I'm really sorry, but do I know you?'

'That's all right; I'm Elizabeth and this is my son Cameron. My best friend was Suzy and we are devastated by what has happened.'

On hearing her name, he turned away from them; a tear made its way down his face. 'It feels like the end of my world. I miss her so much.'

'We all miss her. Look Phoenix, we are going to leave now but I just want you to know we are thinking of you. We will visit when you've settled in at home. We've been friends for many years and we'll be there for you. I know Cody would have wanted us to do that.'

'Sorry the memory is not that good, who's Cody?'

'You know Cody; he was your friend, my husband.'

'Oh, I see. I can't recall him. You and your son are being really kind to me and your Cody sounds like a good guy. Why not bring him in some time?'

Cameron put out a hand and touched his mother's shoulder and said, 'We should be off now, Mum.'

Just as they were leaving Dale offered to show them out and Cameron whispered, 'Do... do we have to tell him my father has also died. Won't that finish the poor guy off?'

Dale bit his lip and replied, 'No, I'll tell him, but not just yet. We gotta take one day at a time. Thanks for coming and I'll give you a bell when he's settled in.'

Dale returned to the room. His father was now sitting in a chair and staring down at the floor. 'It wasn't too much for you seeing visitors today, was it?'

'Yes and no. Did that lady say her husband's name was Cody?'

Dale nodded.

Phoenix's terrified voice rang out, 'I know who he is. He was my friend who worked on the site. The man's dead and I was unable to stop him going over the edge. God, I'm in a real mess. I don't remember Elizabeth or her son, but Cody, yes he's there in my mind and I've now got to accept he's also gone.'

Dale moved over to his father to comfort him.

'Hold me, Dale, and please just don't let go.'

* * *

On the morning Phoenix was to be discharged, a police officer asked to see him. Dale was present and could sense his father was unsettled. All the time he was talking, Phoenix ran his fingers through his long hair that he'd refused to tie back.

'I am pleased to see you are recovering well and won't hold you up any longer than necessary. We have had to wait until you were out of danger before asking a few questions.'

'What sort of questions?'

Looking down at some notes in his book the officer said, 'Nothing to be concerned about, sir. I only want to keep you informed of recent matters referring to the case on Cody O'Brien who, as we know, sadly died from a fall. The case was reopened following an allegation from a Gray Wakeman who claims he witnessed you arguing with Mr O'Brien on the morning of his death.'

'I don't know this guy you are talking about.'

The officer tried again, 'He was the guy who attacked you, sir. Do you not remember him?' How about you tell me what the row was about with your friend?'

Dale intervened. 'He's still suffering with loss of memory, is this really necessary?'

'We are just trying to get a handle on events that led up to the incident. Please be assured the inquest was satisfied that the company safety and health practices were in order. The death was registered as accidental. With this new evidence from Mr Wakeman, we have to follow up all leads.'

Phoenix snapped, 'I don't know why that man hit me, and no, I wasn't arguing with my mate. It was banter and if only I had been present, I might have been able to save him, but I wasn't.'

'I fully understand that, sir, but I'm only doing my job. So, you have nothing to add.'

'No, nothing. But you can tell me what's happening to this guy. Is he locked up? He can't go attacking people and get away with it. You guys ought to be out there making sure he goes down for a long stretch.'

'He was convicted of assault.'

'I can't even remember him attacking me.'

'When are you going home, sir?'

With a puzzled look on his face Phoenix said, 'Not sure – when is it son?'

Dale frowned. 'I keep telling you it's this afternoon. You look tired, so I think I'll ask your visitor to leave.'

As the police officer turned to go, he said, 'I wish you all the best and a return to good health. You must be looking forward to getting back home and seeing your wife.'

Phoenix rushed out of the room and Dale followed leaving the confused man wondering what he could possibly have said to cause such a reaction.

Chapter 13

Settling back into the apartment was never going to be easy for Phoenix. Time dragged as memories of Suzy flooded back leaving only sadness as his closest companion. For the first week Dale planned to stay with him before Marlene and Donald took over. After that he hoped his father would be able to cope on his own.

Phoenix's initial problems with long-term memory were mostly short lived; however, he was still unable to recall attending Cody's funeral. He was keen to see Elizabeth and Ethan again and Dale was happy to know he had friends looking out for him.

Grieving for Suzy would continue for a very long time and everywhere Phoenix turned in the apartment there were reminders of her – photographs, clothes, makeup and toothbrush – everything just as she'd left it. It felt like she had only popped out for a few moments and would return shortly. He was grief-stricken and talking to her continually as he went from one room to another. On one occasion, he hung out her work clothes and on realising his mistake returned them to the closet.

There was so much to do in paying bills and chasing up Suzy's life assurance. Phoenix's chances of returning to work any time soon were remote. With no pay check coming in he knew he would need to look for a smaller place to live.

At the end of the first week of being home, he was anxious to visit Suzy's grave and Dale made sure he was wrapped up warm. The weather was awful and when they arrived at the cemetery gates they queued as a funeral car slowly drove up the narrow road towards the mourners who must have been wet through.

'Nearly there, Dad. Are you going to be okay?'

Phoenix nodded vigorously. 'I have to be. I've come to pay my respects to Suzy. I keep asking why did this have to happen to me? I blame myself for what happened to her. If only I'd not been in hospital.'

'What do you mean? Come on, Dad, you couldn't have loved her any more than you did and still do.'

Phoenix's bottom lip was trembling as he confided in Dale. 'There are things you don't know about, like all my problems at work, and me not happy with her being in that advertising agency. The poor woman went through hell with her boss. His name is coming to me; now just give me a second. Oh yeah... it's Logan and one day he won't know what's hit him. The guy sucks.'

Dale hesitated before replying as he recalled the smart man at the funeral and wondered just what went on.

'That's terrible. Did you ever meet him?'

'No, but I know where he works.'

'Best you put all of that behind you; it won't help one bit if you have a go at this guy. He wasn't responsible for Suzy's death and the last thing you want is the police knocking on your door.'

'I suppose so, but just remember son, what goes around, comes around.'

'Give me strength. If I had a dime for every time you've said that, I'd be a millionaire.'

'Oh yeah, well you have to understand how I feel.'

Dale switched his attention to starting up the motor. 'Here we go. I'll park up in that space. You will need to come under my umbrella as I don't want you getting wet.'

'Tell me Dale; is this the same place Cody's buried?'

'Yes, but let's make this our day for visiting Suzy and come back some other time to show you his grave.'

As Dale helped him out of the car, the persistent rain was already wetting their coats. He opened the rear door and pulled out the roses for Phoenix to place on the grave. They walked slowly and Dale glanced over to the hearse and funeral home men who were wheeling a black casket on a trolley. He kept talking to his father telling him to watch out in case he slipped on the wet ground.

The grass was long and muddy and was soaking their shoes. Dale's eyes scanned the graveyard trying to remember where Suzy was buried. He suddenly came to a halt at a sad mound of earth with a puddle on the top. It was upsetting seeing the dead flowers that lay strewn across the muddy grass. His attention was drawn to the tiny wooden cross with the blue bow that lay at an angle.

Phoenix stared blankly down to his wife's final resting place and at her name on the metal plate. When he finally looked up to Dale, there were tears in his eyes.

'I can't bear to think of her in the dark, all cold and alone down there in a box. Why did you bury her? She particularly stated she wanted to be cremated. It wasn't her wish to be buried. You've let me down big time.'

'How was I to know that? There was no mention in her will of instruction for cremation. We were dealing with a tragedy and I was doing my best. I'm really sorry.'

'Why didn't you tell me about her will? What else haven't you told me? I knew her wishes and I can assure you it wasn't to end up in this awful place.'

'But you were out of it Dad. The funeral was when you were still in the coma. And, just for the record, I did show you the will.'

Phoenix leant down, ignoring his coat that was trailing in the sodden ground. He placed the bright red roses on the raised earth having first pushed the old flowers to one side. Straightening the cross, he patted the wet earth with his hands.

Phoenix's sorrowful voice competed with the heavy sound of rain on the umbrella. 'This is no place for a lady and I wish it was me down there.'

Dale grimaced and helped him stand up, then scooped up the blooms that had perished on the cold cemetery ground. He glanced at the wording on one of the cards that was protected by a plastic wrapper 'All my love, forever Phoenix.' They were the ones Dale had ordered and personally placed on the grave. He passed over a single rose.

'I sent these on your behalf.'

Phoenix snatched them from Dale's hands, 'Give them here. Don't you touch them.'

Ignoring Dale's efforts to shield him from the rain that had turned to a heavy downpour, Phoenix once again bent down and touched the pile of wet mud before carefully placing the flower on the earth. He stared at his dirty hands and told Suzy he would be back soon.

As they walked away, he kept turning around and had to be reminded to be careful with the uneven ground and slippery grass. He was saying crazy things about lonely graveyards and how unfair it had been burying Suzy in a hole.

'I can't leave her here. Do you hear what I say Dale? I want her cremated and I'm going to scatter the ashes in some woods on the Old Blossom Road in Ohio. I'm thinking we will need to speak to the funeral home about exhumation.'

'Just hang on there; you know we can't do that. I'm not happy to even think about such a horrible thing – it's macabre and it's going to bring you a lot of sadness.'

'And I'm not living with sadness already? I want to do the best for her, and it's not down there.'

Dale raised his voice, 'Suzy's funeral was conducted with so much respect and we did our best for her. In time, we'll get a decent stone and you will be able to come and visit. But I wish you hadn't said all that back there. You are still recovering and confused, so I don't want you getting ideas like that again.'

As they reached the walkway Phoenix suddenly said, 'I've changed my mind.'

Dale was relieved to hear him say this and said it was for the best.

'No, what I meant was before we go home, I want to see where Cody is.'

Dale frowned and pulled on his coat collar to keep out the rain. 'Are you sure? You look soaked. I was trying to limit how distressing it would be for you being here. You really don't remember coming to his funeral, do you?'

'I'm afraid not; now let's head over to where he is.'

Dale hadn't attended Cody's funeral, but fortunately he had already asked Elizabeth for the location of her husband's grave. She told him it was visible from where they buried Suzy.

It only took a few moments to reach the white marble gravestone with Cody's name picked out in black lettering. The grave was immaculate with iron surrounds and stones laid the full length of the plot. There were fresh flowers and it was evident Elizabeth had recently visited.

Phoenix remained strong as he patted the stone and quietly mouthed, 'Rest in peace Cody, you were the best friend a man could ask for.'

Dale bowed his head in respect and waited for his father to say he was ready to go. Back in the car he wiped the inside of the windshield to clear the misted-up glass before driving out of the cemetery gates. Neither said a word. The thought of interfering with Suzy's body was what nightmares were made of and he prayed his father would see sense.

* * *

Later on, Dale phoned Donald in Ohio and nothing could have prepared him for his reaction. 'I'm sorry to worry you, but my Dad's saying some crazy things and I don't know how to deal with him.'

Donald's kind voice soothed Dale's troubled mind. 'That's okay; you take your time telling me. Tell me what's worrying you and remember there's nothing we can't fix.'

Dale took a deep breath and went for it. 'He says Suzy definitely wanted to be cremated. He's really cross and mentioned exhumation.'

Donald's voice exploded with, 'No-one is going to dig up our daughter. I'm hurt you called me as you could have saved me from this horrendous idea. I'm beginning to think your old man has always had a screw loose. I've reached the end of the line trying to help him.'

Dale wished he hadn't made the call and desperately tried to think of something to say that wouldn't upset Donald any further.

'Are you still there, Dale? You've gone all quiet on me.'

'Sorry, yes I'm here. I just don't know how to handle Dad when he's like this.'

'So you keep saying. My advice to you is to man up and deal with things at your end. We can't keep running every time he has a setback. We'll be with you for Christmas – isn't that enough help? After that, you are on your own.'

Dale switched hands to hold the phone in an effort to control his shaking. 'I totally agree with you, I handled it badly. Please forgive me.'

Donald shot back. 'What's doing my head in is his misconception of Suzy's wishes. Our family has always gone for burials. Suzy told us she was happier being able to visit the graveyard. It helped her to come to terms with the grief. So, there is no way she would have opted for cremation.'

'You are right Donald, there was no mention in her will and I'm sorry for upsetting you.'

'Upsetting me…'

His voice trailed off and there was silence at the end of the line. When he did speak, his harsh tone worried Dale, 'There's no way I can mention this to Marlene – it will finish her off. We've done our share of looking after your dad and he's not even our son. After we see you at Christmas it's up to you – do I make myself clear? Now if you don't mind, my wife and I just want to get on with our lives.'

'Yes, I understand. I should never have put so much pressure on you. Please don't shut me out of your life. We may not be related by blood, but I have always thought of you as my grandfather. Marlene and you, well you are my family, and I don't want to lose you.'

Donald ended the call and was soon joined by Marlene.

'Who was that darling?'

'Just Dale, he sends his love.'

'And Phoenix, how is he?'

'Oh, you know, up and down. Crazy as usual.'

'That sounded cruel, Donald.'

'Sorry, it's just such hard work caring for him and his son. I think it's time Dale stepped up to the mark. All this misery is like bad weather that I wish would go away.'

* * *

Back in New York, Dale joined his father in the lounge.

'Can I turn the TV off as I want to speak to you?'

Phoenix clicked the remote and patted the couch.

'Sure thing, you know you can always talk to me.'

'I'll cut to the chase. I've spoken to Donald about your feelings on Suzy being buried.'

Phoenix put a hand to his head. 'Oh Jesus, why did you do that?'

'He said she would never have even thought about what you said.'

'And what does this guy know about my wife's last...'

'Just that there was nothing in the will.'

Phoenix looked puzzled and scratched his head, 'Yes, her will and that's something I want to see. Where is it?'

'I gave it to you just the other day and you said you had read it. It must be in your room.'

There was a look of sadness on Phoenix's face as he screwed up his eyes. He conceded, 'Oh yes, I must have forgotten. It's me not thinking straight again. I saw red when that pile of wet earth came into sight. I wanted to do better for her than that. Why I even mentioned it is beyond me and I'm sorry for what I said. I know it will take a while before we can erect a stone in her memory, but I'm going to make sure it's done properly.'

'Sure thing, we'll get a memorial stone, something special. I think it takes about a year for the ground to settle.'

'Should I ring and apologise to Donald?'

Panicking, Dale quickly said, 'No, no, no – please leave that to me and when they come here everything will run smoothly.'

'Tell me son, when is this pain going to leave me? It's like the future has been ripped away. I wish I could go to sleep tonight and never wake up again.'

Dale told him not to say things like that. He added that he would always be there for him. In a relatively short space of time his father would have to fend for himself and with these bouts of depression he wasn't sure if he would cope. He planned to speak with Elizabeth who had frequently offered to keep an eye on him.

He still had to tell his father that Suzy's life assurance was a poor pay out. After settling the funeral costs there was a minuscule monthly income. It wouldn't be enough to support him. A move to a smaller place with lower rent was on the cards and he knew he'd have to help with the search.

* * *

Later Dale plucked up the courage to ring Donald again and heard him sigh loudly.

'Yes, Dale. Twice in one day — what is it now? You'll have to be quick as my dinner is on the table and there's a ball game about to start.'

'I wanted you to know that I've spoken to dad and he regrets what he said. He promises me there will be no more silly talk. In future I won't be taking advantage of your kind help. Now, you must get back to your meal.'

Donald steadied himself on the lounge doorframe. As he was about to say goodbye, he glanced over to a photograph on the hall wall. The image was of Suzy hugging Phoenix with Dale standing close by. Dale was family and always would be, he couldn't deny that.

'Thanks for the update and I'm cross with myself for being so hard on you. Yes, we are still going to step back from helping so much as we are worn out. But you listen to me young man, I am proud for you to call me Grandad.'

After the call Donald took another look at the photograph of his daughter who was gazing lovingly into Phoenix's eyes. Donald kissed one of his fingertips and touched the image of Suzy's face before whispering, 'Sleep well darling, we have everything covered at our end.'

* * *

Christmas Eve afternoon saw Phoenix, Ethan, Donald, Marlene and Dale celebrate as they dressed the tree and placed presents beneath it. The Christmas cookies were from a local store as Suzy wouldn't be baking her wonderful cakes any longer. Phoenix had too much to drink and Dale gave up trying to warn him of the dangers of mixing liquor and medication.

When Phoenix welcomed his friends into his home he said, 'I'm sorry I was a bit hazy on remembering who you were when I was banged up in that hospital. That's what a crack on the head does for you. How could I ever forget you guys? How are you all?'

In unison there was a chorus of replies as they competed to talk to him. Much hugging and shaking of hands followed.

Turning his attention to Ethan, Phoenix was anxious to talk to his friend.

Ethan was first to speak. 'It's great to see you again. I can't tell you how sorry I was to hear about your wife.'

'Thanks, I miss her so much, but I have come to terms with the fact she's never coming back. Somehow, I gotta get my life going again – it's what she would have wanted. I've been acting like a real airhead and I'm not that guy. You didn't even meet Suzy, did you?'

'Yes, I did, when I visited you in hospital. She was a lovely lady and she loved you so much.'

'You came in to see me. I can't remember you coming in. But then again, I was probably still out of it. Tell me Ethan, how's work and is the building finished?'

'Yes, our job there has come to an end and I'm on a new site, a much larger scraper than the last one. Oh, before I forget, Amy the supervisor is also working there. She's put on a fair bit of weight and I wondered if perhaps she was pregnant, but she's still a looker. She often asks after you.'

'Sorry, I don't remember her.'

Ethan lowered his voice, 'You know, the girl with the big ... I mean great figure. You could always come and work with me again; our place needs more people.'

'Me, oh no, I've had enough of working on sites. The height and memories are enough for me. I don't know if I told you, a few years ago I was out of work before Christmas and drove a delivery wagon. When I'm fit, I might go back to doing that again.'

'You're not Santa Claus, are you?'

'Get outta here, won't you?'

Phoenix spent time talking to Elizabeth who insisted he came over for dinner one evening. He made a short speech about Suzy, and then moved swiftly to thanking Donald and Marlene and every word resonated with the couple who were pleased to see him looking so well. A toast was made to everyone present and then it was time for the guests to leave. Ethan promised to call in a few days to arrange lunch at a new diner he had discovered off Delancey Street.

* * *

That night lying in the bed Phoenix had shared with his wife, he held one of her nighties against his face. The warmth of the material, and knowing she'd worn it, felt like she was right beside him. In one of his dreams she'd drifted back into his life as if nothing had occurred. There had been no car accident and she was worried about him coping on his own. She was so beautiful and he longed to hold her, only he couldn't move a muscle. Then, suddenly she was gone again. He was convinced she had come to say goodbye.

He knew life would never be the same without her, but he'd hang onto the thought that, as the seasons turned, the pain would ease. He had to move on. He was certainly going to be busy over the next few weeks seeing his friends, plus the appointments with the memory clinic and his doctor. He acknowledged that soon his son was going home, as would Donald and Marlene, leaving him to face the future on his own.

* * *

On the day of the visit to the memory clinic, Dale sat with his father who, annoyingly, kept cracking corny jokes and tried to share them with other patients. It was mainly elderly people waiting to be called, many of whom were accompanied by family or carers. Phoenix ignored the fact that possibly the men and women sitting close to him were suffering from dementia. One woman, who was quite senior, kept repeating the same words loudly, 'When would Robert be home from school.' The young man, conceivably her carer, who accompanied her, smiled every time she spoke out and patted her arm.

Phoenix kept talking to the lady saying the staff in the centre had terrible memories and often forgot to come into work. The woman raised her head and again asked when her son would be home.

Grinding his hands together, Phoenix stood up to leave. 'Oh, for God's sake Dale, can't you see we are in the wrong place. This lot have had it. I'm outta here.'

A number of people looked up and tutted; it was obvious that many of those waiting were struggling to find the right words or remember things and were not at death's door.

'Dad, sit down. How could you say those things?'

Phoenix stared ahead not saying anything.

Embarrassed by his father's outburst, Dale apologised to the sea of faces.

Close by, a man with a balding head, who was still wearing his coat despite the tremendous heat in the building, frowned having clearly heard the remark. He returned to his book: *The Politics Behind the American Civil War.*

The receptionist on the front desk informed them they were next to see the doctor.

On hearing this Phoenix whispered, 'If you don't mind, I'll be going in on my own. You wait here.'

The doctor stood in the doorway and repeated Phoenix's name.

The young woman with the cheery smile, who was obviously pregnant, introduced herself and Phoenix spoke with her. She raised her eyebrows and then laughed. She must have seen the funny side of the comment about the consequences of forgetting to take her pills and so much for working in the memory clinic.

In he went and the door closed leaving Dale wondering where all the poor behaviour was coming from; not that long ago, his father would have been courteous to people. He was a considerate man who opened the door for others or became upset on hearing their problems, but not today.

Tomorrow Dale was returning to Orlando with the knowledge that Donald and Marlene would only be staying for a short while longer. Wasn't this a prime time for him to step up and take responsibility? But he had to return home as his company had become totally frustrated with his absence from work. At first, they had been sympathetic, but now their patience had worn thin. The day before Christmas they confirmed by e-mail that a meeting with their HR Director had been scheduled. He suspected they were either going to give him a hard time or lay him off.

His attention was brought back to the room by a woman who was shuffling her feet which made a noise on the wooden floor. He glanced at the full waiting room and understood just how frightening it must be to feel lost and unable to express yourself. He wondered if his father had been taking his medication and was concerned with the amount of liquor he was downing. If he'd stalled on taking the tablets, it was probably the catalyst for the quirky behaviour this morning.

He thought of the strained conversation he'd had with Donald and acknowledged the pressure he'd piled on him and his wife and just how worn out they must feel. There was also the cost of all those flights; they couldn't keep coming over. His mind was made up; he was going to suggest they cut short their stay.

A call to his company would end his employment and he'd insist they released him from working out his notice. He'd start searching for work in New York in a sales or marketing role to bring in enough money to keep his father and himself. If he had to take a driving job or work in a shop, so be it. A move to a smaller apartment for them would be necessary. He'd already reduced his life savings to practically zero having paid the hospital bill. Whilst he wanted no thanks for covering this, it was odd his father still hadn't mentioned the cost of the treatment.

Dale's back stiffened when he felt a tap on his shoulder.

'Are you going to sleep in all this heat? Come on let's go.'

Dale thanked the girl on the desk and thrust his hand into his pocket to pull out the car keys. He managed to drop his wallet on the floor, and that's when he remembered Tara. Only that morning he'd extracted her photo from the holder when he vowed never to contact her again.

Their argument was too upsetting to think about. She was now history. As for her agreeing to reverse her decision and come back to him and live in New York, well he knew it was never going to happen. The falling out was due to them not seeing enough of each other and her sudden lack of compassion for his father. Her ultimatum to spend more time with her, or for him to stay in the city, annoyed Dale and he chose the latter. He couldn't comprehend how the love of his life had turned into such a hard person. In no uncertain terms, he told her it was over. She was shortly to move out of his house to an apartment downtown. An e-mail a few days ago from a friend spelled out she had been seeing one of his old college buddies.

Dale managed to keep the news about Tara to himself as he feared the last thing his father needed was another shock, but he would tell him in a day or two.

As they reached the parking lot, he asked how it went with the memory lady. He deliberated on whether Phoenix had been amenable and answered her questions.

'She was ace that lady; she had real class. I admit there were a few awkward moments when I struggled to find an answer. I'm still trying to figure out how anyone can remember the date for Labor Day – my mind went blank. Also, the President's name, I said Obama. Who is this Trump guy? Anyway, the good news is I'm on the mend, so don't have to go back for any more sessions.'

Dale yawned loudly, 'That's awesome. As for Donald Trump, it all happened a long while ago. It's a strange and scary story that just keeps rolling.'

As Dale unlocked the car, Phoenix looked concerned. 'You look worn out son. I can drive if you want.'

'That's kind of you, but I'm fine. We'll head back home to grab some lunch. Later we'll walk over to see Doctor Creedy.'

'Creedy. Oh, for the check-up with her, I'd forgotten about that. I suppose today, it didn't help with me being so rude to those old folks. That crazy woman kept asking me when her kid would be home. I suppose I just lost it.'

'It wasn't one of your better moments.'

'Hands up, I was out of line. But just now I'm worried about you; you look washed out. What's up?'

'Me, I'm fine. There is something I wanted to mention – Donald and Marlene are cutting their stay short, so for a while it will just be me and you.'

Phoenix frowned as he said, 'Are you sure about that. It's nothing I've said or done is it?'

Dale shook his head, 'No, but you will just have to put up with me staying with you.'

'You are not thinking straight. Your job son, what about your job? You'll lose it if you stay with me any longer. I can manage on my own. Why don't you let me drive? Give me the keys.'

Dale's voice rose, 'No, get in the car, I'm the one doing the driving, you just enjoy the ride.'

Phoenix climbed in and drew the seat belt around his now much thinner body and said, 'And Tara; I'm not sure she will be too happy with you extending your stay with me.'

On hearing her name Dale ignored his father and that's when Phoenix got annoyed and unbuckled his seat belt, 'Give me the bloody keys, it's my car.'

'No, now stop shouting and calm down. Put that belt back on. The hospital definitely said it was six months minimum before you could drive and your insurance won't cover you.'

'Nobody is going to know. I'm fed up with being told what to do. Whose side are you on anyway?'

Dale was taken back and concentrated on moving the car away from the sidewalk. He'd only gone a few blocks when Phoenix said, 'I asked you a question.'

'Yes, and I'm tired and don't want to fall out with you.'

Phoenix suddenly switched his attention to something else and tapped a finger on the driver mirror. 'There's a police car behind you with flashing lights. You'd better pull over. What speed were you doing? I knew you should have let me drive.'

Dale sighed, 'Oh bugger.'

He parked up and was amazed when the car zoomed past and took a right a few blocks up.

Phoenix burst into laughter and Dale playfully punched his father's arm. 'That's not funny.'

'I know, but you should see the look on your face. Now hold on a moment, they are back again and coming up behind us, but this time they haven't got their flashers on.'

'What.'

'Just kidding son. How about you get that ass of yours into gear and get us home as I'm starving.'

* * *

Back home Marlene was preparing lunch and Dale seized the opportunity to talk to Donald. The relief on the older man's face was evident as he readily agreed to change

150

their flight plans. Dale informed him he was to move away from Orlando permanently to be with his father.

Over a hurried lunch, Phoenix kept saying he was going to ask the doctor to sign him off so he could look for a driving job. He had to be reminded of the hospital guidelines and sulked through the remainder of the meal.

Not long after they had finished eating, Donald rang the airline to change the tickets for the following day.

* * *

An hour later Dale sat with his father as he underwent a medical with Doctor Creedy. She repeated again how sorry she was to hear about his wife dying before switching the subject to how he was coping being back home.

Phoenix pretended there were no issues saying he felt so much better. Dale prompted him to talk about his medication. He simply shrugged his shoulders and asked if he could be signed off early to return to work. The doctor shook her head. She observed her screen and asked about his next visit to the memory clinic that was coming up in three weeks' time. Dale was confused as Phoenix had said there were no more visits scheduled?

Dale pulled a face before challenging his father who coughed and said he must have misheard. He stood up and walked out of the door without saying goodbye. Dale apologised to the doctor who promptly reminded him that his father had planned appointments with her too.

Out in the street, Dale reminded his father that Donald and Marlene were leaving in the morning and they would be taking them to the airport. He was cheery and remarked on how kind they'd been and was sorry they were going. As they reached the steps of the apartment, Dale's heart went out to him as the vacant expression on his face matched the words he muttered, 'You won't leave me, will you son?'

* * *

Airport farewells were always difficult for Dale as he recalled the number of times Tara had accompanied him and her promise of never-ending love. Saying goodbye to Donald and Marlene was a brief affair as Phoenix insisted they go straight through to security.

* * *

Sleepy and sipping coffee, the two men gazed at the Christmas tree that was due to come down in the morning. Dale ran his finger along the back of a wooden chair next to his seat and stared at the dust that had built up. He acknowledged that the cleaning of the apartment had featured low on their list of priorities. The place was a mess and he'd have to draw up a rota; he certainly wasn't going to do all the housework on his own.

Phoenix rose from the couch and went over to a box under the table insisting they talk about finances.

He waved a document in the air. 'This came this morning addressed to Suzy. I never knew she had savings in this bank. They are writing to say the interest rate is coming to an end and there are suggestions for reinvesting the amount. Here look for yourself.'

Dale hit the TV control mute button to study the statement and his voice rose, 'Wow, there is one hundred and eighty thousand dollars here! But, hold on, why didn't your lawyer, who handled her will, mention these funds?'

Phoenix smiled and excitedly said, 'I can only assume it's the money from her granddaddy's estate she kept talking about. She never told me how much it was; I just thought it was a few thousand bucks. Her family are wealthy but don't like to talk about money. Suzy always had her own bank account. This figure is unreal. It must have been her safety net and she hid it away in a bank. Bless her; I'd probably have blown it all if I'd known about it.'

'No need to shout Dad, I'm not in the next room. This is going to help hugely with getting you back on your feet. I would, however, say it is going to be complicated for the lawyer to sort out the legal matters before they sign over the money to you.'

'Why? Correct me if I'm wrong, her will states she left me everything.'

'Yes, but this money has only just showed up. The tax department will want to check she's paid her dues as well as yours. Then our legal guy will transfer the funds to your name. It's complicated and will take a while to sort.'

Phoenix was now on his feet and waving hands in the air. 'I know all that. The thing that pleases me is you won't have to move to New York. Go home and patch things up with Tara. I'll get the money when it's due, so no sweat.'

'No, I'm starting a new life here. Tara and I are history. Tomorrow I'll bell my company to hand in my notice. I will also contact the real estate office to hand back the rented house and I'm going to find work here. For a while my place is with you.'

'That makes me so happy; we make a great team. Even with all this dough, I'm still going to move apartment as I need to draw a line under all that has happened. I want to find happiness again. What saddens me is you splitting with Tara.'

'I've come to terms with that already.'

Dale watched his father reading the document over and over again. He thought about some of the things that had been happening. The tempers, mood swings and gentle return to being amenable again. It was a real roller coaster ride and he wondered how much more pressure he would be able to take. Then he thought of Suzy and instinctively knew she'd have wanted him to look out for Phoenix.

* * *

On calling his company, Dale listened to their suggestion for him working a three-day week whilst he resolved his problems. After that a discussion would be scheduled for him to resume working full time. Dale thanked them and explained financially this would be impossible with all the flight costs. He then dropped the bombshell that he was making a new start, moving to be with his father and resigning with immediate effect. The HR Director tried in vain to persuade him to reconsider.

In a last-ditch effort to retain their best account manager, she offered him a sabbatical period of one year. It would be unpaid, but there would be a job for him when he returned. Dale figured he'd made up his mind and advised that an e-mail would follow shortly to confirm his intention to leave. She reluctantly acknowledged they'd lost their top man who'd helped catapult the company into new and profitable markets. She wished him well.

Dale reached for his iPad and began his search for work. He knew it was going to take time to land the perfect job and, for the meantime, he planned to take something temporary. There were various recruitment companies in the city and he randomly chose one from the internet. His eyes were drawn to a listing for an operations manager based in Queens. He uploaded his resumé and carefully read the relevant information on the kitchen furniture company. Initially he was concerned at the low pay that was on offer. What did interest him was there was no evening or weekend work involved. He was sure this agency would question why a career-driven person earning high bucks had resigned from a top job.

Two hours later he got a call and underwent a preliminarily discussion with a young man from the recruitment firm. He answered all his questions including reasons for moving to the city. He also gave a commitment to work hard. The date was set for the following morning to be interviewed by one of the directors of the company.

* * *

Thursday morning and, rushing to get ready for his meeting, Dale shouted from the bathroom that he didn't want any breakfast. He could smell burnt toast and hear the high pitched shrill of the kitchen smoke detector as his father struggled to disarm it. He tightened his tie and applied aftershave before having one last look in the mirror.

On entering the kitchen, he glanced at the enormous pile of blackened toast that was being scraped over the trash can; much of it on the floor.

Opening a window to let out the smell, Dale frowned. 'It's like you've had a bonfire in here. What made you use so much bread – look at the state of this kitchen?'

'The toaster must be faulty. Sit down and I'll have another go. You must try some of this marmalade.'

Dale observed the knife his father was waving around in the air that was covered in butter and burnt toast crumbs.

'No thanks; I'll catch a snack later. Do I look okay in this navy suit or is it too formal for working in an office?'

'You look swell son. I'm that proud of you and hope you get the job.'

'Let's not get excited, it's just a temporary thing to get me back into work.'

He glanced down at the ruined toast and said, 'Following your attempt to make breakfast this morning do me a favour and get this mess cleared up.'

'What do you mean?'

'The cremated toast; what else do you think I'm talking about? If it were any blacker it would have caught fire. We don't need a new toaster, just turn the setting down.'

In a dismissive voice Phoenix muttered it wasn't that bad. He also wished him luck with his meeting.

Dale nervously emphasised the fact he had no experience in the kitchen market.

'You'll fly through the interview. Just a thought, while you are out in Queens, how about you see if there is a letting agent to find us a new place to live. But it's gotta be in a reasonable area and not too costly. Are you sure you don't want breakfast? I could do you an egg.'

Dale vigorously shook his head. 'You have taken your medication this morning, haven't you?'

Phoenix looked deep in thought. 'Yep, I've taken them. Two blue ones and the white one or was it green? You get off and I'll see you later. I have a busy morning making contact with the lawyer on Suzy's money and Ethan is popping in to see me. I'll introduce you to him when you get back; I worked with him on the scrapers. He's an ace guy.'

Dale sighed. 'Dad, he was here on Christmas Eve and I met him at the hospital.'

Ignoring his son, Phoenix proceeded to load an over-generous spoonful of marmalade onto his toast, having forgotten first to spread butter on the surface.

Grabbing his coat and briefcase Dale left the apartment wondering what had possessed his father to make so much toast.

Chapter 14

On the subway ride to Queens, Dale read the printouts for Talbots Home Improvements, acquainting himself with the company and their market status. There was no escaping the fact that this was a small concern and the internet revealed a business that was under new ownership. The headcount was twelve; his old company employed four hundred staff of which thirty reported to him. One worrying factor was this company's customer base was predominately set up to service the trade sector. There was a relatively small percentage of retail and no mail order activity whatsoever. The question that begged an answer was, why weren't they reinventing themselves and pushing the boundaries for new sales?

There were two directors, William Soham and Rachel Burrows; the latter was the person Dale was to see. Having viewed their website earlier, it cast a shadow on whether this was a worthwhile company to work for.

What was he doing jumping at the first job that reared its head? Relevant to his career track record, there were a number of national paper suppliers in the state of New York that he could have called first. However, now he'd secured the interview, it would be rude not to show.

Housed in an old industrial unit in the Ridgewood area of Queens, the red brick building came into sight. Graffiti depicting ferocious tigers adorned the warehouse doors and walls with a green snake curling its way to the roof. There was a terrible smell coming from some bins that had the lids missing and discarded pizza boxes lay on the concrete base. The property was in a state of bad repair with one of the rusty air conditioning unit covers hanging precariously from its hinges. He observed the faded blue plastic company sign that had seen better days and decided, if he got the job, he'd have to update their image.

Dale rang the intercom and almost immediately heard the clatter of someone noisily descending the stairs. A young man with a shaved head and dressed in jeans escorted him up a creaky wooden staircase to level two where he was shown into a large office. On the blue painted walls hung evidence of their product range and he was impressed with their marketing. He did, however, question why this company chose to work in such a poor building. The inside looked acceptable, yet the exterior was another matter. A draughty window afforded a view of a rusty-looking fire escape and pitted brickwork of the adjacent warehouse.

He nervously crossed his legs and straightened the tie that was making his neck sore. Within a few minutes of waiting, in walked an attractive woman with short blonde hair, who he gauged to be in her early-fifties, impeccably dressed in a smart skirt and sweater. Dale stood up and put out a hand to introduce himself. He observed her perfect skin and trim body. His eyes scanned her fingers to see if there was a ring and he was surprised not to see one.

Rachel Burrows asked him to sit whilst she settled behind the desk moving folders around her immaculate workspace. Picking up a document from the recruitment firm, she quickly read the details and highlighted various lines of text with a green marker pen.

'Thank you for coming and do you mind if I call you Dale? I see you have experience in management with a paper supplier in Orlando. What brings you to New York and to our company?'

'I've relocated here and am keen to get back into work. I have a great track record in sales and running teams. Not long ago I lost my stepmother and I intend to look out for my father, so working in the city will be ideal.'

She sighed and kindly said, 'I'm sorry to hear about your loss; these things are never easy. My father passed last fall and I still miss him.'

Dale warmed to her soft voice. 'Thank you and yes, it is hard, but I am ready for a change from working for a major company. I am interested to learn more about your business as I may have something to offer in increasing your sales. Am I correct in saying your core product range includes kitchen furniture carcasses, cooker hoods and laminate splashbacks?'

'Yes, but our sales in this sector are low due to massive competition. We deliver in a thirty-mile area around New York, though many of the builders tend to collect.'

Dale took off his glasses and smiled. 'I was interested to read the recent internet article on your company. It praised your attention to customer service and that impressed me. I also note you are sole distributors of the Hayver Range and your year-to-year sales have increased by six percent.'

'I gotta say that you have done your homework. Perhaps, what you didn't see on the net was the previous owners practically bankrupted this business. My partner and I bought the company five years ago and net profits are up for the last six months. We have plans to move from this awful building to a new purpose-built unit.'

Dale was suitably impressed.

'We are going to strengthen the retail side of the business. The new office manager will have to be able to multi-task and share our vision. The question is, Dale, are you the guy we are looking for?'

Dale nodded his head and thought to himself that she certainly knew what she was doing; but did she say partner? He took a chance and included the word husband in his acknowledgement for all their hard work.

'Good God, no, William is not my husband. We met at Harvard Business School and on graduating worked for the same company. The two of us sunk our savings into this business and are finally turning a profit. Now, what makes you think I'd be interested in you running the day-to-day operations here?'

For some unknown reason Dale flustered his reply which was unusual for someone who normally excelled in pitches. He stumbled through a few sentences and eventually stopped talking.

Leaning forward over her desk she smiled at him. He couldn't help but notice the straining of the material of her blouse and the hint of the white bra that came into sight. He felt uncomfortable and stared over to the window.

'Relax, interviews are always difficult.'

He wanted the floor to swallow him up. Normally he was confident as selling was his forte. What was wrong with him today? There was a nagging voice in his head that told him to stop looking at the pretty lady and get his act together.

Rachel glanced back to his application form and Dale noticed how serious her face had become.

'I see from your CV that you were a big shot, quite a mover and shaker. I'd hate to take you on only to lose you if a better position came up.'

'Once I commit myself to your business, I'm in for the long run.'

He studied the way she moved her lips and the hint of a smile that was forming. He was cross with himself once again for staring and brought things back to earth by asking for more details on the vacancy.

After a lengthy discussion, they took a tour of the premises that included a plethora of small offices, a large storage area and trade counter. He met a number of the staff and learnt more about their industry. He was forming a picture of the company and beginning to see working for them as a challenge. This was a small enterprise with big plans and he was interested in giving it a go.

Their meeting was disturbed as his cell phone vibrated madly and let out its screechy call sound. He cursed not having turned it off. He was dismayed to see his father's face on the missed call screen.

'I'm really sorry. It's my father, I told him not to ring me.'

'The rule here is no private phone calls during meetings.'

'Really sorry. It won't happen again.'

They were interrupted by a man standing in the doorway.

Rachel introduced her business partner, a man who Dale gauged also to be in his fifties. Wearing a poorly fitting suit and in a hurry to visit a client, he barely responded to Dale's attempt to greet him. Rachel dismissed her fellow director's rudeness saying William was working too hard.

Enquiring about when a decision regarding the job would be made, Dale was told they had seen a number of applicants and would be in touch shortly.

As he was about to leave, she retrieved his scarf that had become wedged between a chair and a filing cabinet. 'You'll be needing this; it's freezing out there.'

* * *

Back at the apartment, Phoenix was finishing an early lunch with Ethan and they were busy talking about work. Both looked up when Dale entered the kitchen. He produced a loaf of bread from a bag and grinned at his father.

'Well, how did it go son?'

'Oh, you know, early days, but yes, for a small company, I was impressed. They have interviewed a lot of people and will make a decision soon.'

Ethan was unsure what they were talking about. 'I thought you already had a job.'

'I did have, but didn't Dad tell you I am moving in with him?'

Dale's cell phone rang and he put a hand up in the air. 'Hold on, I gotta take this call.'

Moments later, in the privacy of his bedroom, he told Rachel he would be delighted to accept the position and would start in three weeks' time. An agreement was made for him to visit the following day to collect his contract and company manual. She told him there was much work needed to familiarise himself with the complex world of kitchen furniture.

* * *

Struggling to acquaint himself with the product specification manual and sales forecaster documents, Dale turned off the bedside light and sighed. He wondered if he'd grasp enough of the data before starting his new job.

He spent the following morning researching on the net, trawling through competitors in the industry to get a feel for the work ahead. One thing that he should have asked about in his interview was their company's computer software, but that would now have to wait.

His father kept interrupting asking if he required anything and reminded him that after lunch, he had an appointment at the memory clinic.

Fortunately, all went well with Phoenix's meeting. This time, he admitted there were still some things that confused him. Dale was relieved to learn there would be a break until his next visit. Requesting time off to accompany him during his first few weeks of working would have been difficult to arrange.

* * *

Mid-week was garbage collection day and Phoenix duly placed the plastic sack in the chute, made his bed and did some light housework before joining his son for breakfast. Dale was pleased to see him tackling tasks around the apartment. Both were cheery and Phoenix was looking forward to a walk in Central Park with Ethan who had the day off work. They would have lunch in a diner off Upper East Side, and later Ethan would take a ride with Phoenix to bring him home.

When Phoenix left the apartment, Dale was puzzled – where were all his work papers? He cursed his father remembering he'd been tidying up. How many times had he moved things and stored them out of sight? He checked the closet in the bedroom but there was no sign of the documents. He gave up looking and slumped in a chair to check his iPad for messages. His new boss, Rachel, confirmed she wouldn't be present on his first day at the company. Her partner, William Soham, had everything in hand. He hoped the man would be more welcoming than the first time they met.

When Phoenix finally returned home, it was obvious he was drunk, and Dale snapped at Ethan for bringing him back in such a state.

'Dad, how much liquor have you had? I thought we agreed with your medication there could be an issue. As for you Ethan – please leave now.'

Ethan was as intoxicated as Phoenix and feebly waved goodbye. He noisily broke wind and left the apartment forgetting to close the door behind him.

Suddenly, Phoenix raced off to the bathroom and Dale heard the unmistakable sound of him throwing up.

He waited patiently for him to return. With a yellowy sickly mess on his jeans and sweater, Phoenix stood around looking quite helpless. The smell was awful.

'Oh, for God's sake, look at the state of you. Go and take them off and I'll get the washer on.'

Phoenix proceeded to strip off the soiled garments right there in the lounge. He was about to remove his underclothes when Dale stopped him.

With a mixture of embarrassment and annoyance, he mouthed, 'Stop, leave those on and come away from the window.'

Unashamedly he stood perfectly still in just his undershirt and Dale couldn't help notice how thin his father was. It wasn't a pleasant sight glimpsing him in this state of undress and he urged him to go and get cleaned up.

Phoenix stared at the clothes littered around his feet before bending down to retrieve them with one hand, the other was held firmly in front of his mouth. The sickly smell was turning his stomach. Dale went in search of the cool cotton scented air freshener can.

It was a while before his father came back and Dale asked him how he was feeling. He put a thumb in the air and continued buttoning up his shirt. 'What's that smell, have you spilt something?'

'No, I haven't, it's air freshener. Look, I may have a problem here. You haven't seen my work files, have you?'

'Not sure.'

'What do you mean not sure? You have, or you haven't – which one is it?'

'I did do some clearing up and got rid of loads of papers from your room. I threw away those old brown shoes of yours you put in the bin and a bag propped against the closet.'

Suddenly it all became clear as Dale recalled him putting out the garbage.

He shouted so loudly it frightened his father. 'You bone head. My work things were in that bag. What were you doing in my room? Now I'm in a quandary. How can I ask my boss for a duplicate set?'

Phoenix looked tearful and was shaking, 'I'm sorry. Please don't shout at me again. I thought it was trash in that bag.'

Dale knew the garbage would have already been collected and sat heavily on a chair. With a hand on his forehead he wondered how he was going to explain to Rachel that he'd lost absolutely everything she'd given him to study. He could hardly say his crazy father disposed of their company paperwork and could he have another set of documents. He dreaded the thought of ringing her as she was bound to think he was a complete airhead. What a terrible start to the new job.

His reveries were disturbed when he spotted his father turning away to cry and he immediately regretted upsetting him. It was a timely reminder that, not that long ago, the poor man had lost his wife. In truth, he was doing remarkably well for someone who had been so ill and was still grieving.

He listened to the sobbing that turned to louder heart-rending words echoing how he missed Suzy and wanted her back. Dale tried to console him but he pulled away sharply. There was nothing he could say to help. He watched him hurry out to the hallway and then the wailing began again.

Dale was beside himself – just what had he let himself in for? Was it always going to be like this? A few months ago, he had a great job, home and girlfriend, and now his life was a mess. He played with the thought that possibly he was the one who should be seeing the shrink.

He was startled by the ping and vibration of his cell phone. It was another e-mail from his new employer that read: *'Hi Dale. I have some extra pages that you will need to see after you have viewed the section in the manual on rebates for wholesalers. Please see the attachment and ring if you have any questions. Best wishes, Rachel Burrows.'*

* * *

Prior to Dale embarking on his new career, he rang Rachel to tell her he'd lost the company literature. He remembered his stepmother Suzy telling him that honesty was always the best policy. His new boss's calm approach to moving on from a crisis impressed him. She said that on commencing work, he'd get his computer sign on and be able to access the documents online. She insisted he enjoyed his last few days of freedom and she would see him on her return from her business trip.

She was right, it was in his interest to enjoy a little leisure time and he planned to do just that. Along with his father they would revisit New York's tourist haunts and seek out new diners, possibly even a club with some live jazz.

Phoenix gingerly asked him how he got on telling the company about the lost documents. The older man's worried face softened considerably as he learnt it was no longer an issue. Dale also mentioned that for the next few days they were going to have some fun visiting Ellis Island and a stop off to see Liberty. The mention of lunching at Phoenix's favourite diner for his much-loved burger and fries pleased him. He also asked if they could visit his wife's grave. Whilst he knew it was too early to arrange erecting a stone, he admitted he was anxious to get on with it.

* * *

Driving to the cemetery, Dale listened intently to his father's plans for the future, especially that he was finished with working on construction sites. His intention was to seek employment with local delivery companies. He was surprised to hear him say that possibly once a week he would help out at a charity for the homeless. There were a number of soup kitchens operating in church rooms in downtown Queens and, surprisingly, even around Manhattan. He said people had been inordinately kind to him and this was his chance to do something worthwhile. Dale was moved to hear him talking like this and agreed it would be a great thing to do.

As they drew closer to their destination, he plucked up courage to enquire. 'Dad, you haven't mentioned Suzy's savings for a while and I was wondering if you had any plans once the money comes through.'

'Well, those forms you helped me fill out got me thinking. I'm not going to be impulsive and blow the lot. I can hear Suzy telling me to not rush into spending it. It's such a lot of money and it stays in the bank for a while. It's gotta to be somewhere I can get it out quickly in case of emergencies. You and I can survive on whatever we earn, can't we?'

'Too right we can. I like the way you are thinking and whilst it's not going to be easy with all this grief, we have to remain positive and build our future.'

'And that's another thing, son; there will come a point when I want you to pick up your life and leave me. I'm sure you will find a new lady and fall in love again.'

Dale had trouble imagining meeting someone he'd fancy again. He acknowledged there would come a day when his father would be strong enough to go it alone, but not just yet.

On reaching the cemetery, they parked up and Phoenix was overjoyed to spot Elizabeth waving at them. They crossed over to her and exchanged greetings, each glancing down at the flowers they were carrying. The magnificent blooms were soon to be laid on Suzy and Cody's graves and would surely cheer up the miserable graveyard.

Today, although there were dark clouds racing along the sky, it was still pleasantly warm. For a few moments the weather became the topic of their conversation. Elizabeth said it was time for her to tend to her husband's resting place and kissed Phoenix on both cheeks. She wished Dale luck on his first day at work adding she was looking forward to coming over for lunch with them the following week.

The stroll over to Suzy's grave was a silent affair as they dodged puddles and stray tributes that had been carried by the wind. They skirted around the muddy areas of a newly dug grave covered partially with a wind-torn tarpaulin in preparation for a burial. Phoenix bent down to look into the dark wet hole and shook his head.

Up until now he had remained remarkably calm but then broke down as Suzy's miserable grave came into sight. Sadly, it looked like someone had trodden on the raised earth leaving part of the ground flattened. There were new flowers and Dale leant down to read the card.

'Look at this Dad. Don't they look beautiful? They are from Elizabeth; she must have placed them just before we arrived. Wasn't that kind of her?'

There was no reply and Dale quickly laid their flowers on the ground. He stood up to observe his father hurrying away.

Before leaving the graveside, Dale attempted to move some of the muddy earth with the side of his shoe. Packing it back into a mound, he felt happier leaving his stepmother's plot tidier than they found it. Now it was time to support his father.

* * *

Later that morning, having returned to the apartment to change into clean shoes, they set off for Battery Park to take the ferry to Ellis Island. They went through security and rode on the top deck, which afforded an incredible view of the forest of skyscrapers. With the vessel riding the choppy waves, Phoenix stared over to the statue. He told Dale it had been years since he last saw Liberty up close and had forgotten how green she looked. As they drew near, the enormity of the magnificent structure of the lady with the torch was breath-taking. There was a brief stop to allow passengers to alight before the ferry headed for Ellis Island.

Walking in the drizzle wasn't going to spoil their afternoon and they were soon inside the main immigration hall viewing the memorabilia of those who chose to make their lives in the new world. They climbed the steep steps that led to the upper floor to wander through the various exhibit halls. On the lower level they ate a sandwich in the restaurant before leaving to catch the ferry back to the Statue. Phoenix was happier walking around the base of the monument than going up. There were a few photos taken on Dale's cell phone and it was time to go home. Both men agreed it had been a great afternoon and went below in the boat to shelter from the drizzle that had turned to heavy rain.

* * *

The next morning, showered, shaved and dressed in his new suit, Dale applied his favourite designer aftershave. Glancing in the mirror, he straightened the white handkerchief in his jacket pocket, then moved it again. He wondered whether his appearance was too formal for his first day.

Making his way to the kitchen to join his father for breakfast, he hoped there wouldn't be any issues. With a degree of apprehension building up about leaving him alone on his first day, he was pleasantly surprised to see him so calm.

There was no mound of burnt toast or him saying crazy things. He was presented with a fine-looking cheese omelette and a cup of coffee. He cautiously ate his breakfast, fearing he'd drop something on his white office shirt. He must have checked his watch at least three times and, at seven forty, told himself this left ample time to reach Queens. He quickly examined his father's cell phone to ensure his number was still stored in case he needed to leave a message.

As he said goodbye, he was reprimanded for not cleaning his teeth and swiftly returned to the bathroom. He heard his father saying not to worry about leaving him on his own. Dale desperately hoped the day would pan out well. He could cope with anything on his induction to the company, but was his father going to be okay? How he wished Elizabeth hadn't been working and was free to pop in. He'd just have to get home as quickly as he could.

It was a strange farewell as his father put out his hand to shake and then ushered Dale out of the apartment. He stood outside in the lobby fingering the poorly varnished brown oak door and heard the unmistakable sound of the safety chain being secured. With one eye on the lift button and the other on their apartment door he told himself, it was now or never, he had to leave or he'd be late.

* * *

Rachel's fellow director, William, a tall thin man with overlapping front teeth, was dressed casually in jeans and suit jacket. He opened the door only to fail to recognise Dale and there were a few moments of confusion. At first, he was resistant to inviting him in, having confused him with a salesman. He told Dale that he needed to make an appointment. It was only when he announced he was their new operations manager, that he was permitted to enter the building. The man looked so much older than at their brief meeting at the interview. His haggard face and furrowed forehead hinted this was someone who had the troubles of the world riding on his shoulders. His vagueness concerned Dale as the man continued to question him.

'You say operations manager – what did you say your name was?'

'Dale Harrison, sir, your partner Rachel Burrows hired me; we met on the day I came for my interview. I understand that Miss Burrows is away today and I am to report to you.'

It was a relief when William began to realise who he was. Dale witnessed the start of a smile forming.

'You'll have to forgive me; I got confused. I thought Rachel was hiring an office manager and you threw me with that fancy title. I do most of the day-to-day operational work and I'm being pulled in all directions. Now, Dale, welcome to Talbots Home Improvements. Come up to my office and we'll get you acquainted with what we do.'

Dale cringed when he heard the company title that was definitely something he intended to rebrand. The word *home* concerned him; weren't they predominantly middle men selling to wholesalers and not to end users?

'That's not a problem, sir. I'm sure this is a busy outfit and keeping tabs on the market is not easy. That's part of the reason I'm here to learn about your business and give you a hand.'

As they climbed the rickety staircase, William suddenly stopped in his tracks. 'I just forgot I need something from my car. You go up and walk past all the green doors and my office is on the left. It has a picture of an owl below the glass panel.'

He squeezed past Dale and made his way back downstairs, slamming the front door behind him.

As Dale walked past the green doors, he was secretly having a conversation with himself. *Bloody owl on the door, what have I let myself in for. He sounds as mixed up as my dad.*

A young lady, probably no older than eighteen, greeted him and Dale said hello back.

'Are you lost; can I help?'

'Yes please, I'm Dale and I'm looking for an owl; actually, I'm looking for a door with an owl on it. I have been told to go in and wait. I'm the new operations manager.'

He could see she was puzzled – the role operations manager was obviously a newly created title and totally unsuitable for this small company.

'Owl you said, that will be Mr Soham's office.'

She started to giggle and he followed her up the corridor. On reaching the last office, she came to a halt and there was the image of a sorry looking bird of prey. The crudely painted owl on the woodwork appeared to be watching their every move.

Opening the door, she showed him into the office. 'I'm Carrie – would you like a drink.'

'Thanks, that would be awesome – black please.'

Leaving him alone in the cramped office he observed the mess on the director's desk. Documents strewn all over the place with two of the drawers partially open, exposing further mayhem. A calculator, with its plastic cover removed from the back minus the batteries, sat on top of a folder labelled: invoices unpaid.

The rest of the office was just as untidy. Who was William, and what made him tick? All the signs suggested he was a clever man, but he seemed lost in his own little world. Where was he right now though? Purportedly retrieving something from his car and yet a good ten minutes had flown by.

Then the door creaked open and Dale sat upright in his chair expecting William to enter and in came young Carrie with his drink. Accepting the hot china cup, he took a quick sip and asked if her director would be much longer.

The reply he received worried Dale; it appeared Carrie hadn't seen his car when she looked out of the kitchen window.

'He's probably wandered off and forgotten your meeting – he often goes out.'

A further ten minutes rolled by before the elusive director strolled into the room. Dale scanned William's hands for evidence of what he'd gone to retrieve from his car. It came as no surprise that there was nothing to see.

'Sorry, I got waylaid talking to Damien in the warehouse. I'm glad you got yourself a drink. Now, somewhere on my desk are your induction programme notes that Rachel left me.'

'And my sign on ID for your system.'

'Yeah, that's something she gave me. Just give me a moment and I'll shift some of these papers. It's got to be somewhere. A sign on. Yes, you'll need that.'

Observing William's puzzled expression, Dale just knew he wasn't going to find the much-needed information. He rubbed the side of his head and thought how similar all of this was to his father's behaviour. He questioned if his new appointment was in some kind of a mad house or was he stuck in a nightmare? How could he possibly work in this place? He was beginning to feel cross with Rachel for not warning him that her partner had issues. Perhaps the best plan was to put a call through to her to say he had changed his mind.

The sound of his cell phone ringing interrupted any further decision-making. It was his father. Cursing himself for not putting his phone on silent, he quietly answered the call. 'Hello Dad, yes I'm fine. I'm in a meeting right now. You know it's my first day. Is there a problem? I really have to go.'

He turned back to face William. 'Sorry about that.'

'Let's get one thing clear, we don't mix business with social here.'

Dale repeated the sorry word.

William was clearing a space to operate the mouse for his computer and much of the paperwork now lay on the floor. 'My forte is sales and the software on this thing is ace.'

He tapped the casing of the screen in a proprietary manner and smiled. In a strange sort of a way, Dale was warming to him and asked if he could see where his office was before getting started.

'My partner wants you in with her while you settle in. She's on a business trip and will be back tomorrow. I'll do the introductions and her plan is to have you working alongside our girl who runs accounts. Have you any experience in reading a balance sheet?'

Dale's back stiffened on the hard chair as he replied, 'You could say that as I trained as an accountant and then moved into sales and marketing.'

'Good man. I have some figures to show you on our profitability. If I'm remembering right, Rachel has high hopes for you. I know the way the lady works and she's obviously spotted talent in you. She won't rest until she harnesses that fresh energy. Welcome on board. Just one thing young man – no need to wear a tie. We don't do formal here.'

'Well, Mr Soham, I'm ready to start if you could just show me my desk.'

Raising a hand to emphasise his point William smiled, 'We don't go for surnames in this company – call me William.'

* * *

Back home Dale excitedly related his news about his first day and his father kept raising his eyebrows.

'The guy sounds a case and you say he's got an owl on his door.'

'Yeah, but I have to tell you he knows his business inside out. Later in the day I heard him talking to a client on the phone and I take my hat off to him. He's some salesman and you should see him on the computer. He even got me a sandwich from a deli a few blocks down.'

'What did you eat?'

Dale pulled a face. 'I think it was salami, he chose it. I spent most of the day sitting with the girl in accounts. I can see room for improvements in their invoicing. Now, how was your day?'

'Well, I got a call from the lawyer about Suzy's money. It may take up to a month before he credits my bank account.'

'Main thing is you've got it in hand; anything else happened?'

'I made a few calls to real estate companies to enquire about apartments in Queens. They are arranging for a guy to set up a few to visit this Sunday. I said we'd go over.'

'That's great and I'll show you my work place. Sounds like you've had a productive day. What's planned for tomorrow?'

Phoenix smiled, 'Elizabeth is coming to lunch, only she doesn't know I've booked the Italian off Christopher Street. She deserves a treat after all she's been through.'

Chapter 15

The following day the journey to the office was difficult due to torrential rain and Dale's new suit took a damping. Sitting in front of Rachel's desk feeling dishevelled, she welcomed him to the company. She apologised for her partner losing the note with his sign on details and joked one day she was going to tidy his desk. She also praised the man for his ability to bring in sales along with his marketing skills.

She wanted to know who Dale had shadowed the previous day. Impressed with his photographic memory in recalling customer account detail, she smiled. He told her he'd done a quick calculation and the payment days were running at over thirty-two, which would inescapably affect bottom line profits. Rachel frowned.

She mentioned she was arranging for him to visit their main supplier, then pointed to the small desk in the corner of the room that was devoid of a computer or phone. Handing him a new laptop and cell phone, she confirmed the office he would use was being cleared out and a desk installed.

Their general discussion centred on company activity and moved to stock control. It would appear that this company held large quantities of self-build carcasses, cooker hoods and splashback panels.

Their skill was in seamlessly bringing all the elements together in record time. Companies relied on this relatively small outfit for a fast turnaround. Coupled with William's expertise in selling, it would appear their business was motoring.

One area that Rachel appeared excited to tell him about was her plans for expanding the company. 'Mirrors. We are going to invest in buying stock.'

He was fascinated to learn more about the new venture that was miles away from selling kitchen furniture.

'I have researched this lucrative market and it got me thinking, with our move to larger premises, we will have scope for a showroom aimed at securing retail business and online trading. I want you to oversee the move to the Peters Estate including marketing the new product range. We will be adding an extra three people to the headcount.'

'That's awesome Rachel. This will be the route in for launching a new arm of our company, especially for online ordering. Now tell me more about your forecast for growth. I'll need the figures on your investment plans for me to really get my teeth into moving us forward.'

Dale was absorbing the relevant information like a sponge and all the time asking questions, which obviously pleased Rachel. They must have been talking for about three hours when she suggested they walk over to the local deli.

Over a hurried lunch she asked after his father and he explained things were going as well as could be expected. They agreed that his first month would be a huge learning curve and the best way for Dale to understand the business was the hands-on approach.

Back in the office he mentioned the visit to their supplier that she'd scheduled for him to make on Friday. 'I'm looking forward to meeting the guys at Hazer Sandpiper. Just fill me in with the location as I need to drive there.'

'You won't be driving Dale; it's too far. The New York address is just a local sales centre, where you are going is their head office and manufacturing in

Pittsburgh. It will be an overnight job, so you fly out on Thursday night.'

Dale leant back on his office chair with the torn padding. His thoughts centred on his father. 'You say I'll be away for one night. I could take an early flight Friday morning and be back on the same day. It would save on the hotel.'

'Sorry but our top guy, Bud Phillips, can only see you on Friday morning at nine so it will have to be a stay over the night before. He'll spend the morning showing you around and then it's back home. Jess in accounts will book the flight and organise accommodation close by.'

Professional as ever, Dale answered in a confident manner, 'Got that. It should give me a better insight into manufacturing and managing supplier chains.'

The trip to Pittsburgh was crucial, only then would he begin to grasp the complexities of the market. His initial impression of their company's range was that they stocked too many similar flat packs. It would take him a while to get his head around creating a plan for marketing a *one for all* range.

On the way home his mind was racing asking how was he was going to leave his father on his own? It was too soon to be going away. Perhaps he could get hold of Elizabeth to come over to stay. He ruled this out as it seemed rude to go running to her and he certainly had no intention of inviting Ethan. Should he chance it and leave his father for a night and a day? There was always the uncertainty he might go missing or worse. He reminded himself that there was Facetime for them to keep in contact. Then the worst of scenarios shot into his thoughts – what if he had one of his distressing nightmares and there was no-one there to reassure him?

Thursday soon came around. Dale packed a bag and apprehensively left his father to finish his breakfast. It was hard leaving, but he had to go and prayed there would be no incidents while he was away.

He worked at the office and at the close of day set off for the airport. Prior to boarding the plane, he had a lengthy chat with his father who seemed happy enough about being alone for a night. The flight to Pittsburgh was on time and it was late evening before he picked up a ride to the hotel.

The next morning, Dale was up bright and early. He ate a small breakfast, and set off in a taxi for his meeting with Bud Phillips. On arriving he didn't have long to wait at the front desk before a tall, bald-headed man in a smart suit and red striped tie came down to see him. Dale reckoned he was about sixty years of age and noticed he was frowning.

His first words were. 'Are you Dale Harrison?'

Dale put out a hand to greet him and was surprised when the man took a step backwards.

'You have the wrong day. I have you scheduled in for Friday week.'

In the long pause that followed, Dale tried to collect his thoughts. Rachel definitely said it was today and organised the flights. This was a bad start to the trip.

He decided not to attach any blame to his office and said, 'I am so sorry Mr Phillips I must have got the date wrong. I know you are an extremely busy man. Are you free later on in the day if I change my flight for late evening? I have been looking forward to meeting you.'

The older man looked really annoyed and Dale was sweating profusely as he waited for him to reply.

Bud positioned his grim face close to Dale's head. 'No, that's not convenient. I can do Saturday morning. I normally play a round of golf but I'm prepared to come in and show you around. Then you can get a flight back to New York.'

Dale sucked in breath before repeating the word Saturday. There was no way he could leave Phoenix for a further night. What was he going to do?

Then the man suddenly smiled and roared with laughter. He patted Dale hard on the back.

'Just kidding, you should have seen your face. Didn't that fine lady Rachel tell you I like having a bit of fun?'

What could Dale say to this practical joker who had taken client and supplier relations to another level? It was a poor thing to do to someone you'd never met. He acknowledged the importance of nurturing relations with suppliers, but this man was going to be a pain.

Dale sternly said, 'Well Mr Phillips, I just lost six pounds thinking I got the meeting day wrong. Next time we see each other leave out the jokes as I want you and me to get on. Are you reading me? Let's move on and you can show me your factory.'

Bud had picked the wrong person to have fun with.

During the tour of the works, Dale took notes on the fabrication of the individual sections that made up the carcasses. An idea came to him that involved doing away with assembling units with fasteners. He toyed with a design to employ hinges with lock pins for an all in one pop-up unit. The possibilities for an easy *one fits all* could help them launch a new product aimed heavily at the retail sector.

He received the tour of all tours and at the end of the morning they had lunch. He congratulated the sales director on a slick organisation. He was surprised when Bud mentioned the earlier occurrence and apologised.

On the way back to the airport Dale was pleased he'd seen first-hand the production line. However, whilst he had got over Bud's crazy episode, he still felt cross with Rachel who should have warned him about this man. It sounded like she knew Bud got his kicks from fooling around. He also reflected on his first morning when she left him in the hands of William and the strange things that happened. What was wrong with her? She really should have filled him in with important information like this.

What a first week it had been, the oddest of inductions and now the man from Pittsburgh who thought he was being terribly clever. It really irked him. He acknowledged his new boss rated him, but failing to keep him informed just wasn't on. He thought babysitting his grieving father was exhausting, but this new career was proving to be a whole new ball game.

Whilst waiting for the flight to be called, Dale rang home.

'What do you mean you forgot I was staying over in Pittsburgh? I even spoke to you when I arrived at the hotel. Anyway, I'm shortly to board the plane so will see you early evening.'

'Sure thing, son. I'm cooking your dinner.'

As Dale joined the queue of passengers waiting to be checked onto the aircraft, he wondered just exactly what Phoenix was preparing for them to eat. Serving up meals was normally his job as his father struggled to grasp the basics. His kitchen escapades were, let's just say, interesting and he hoped he'd take care with the stove and not burn the place down.

* * *

The afternoon flight into New York went smoothly. On clearing Arrivals, the first thing Dale did was call home again.

Once back in the apartment the two men hugged briefly. Dale observed his father was unshaven and his breath smelt of liquor. His hair, that looked like it needed a wash, hung loose as he hadn't bothered to tie it back. He was wearing his white dressing gown and not much else, Dale averted his eyes each time the garment fell open. Then there were his old black shoes with the backs pressed down, the ones splattered with blue paint on the fronts. How many times had Dale tried to throw them away and magically they reappeared on the kitchen floor?

'You didn't get dressed today.'

Phoenix ran a hand through his long hair sweeping it away from his eyes.

'No, I couldn't be bothered. This sodding hair is doing my head in. I may shave my head bare; it'll save me time in the mornings.'

Dale smiled at the suggestion. 'You look great with a ponytail; just do me a favour if you have guests here in the day smarten up a bit, won't you? That gown hardly covers you.'

'Give me some credit, son.'

Standing in the hallway there was the welcoming smell of cooking. Phoenix asked how he'd got on with his trip. Dale's account of the crazy man from Pittsburgh made him laugh.

Staring at the untidy apartment Dale tapped his father on the shoulder. 'So, Dad, what did you do while I was away?'

'Oh, this and that. You must be tired; get washed up and I'll put the finishing touches to our meal.'

'Great, I was wondering, what are you cooking?'

'Lasagne.'

Dale was impressed and hurried off to change. When he returned to the kitchen Phoenix had fixed his hair and was warming the plates for their meal. Seated at the table, Dale looked on in anticipation as the piping hot meal was served up.

'This is really good. Did you follow a recipe?'

'Sure, thing, son, I Googled the recipe, only it was a bit complicated. Basically, I did my own thing with a little seasoning from those jars you bought. It didn't turn out too bad.'

'What do you mean not too bad? It's awesome. You are quite a cook. Well done.'

'Spot on, I'm glad you like it. Before I forget, the real estate company has two apartments to show us on Sunday morning.'

Later on, when Dale was loading the dishwasher, he leant down to the floor to retrieve a torn off end of some food packaging. He examined the colourful packet and wording that read, *Super Lasagne ready in minutes.*

He couldn't stop laughing as he pictured the contents of their ready meal being emptied into the cooking tray and a few herbs sprinkled on the surface. Medium to high heat for forty minutes and Phoenix proudly presented the lasagne that looked like he'd made it from scratch.

* * *

On Saturday morning, Dale decided to get on with some housework. He tidied up the lounge coffee table, straightening magazines and his eyes were drawn to a receipt for twenty-seven dollars forty from a gas station. The date was for the previous day. The location was the same district as the cemetery. It was clear Phoenix had used the car and that the insurance would have been void in the event of an accident.

Dale sighed, as if there wasn't enough going on in the new job without all of this. He could put up with the mood changes, but not him driving whilst still being signed off by the doctor.

He tackled his father on the tricky subject. 'When were you going to tell me?'

'What am I supposed to have done now?'

'Don't lie to me please. You took the car and I found the receipt from the gas station.'

Dale felt embarrassed as he witnessed Phoenix acting like a petulant child when he pulled a face before storming off.

'Come back here. I asked you a question.'

There was no reply, not that Dale really needed clarification; he'd driven to the cemetery to visit Suzy's grave.

* * *

On Sunday morning they met up with the real estate agent in Queens. A young man with a stutter welcomed them. It was hard to avoid finishing off his sentences for him and, at times, he limited his explanations to pointing to his company brochures.

They were shown two apartments in a respectable area of town with good public transport links. The first property was an eight-storey building that was currently undergoing extensive repairs to the exterior and roof. The characterless third floor, two-bedroom accommodation was cramped and the tiny galley kitchen overlooked windows to a neighbouring apartment block. The place also smelled damp.

Ruling out this viewing, the next one had more going for it. The attractive tree-lined street, with stores and amenities close by, was of interest. The building dated back to the thirties with large pillared bay windows dominating the red brickwork. This was a four-storey with two penthouse suites that had obviously been added at a later date. The shiny red painted front door was huge with entry by intercom. First impressions were good as they stood around the spacious and well-decorated entry hall.

The agent showed them into the large second level dwelling that was empty but still welcoming. Inside the cavernous lounge, bright sunshine streamed through the tall windows and their voices echoed as they excitedly explored the room. A magnificent oak fireplace came into view and Phoenix proceeded to pat the woodwork. He commented he could place Suzy's antique clock on the shelf and how she had enjoyed winding it each Saturday. The ticking and chiming were always good to hear. Since he had returned home from hospital, he had forbidden Dale to wind the clock. Time had stopped, as had his wonderful wife's life. A new start would see her favourite keepsake being encouraged to work again.

The kitchen was equipped with new units and a stove. This apartment was just what they wanted with an acceptable rent, deposit and tenancy agreement. They were relieved when the agent chose to write down the figures for them to simplify matters.

Satisfied they had found the right place to live, they agreed to the deal and made arrangements to pay the deposit. They signed the initial documents that permitted the agent to make checks and arrange bank collections. Vacant possession would be in one month, this being the required notice on the West Village apartment. A removal company would be employed to move their furniture and Dale would ship his belongings from Orlando.

After thanking the young man, they motored over to see Dale's workplace. The sun that shone through the windshield warmed the interior of the car. Excited about the move, both men agreed the new apartment needed a fresh coat of paint. Phoenix insisted he was going to do the decorating.

Dale parked up and pointed to the scruffy looking large warehouse and offices.

Phoenix's first words were, 'Bloody hell, this can't be it. This dump looks like it's about to fall down and the graffiti is awful. Some of those words are downright rude. Surely you don't work here.'

Laughing, and at the same time wanting to agree with his father, he replied, 'Yes, I know it is a mess but it's better inside. The lady who runs it is talking about moving to a new unit. We are expanding and that's part of my role as operations manager.'

'Sounds like a fancy title to me.'

Dale frowned.

Phoenix's eyes were drawn to a red Ford drawing up outside the premises and out stepped a woman in a black coat with white tights covering her long slim legs.

'Now, that's what I call a beautiful broad. Take a look at the pins on her.'

'Dad, nobody says broad or pins anymore. It's Rachel. She is the director I've been telling you about. I think she's spotted us, so don't say anything embarrassing.'

Rachel crossed over to their car and the driver's window was lowered.

'I thought it was you Dale.'

Phoenix was leaning heavily over his son to get a better look at the attractive woman. It was clear he wanted to be introduced.

'Rachel, this is Phoenix, my dad. We've just signed up to rent an apartment ten blocks down.'

She extended cold fingers to shake hands with Phoenix who lowered his voice to speak. 'The pleasure is all mine. I understand you are the owner of the company.'

'Yes, that right. It's not much of a building but I think you will like the new place we are planning to move to.'

She turned her attention to Dale. 'I'm not usually in on a Sunday. I just need to catch up on a few things. And what about you, how was Bud Phillips? I hope the two of you got on. He's ace, don't you think?'

Dale hesitated, and tapping the steering wheel, he said, 'You could say that. I'm not sure I have the measure of the guy just yet. From what I conclude, he's built that operation up and knows the industry inside out. Yep, I guess it was a good trip.'

'I'm pleased it went well. Bud rang me after you left for the airport and paid you some good compliments. He said I'd picked a gem of a business man and I'd better hang onto you or he'd make you an offer himself.'

After saying goodbye to Rachel, Dale drove home. He listened to his father saying kind things about his boss. He was also thinking again about what a week it had been. And now this guy Bud had given him a positive report back on their meeting. Things were looking up. Five long working days had passed and he was determined to become a mover and shaker who'd change the fortunes of this relatively small company.

* * *

Working eight hours a day, Dale balanced his job with looking out for his father. The move to Queens went remarkably smoothly and it wasn't long before the apartment felt like home. Phoenix set to work on the decorating. The walls took on a warm hue of cream with white ceilings. A deep blue carpet was purchased for the lounge and some new drapes. With all their furniture now in place, it made it a comfy room to relax in. Suzy's clock adorned the fireplace shelf and ticked away the hours. The sound of the chimes echoed through the high-ceilinged rooms affording a homely feel.

In the first month a number of neighbours called round to make their introductions. A mixture of people lived in the building. An Argentinian woman, with long, silver-grey hair and round, John Lennon style glasses perched on her nose, told them she had been widowed four years ago. Paulina's calm demeanour resonated with Phoenix as she revealed her passion for helping the unfortunate who lived on the sidewalks of the city. He let drop he was considering assisting in this field prompting her to relate many heart-rending stories of the rough sleepers. She suggested she could take him along one evening. Phoenix said he would think about it. Maybe he wasn't quite ready to experience more sadness just yet.

Other visitors included a couple who worked in finance, two gay men who brought flowers and an invitation to a drinks party. A young man, with a bushy beard and long hair, who spoke with an English accent, told Phoenix he was writing a novel and had writer's block. Phoenix was soon to regret asking him about the content of his story. A long, dull tale was unleashed resulting in the writer offering to show him his work. He divulged the fact that his parents were financing him whilst he completed his book. Phoenix swiftly switched the conversation to the apartment block.

Chapter 16

To say working for Rachel and William was a struggle would be an understatement. Four months along the line and there existed a problem. Conflicting instructions were often the bane of Dale's busy day. William would brief him, only for Rachel to tell him to ignore her partner. To an outsider, the two owners were just colleagues, but tell-tale signs convinced Dale they were an item. The overriding worry was that the running of the business should not be affected by their poor decision making. The pair were poles apart in their vision for the new office and warehousing and, as for the marketing of mirrors on a retail platform, well it was like they had both given up on the venture. Dale's eagle eye for accounts detected there was no scope to earmark funds for the move, leaving him frustrated and determined to tackle Rachel head-on.

He turned his attention to the day-to-day operation by reforming the quoting system thus linking it to the sales planner data. Upgrading the software to expand the package was going to be costly and he'd need sign-off for that expenditure. Perturbed by Rachel's reluctance to agree to changes, he wondered if she was thinking of selling up. What was wrong with the woman? During his first two months of working there, she had been so supportive of him and now there was a problem. She'd moved him to an office down the corridor and her diminished enthusiasm for everything certainly worried him.

The move was definitely on hold and Rachel kept telling him it was just a glitch. Where had all the dreams gone? Overnight the curtain had fallen and Dale struggled to understand the sudden change.

One morning, at the start of work, he knocked on her door and Rachel offered him a drink from her coffee machine. The office was untidier than usual and he cleared documents from a chair before sitting down. In a disinterested voice, she asked what he wanted.

His voice quivered as he went over the rehearsed words. 'I hope I haven't upset you in any way, but just lately you seem too busy to talk to me. We've had the best quarter for two years with sales and net profit riding high. I'm pleased with our progress. Are you not happy with the figures? I have to ask if things have changed? Is there something I should know?'

Rachel shrugged her shoulders. 'Like what, Dale?'

'Well, for starters, the move appears to be off.'

Sipping her hot coffee, she appeared deep in thought and remained silent.

Dale considered the possibility she was downsizing the company and no longer required his services.

It was then that his cell phone rang and he frowned on seeing it was his father calling. How many times had he told him not to ring whilst he was at work?

Rachel snapped, 'Not your father again. I get fed up with you taking calls. I keep reminding you we are here to work and he keeps on calling. Keep your private phone calls for your leisure time.'

Dale put a hand up in the air. 'It's not all the time, but I agree I need to rein him in.'

Her mood lightened, 'Sorry for biting your head off. How is he?'

'We get good days and then he goes off on one. This morning I couldn't find a tie to wear as he'd taken them all to be cleaned. It's a good job I'm not meeting clients today. And the previous weekend he lost the key to his wife's clock and got extremely emotional. Finding a horologist on a Saturday afternoon wasn't easy, but I got him a replacement winder. I tell you, it's a strain sometimes.'

Rachel's face was full of sympathy and, although Dale didn't want to upset his boss, he just went for it. 'Rachel, I have to ask you to level with me. Give it to me straight – what's the problem?'

She immediately responded, 'As you said, we are doing well, but, yes, I've taken my eye off the ball.' Her face looked so tortured and he noticed her eyes were welling up. 'It's William; he's met someone else and wants out of the business. So now you know why I can't take the company forward if I have to buy him out. Finding another partner could take forever.'

'Oh, I see. I'm sorry he's hurt you so badly. I thought you said at my interview you were just business partners.'

Rachel closed her eyes for a brief moment. 'I didn't want you knowing about my private life. I've always kept work separate from my leisure time. We didn't live together; it was complicated. I really loved him.'

It was upsetting seeing her cry and Dale's first reaction was to comfort her however his inner voice warned him to remain professional. He offered to leave the room.

'No, don't go. Please give me a moment. I might as well tell you that William has already left the company. I don't know if I should ring the bank to stop him taking out company funds.'

Dale's face reddened as he acknowledged the ramifications of a partner emptying the account. 'I suggest you do that right away.'

'Got that,' stammered Rachel.

Dale observed her hair, that normally looked so tidy, was dishevelled. She looked worn out and kept closing her beautiful blue eyes. He'd never noticed the colour before. Wearing jeans and sloppy jumper was unusual for Rachel who normally took such pride in her appearance.

He made a concentrated effort to stop staring. He was racking his brain to say something that would demonstrate his loyalty to her and the company.

'With losing William, I can handle our sales. This company doesn't need to cease operating because someone leaves.'

Rachel suddenly looked hopeful again, she was stirred by his determination to overcome the hurdles. 'Thank you, Dale, and please be assured I have every confidence in your ability. The difficulty I have is in buying him out.'

'What about a bank loan?'

'It's a large sum and I'd probably only get half of the money. I have assets in shares, but can't raise anywhere near that amount. He wants two hundred thousand bucks.'

'Oh, that's a shed load of dough. The guy will just have to wait until you can get the funds together.'

Dale took off his glasses and rubbed his eyes. He was shocked matters had escalated to this level. His mind toyed with the necessity for Rachel to secure the money and then he'd make the changes to the firm that would give them a chance to carry on trading.

In a confident voice he rolled out his plan. 'For starters we reduce the headcount and I start shaking up this business. There are two potential clients we'd love to get into bed with, so let's offer them a deal they can't refuse.'

He checked he had her attention before continuing. 'We put the move and the mirror launch on the back burner. You need to get on with selling those shares and have your lawyer offer William a part payment. That will give us breathing space. First though, you gotta put a hold on that bank account.'

Rachel sat upright in her swivel office chair and drew out her bank book from the desk drawer. 'Thank God you applied for the job. I really appreciate your help.'

'Don't thank me; we are not out of this mess yet. I have everything riding on this job. I've turned my life upside down to live in New York with my dad. He's still grieving and, on top of that, we've just moved apartment.'

'It really must be hard for you.'

He quickly returned to the matter in question. 'So, I'll concentrate on sales. How does that sound to you?'

Nodding her head in approval, he was pleased she was now thinking about the business again.

Dale smiled at his boss. 'I have something to say to you. I can't buy into your company, but I want you to make me your new business partner. I will hold no shares, but will have the opportunity to build up this firm until I can raise sufficient funds. I know we can do this together. I want you to shake my hand on it.'

A look of astonishment lit up Rachel's face as she struggled to get out her words, 'W... w... well yes – I don't know what to say. You have only worked here for a relatively short time but instinctively I know you are the guy to help me.'

'I ask only one concession. I get William's office and his ruddy owl painting on the door goes.'

She laughed. 'Okay, I agree. He was no artist. It's awful, isn't it?

After the handshake that sealed their new partnership, Rachel mentioned that William was history. She was moving on.

* * *

That night Phoenix listened as Dale relayed the news that he was to be made a partner in the company where he worked. He hadn't bought into the business but hoped to one day.

Phoenix poured himself more wine ignoring Dale's empty glass. 'You say a partner, that's awesome. I'm amazed all this happed in just a few months. I can sense your excitement to rescue this business. I'm also relieved to know their accounts are in reasonable shape. It's buying out this creep William that hurts. I told you he sounded like a mad man. To run a business, you need calm heads like yours and mine. Now me, I would shake that business up.'

Stifling his urge to laugh, Dale coughed and said, 'I'm on the same page as you Dad, only he wants his investment back quickly. She has to sell some shares, but that won't cover it. She is instructing her lawyer to put forward a payment plan for the balance.'

Phoenix raised his voice to make his point. 'So, as a company they are sound and you are going to turn around their fortunes? It sounds like an incredible stroke of luck you getting that job.'

'What do you mean?'

'I have every confidence in your ability to run the company and it will be a lucrative earner for us both.'

'And your point is?'

'I want to buy you in as a real partner. No strings attached, I'm giving you one hundred and twenty thousand bucks from Suzy's money. It's sitting in the bank earning next to no interest and I'm going to invest in you. It's what Suzy would have wanted me to do.'

Dale was stunned to hear him say this. 'Oh no, you are not. That money is yours and you may need it for the future.'

'I've never been surer about anything in my life. I still have plenty left, so that's what we are doing.'

Acknowledging that this was an incredibly kind and generous thing his father was offering, he hugged him and whispered his thanks.

Phoenix then had some news of his own that he was anxious to share. 'You know Paulina, the Argentinian lady; well, she has invited me for lunch. Now don't go reading anything into this as you know I don't want anyone except Suzy. I like this lady and I'm keen to learn more about helping the homeless.'

'Wow, it really has been quite a day.'

'You could say that. Do you have Rachel's number?'

'Yes.'

'Well ring the lady with your offer of the money.'

Five minutes later Rachel took a call from Dale leaving her thrilled with his news. She informed him that her lawyer would draw up the papers. She sounded upbeat saying she'd already spoken to her financial advisor about selling her shares. She stressed that soon William would be out of her life.

On saying goodbye to Rachel, Dale put a thumb up in the direction of Phoenix who glanced up to the ceiling and Dale heard him whisper, 'Thanks Suzy.'

Chapter 17

When Phoenix was finally deemed well enough to work, it proved more difficult than he initially thought to land a job as a driver, due to his age. However, there were still vacancies on Ethan's site, so he attended an interview and landed a welding position. Dale was concerned but deep down knew he couldn't dissuade him.

Phoenix, relieved to be back in work, enjoyed every moment of it. The heights no longer bothered him and it appeared he was at long last back on track.

* * *

Dale's busy life saw him putting in longer hours to assist Rachel with restructuring the company. For the meantime, the move to the new premises had been postponed. The exterior of their works was tidied up with a fresh coat of paint. A smart sign incorporating the new company logo improved the appearance of the building. They hoped the graffiti artists would give them a break and not spoil their newly painted walls.

Areas that were addressed promptly were the new company name and website. Dale spent three days a week out on the road visiting prospective customers and gradually drew new companies into their net. He negotiated a twelve-month lease for their building that reflected a reduction in rental costs. Diversification was essential for seeking out new markets and he was the man to bring about change.

His investment in the company went towards paying William off and the balance from Rachel's shares was allocated for the final payment.

Dale got his father, on his days off, to help out with putting up some shelves and moving furniture around, and made sure he got paid for his efforts. The finishing touch for his office was in hanging a new door. At long last the annoying owl was destined for the garbage.

During Phoenix's few days working at the company, Rachel made a fuss of him and took him out to lunch on his last day. Dale put it down to them being the same age. Her life was her work and she showed no signs of wanting to date again. However, he was aware she kept in touch with William, often speaking to him on the phone.

* * *

The day William turned up unannounced at the office was hard for Dale as he was trying to have a meeting with a prospective client. Judging by the raised voices coming from his partner's office, the air was electric. On hearing an almighty thud, he quickly apologised to his visitor promising to return as swiftly as possible.

When he reached Rachel's partly open door, he was horrified to see William holding her wrists. She looked terrified. On seeing Dale, he released his grip and stood back from her.

'It's none of your business – get out,' William shouted.

'No, you looked like you were hurting her. Rachel you come over here and I'll get rid of him.'

She was now by his side and trembling with fear.

'Did he hurt you?'

'No, but he won't leave me alone.'

William, who Dale had always seen as a bit of a softie, turned out to be a really nasty bit of work. He was surprised to see him wearing a suit and for once his grey hair was neatly combed.

'Look William – please leave.'

William spat out his insult. 'Oh, don't you two look cosy. Is there something I should know?'

Dale was disgusted with the suggestion and shook his head.

William pushed past them and noisily left the building. When the thud of him slamming the front door came, they both sighed with relief.

Dale was not prepared for what happened next when Rachel hugged him really hard and showed no signs of letting go. She was crying and he felt her tears wetting the collar of his white shirt. He pulled away sharply.

'What are you doing Rachel? This isn't professional. We work together and I've got a client back there who must think he's come to a mad house.'

It was like she wasn't listening, staring blankly at him.

'Speak to me Rachel, level with me please.'

'You just don't understand, do you? I'm practically running on empty and at my wits end. There is no way I want him and he says we should give it another go. He's history Dale and I just wish I'd met you before and not him.'

Dale stood back from her. He was shocked and wished she hadn't said that.

'Please don't talk like that. For the record, I'm not interested. Do I make myself clear? Remember, we are colleagues and outside this place we go our separate ways. We have a business to run, so get a handle on your personal life.'

He was concerned she was thinking about him in this manner. He hadn't given her any reason to believe he had feelings for her. The last thing he needed was a woman old enough to be his mother coming on to him. All he wanted to do was carve out a living and he could do without these distractions.

He sensed her embarrassment and, if he wasn't mistaken, she was about to cry again.

Then he remembered his visitor who he hoped was still in the office. There was no getting away from the fact he would have overheard the turmoil just a few doors along the corridor. This was, without doubt, the worst of days; as if he didn't have enough on his plate without Rachel piling on her problems.

As he walked the short distance to his office his cell phone rang and, on checking the caller display, he cursed his father for his timing.

'Not now, dad, I'm in a meeting,'

'It won't take a moment - I'm buying the paint for the hallway – I just want to know if you'd prefer plain white or pale green for the woodwork?'

Angrily, Dale hissed down the phone, 'Go for the sodding green.'

* * *

Recently Phoenix's mental state was nigh on perfect and Dale prayed nothing would change this. The memory clinic appointments had definitely helped, so the doctor had given him the all clear.

Dale decided not to tell him about Rachel making a move on him. He didn't want him worrying after having pledged so much money to buy into the partnership. After that particularly trying day at the office, he warmed up their pizza with the extra peperoni and chilli but soon became concerned when his father said he wasn't hungry. He had his own bad news to relate. Ethan had left his wife.

Phoenix tentatively broached the subject of Ethan coming to stay whilst he sorted out a new place to live. Dale's initial hesitation was down to the fact that there were only two bedrooms. There was also the issue of maintaining a tidy apartment. Phoenix, at the best of times, led a disorderly life with the brunt of the housework falling on his son. And now, with the threat of another messy person invading his space, he couldn't say he was that keen. He shuddered at the thought of this builder friend breaking wind in their home, something that had happened a few times before. Phoenix thought it hilarious.

Concerned for Ethan, but still anxious about this new arrangement, he muttered, 'Oh, that's awful news. Is his wife all right?'

A wry grin lit up Phoenix's face. 'Not sure, but I do know he's dating this girl from a liquor store. The guy needs a roof over his head and I'd like to help out. It will only be for a month. He'll sleep on the couch and won't be any bother.'

Dale visualised the couch they'd only recently purchased becoming grubby and worn out. His orderly life was going to be disturbed. What if this man snored or shouted out in his sleep? He pictured their apartment taking a beating. However, he wasn't going to upset his father.

'A month, you say. Just make it clear it's only a temporary arrangement. You also need to put down some house rules; I don't want to come home after a hard day's work to find the place in a mess. And for the record, no more farting.'

Bursting into laughter Phoenix pouted his lips and made a rude noise.

'That's really not funny. I don't want him ruining our new couch.'

Still amused by his son's comments, Phoenix nodded in agreement. 'I'll make sure he keeps a hold on things.'

He giggled when he said this and Dale told him to stop being so childish.

Now in a serious mood, Phoenix said, 'I ought to mention; there might be the odd time his lady friend stays over. That will be okay, won't it?'

'No, that won't be all right. I draw the line there. With him camping out in our lounge, I'm not tiptoeing around with two people getting up to heaven knows what.'

* * *

Ethan's first evening in the apartment soon came around. To Dale's relief, he brought with him a new sleeping bag, pillow and blanket to cover the couch. He'd also prepared their meal, mixed canned beans with microwave spicy rice, washed down with an ample supply of bottled beer.

On seeing the dreaded beer, Dale frowned at his father.

Over the meal, Dale listened intently to a tale that differed from Phoenix's account of the breakup of the relationship. It appeared Ethan's wife had been playing the field for some time. There had been an almighty row and now he'd linked up with his new lady friend. Divorce was on the cards for Ethan.

Ethan insisted on doing the washing up and when Phoenix went off to the bathroom, he got Dale's attention. 'I wanted to thank you for letting me stay. Also, I'm going to pay my way, so here's two weeks rent as a starter.'

'Thanks Ethan, that's much appreciated and I'm sorry to hear about your wife.'

Ethan's smile turned to a grin. 'Well, I'm not. Now what I really wanted to speak to you about is your father.'

'Oh yes, what's bothering you?'

'It's the things he's been doing at work that concern me.'

Dale felt a shiver run down his spine. 'God, what's he been up to now?'

There was a pause and for a moment he wondered if Ethan had changed his mind about revealing terrible news.

'You do know his supervisor had words?'

'No, he didn't say anything to me?'

'Yeah, he was acting strange last week standing close to the edge of the building. It's like he ignored me when I urged him to stand back. I was worried he was thinking about Cody again. It's not safe what he was doing. The supervisors also noticed him gazing down.'

'Oh Jesus. What level were you working on?'

'High enough.'

'And what did the supervisor do?'

Ethan nodded his head. 'Oh, he waited for your dad to return to his welding work. He was satisfied with what he told him about it being a one off, but I did notice him making a note on his pad. I bet it goes on his record. Phoenix said he was just looking down at the street and didn't know what all the fuss was about. Of course, it wasn't the first time he had done this.'

Dale whispered, 'Bugger, here we go again. Just as I thought things were going well. I might have to get him an appointment with the doctor or the guys at the Woodside Clinic.'

'Do you mean the shrinks? Look, let's not upset him with talk like that. Your father explained to me why he was looking over the side…'

Interrupting, Dale placed a hand on his quivering lips. 'W… w… what did he say?'

'He was getting nervous about working up high and was just checking to see if he could cope with the height.'

'Bloody hell,' muttered Dale.

'My reaction too at first, but I don't think he intended to do anything crazy. He was just trying to come to terms with being up there.'

Dale closed his eyes. 'Great, so he goes and stands on the edge of a building. If only I'd talked to him more, but I was wrapped up with my own business.'

Ethan stretched out his hand and patted Dale's shoulder. 'Don't beat yourself up. I'm convinced he's not going mad or anything.'

'But how can you be sure?'

'Only that more recently he seems to be in a better frame of mind. I'll keep an eye on him.'

They heard Phoenix opening the bathroom door and Dale decided against confronting him with Ethan's revelation.

When he joined them, Ethan held up a can of beer for his friend. 'Do you want one of these? How about you, Dale, are you going to join us? These little beauties really pack a punch and I can vouch for that.'

Chapter 18

The days that followed saw Dale keeping out of Rachel's way as much as possible. They kept their discussions brief and there were, unquestionably, moments of unease between them. Rachel suggested she take some holiday to give her time to think. What was there to think about? Dale had made it perfectly clear where he stood.

She was to be off for a week and he relished the prospect of running the firm alone. The new computer software was being installed on Thursday and he should learn from Market Zenet whether they'd won the new contract. If the business came their way, the necessity for finding larger premises in the following year would start all over again. This time a bank loan would definitely be required.

One evening, Dale was about to go home when Rachel asked him to assist her in her office. It was apparent she was having a spring clean before taking her leave. Dale readily put his back into moving the heavy garbage sacks.

'What have you got in here, they weigh a ton?'

'Oh, it's most of William's stuff. Old trade catalogues, magazines and golf balls.'

'Won't he want them?'

'No, I don't think we will be seeing him again.'

Dale put down the two bags he was carrying and said, 'Let's clear the air. Since that day William acted like a real jerk, it feels like you and I have been walking on broken glass. Level with me, are you over him?'

'Yep, but what I didn't tell you was that last week he turned up at my apartment drunk as a skunk. He was demanding back the present he gave me for my birthday.

I reminded him there had been no gift and he was confusing me with the girl he'd shacked up with.'

'Mmm, did you tell him to get lost?'

'The guy actually cried there and then in the lobby of my apartment building and people were staring. I felt humiliated and, do you know Dale, I couldn't give a damn what happened to him.'

'Good on you.'

'And as for clearing the air, I want to say sorry for telling you I had feelings for you. You are right this is a business we are running, not a dating agency.'

'Let's say no more.'

Dale disposed of the garbage in the container in the warehouse and returned to the offices to say goodbye. Rachel was pulling on her coat and got an arm stuck in the sleeve.

'Help me please.'

As ever a gentleman, he went to her aid. She turned her head round to thank him and he must have been too close. Their heads briefly came into contact. It was a soft blow and Dale found himself gazing into her beautiful blue eyes. The smell of her perfume was strong and exotic. It all happened so quickly with Rachel gently kissing his lips. He froze on the spot.

He found himself responding and placed his arms inside her coat. Through the thin fabric of her shirt he could sense her warm body and feel the clasp on her bra. His mind was spinning. How good it felt holding Rachel and her responding to his touch.

This time Dale kissed Rachel and held her tight. He could feel her breasts tight against his chest. They were interrupted by the sound of a car horn and he pulled away.

'Sorry, the street door is unlocked. Let me see who is out there.'

Dale moved over to the window. It was dark as he glanced down to their warehouse area. There was his dad's car and he was standing on the sidewalk. On catching sight of Dale's face, Phoenix waved madly.

'It's my Dad. I forgot he was picking me up. We arranged to go out for an early dinner; I've got to go. We don't want him coming up here.'

'Slow down there. You have lipstick on your face and I'd better clean it off.'

Taking a wipe from her desk drawer, she smoothed off the tell-tale sign and told him she'd see him soon.

He held Rachel's hand and said, 'We need to talk. Are you still going to take time off work?'

'Oh no, I think you and I have some unfinished business.'

Then the tooting of the horn started again. His father was getting impatient.

Rachel smiled and told him she'd lock up and he kissed her forehead.

'Slip the catch on the door. I've changed my mind about going home just yet. I'm going to go over some of those quotes of yours. It will be great if some of them turn into orders. Off you go and I'll see you in the morning.'

Dale joined his father in the car and was surprised to see Ethan.

Phoenix hurriedly told him that his friend was treating them to dinner. Ethan had some news to convey, he was moving in with his new lady friend. Dale was pleased to hear him say this. He'd only been with them for a few days and already the apartment was beginning to look untidy as his father's builder friend camped out in the lounge.

Ethan enquired how Dale's day went.

Glancing up to Rachel's office window Dale replied, 'Yes, one of the best, thanks.'

* * *

The next morning Dale listened to the warehouse manager's explanation on the current damage to stock caused by a new employee's carelessness with the reach truck. It was the second time in a week. Moving goods around their storage area was a dangerous business and Dale didn't wish to fall short on safety and health regulations.

'You being the boss, I want to know if we can we legally terminate her employment?'

Ignoring the question, Dale kept looking towards his office window. 'Have you seen Rachel this morning?'

'Well no, but I took a call to say she'd be in around midday. Now, what do you want me to do with this new girl?'

Dale couldn't stop thinking about Rachel. Several times he stood up from his desk to look out of the window hoping to see her car, only to be disappointed.

The warehouse manager reminded him of the stock loss and this time Dale responded with, 'Once, I can put up with, but this morning's accident must be another thirty bucks in the trash can. I'll let her go before she breaks more stock or, worse, injures someone.'

Just before lunch in walked Rachel, and judging by the store bags she left by her desk, it was clear she'd been shopping.

'We need to talk; I've been thinking about what happened.'

Dale moved away from her. 'Not now, someone might come in. Why didn't you call?'

'I left here quite late last night and decided I needed a break. This morning I lay in the bathtub for ages then went into town to buy clothes. Haven't missed anything have I? Except you, of course.'

Trying desperately to stitch the right words together, it all came out wrong. He so wanted to talk to her about the previous evening but was scared as there was bad news he needed to convey.

'That new girl damaged some stock and she's getting her cards.'

Shaking her head Rachel's voice rose to one of annoyance. 'Not again.'

'Worse than that, I've been dreading telling you that we picked up a bad debt. Reazel Small have gone into administration.'

He could sense Rachel's anger. 'I knew it. Bloody hell Dale, I warned you about dealing with them and you said we should take a chance. Now look what has happened. That's twenty-two thousand dollars up the creek. I'm beginning to wish I hadn't come in.'

'I'm really sorry. They had been paying on thirty-six days and last month dragged their feet. My only hope is we win that tender this week, it will more than compensate for our losses.'

With a hand on her forehead she muttered, 'God, I could do without all this. We'd better win that new business and you watch their payment days like a hawk. You print off the outstanding invoice data for me and I'm going to go through it with a fine toothcomb. One more debt like this and our cash flow situation is going to grind to a halt. And that girl, how much did that cost us this morning?'

'She took the corner off a unit – thirty dollars max.'

Rachel sighed. 'Only thirty dollars you say, today that's a fortune in my books.'

Dale's heart sank, only last night she was cuddling up to him and now she was bad-tempered. Wasn't this a prime example why office romances were never a good idea?

The air was sour and there was no mention of their moment of happiness. Had she decided it was a bad idea and was embarrassed? He couldn't blame her for sparking off; after all he had taken one hell of a chance with the company that went bust.

The rest of the day was hectic and he was downhearted praying nothing else would go wrong. Opening his inbox, he read with dismay an e-mail from the company he was pinning his hopes on. They had been unsuccessful.

Uncertain that Rachel could take any more bad news, he entered her office with trepidation. She could tell by his grim face there was a problem.

'We didn't get it, did we?'

Dale put a hand in the air and apologised.

She appeared to be more in control and the tension that had built up earlier dissipated.

'You are normally the strong one Dale. I've been doing some thinking – let's draw a line under today. It's a good job our sales are good. We'll offset that debt with some of the profit we've been making. It's a blow, but hey, we are still open for business. I'm sorry I lost it with you earlier and you got the brunt of my temper.'

'That's okay. I took a chance and even calculated risks go wrong. I just wish, after last night, we hadn't had to go through all this anxiety today. I went home so happy and dreamt about you and now …'

Rachel took a deep breath. 'Let me stop you there. Last night should never have happened. It doesn't change the way I feel about you. I'm just not ready for a relationship at the moment. I don't know what came over me.'

'Oh, don't say that. I won't put any pressure on you. Please, let's take it slowly.'

'I am very fond of you, but I've got my sensible head on today and it's telling me to slow down. This ain't no two-way street. For the meantime, we carry on and concentrate on our business. That way we will be able to cope with anything work throws at us. You do understand, don't you?'

Inside Dale was hurting and felt he'd been dealt a harsh card, but he wouldn't stop loving her.

Chapter 19

Suzy's memorial stone was finally erected thirteen months after she died. Phoenix had kindly allowed Donald and Marlene to choose the wording. The Italian white marble was inscribed beautifully with two blue jays circling her name; the blue jay had always been Suzy's favourite bird. Brightly coloured flowers adorned the base and the warm summer breeze made their visit more bearable.

It was an emotional morning as Suzy's parents stayed behind to pay their respects.

Phoenix glanced over to Cody's grave and then back to his wife's resting place. The tears welled up as he acknowledged that the feeling of loss wasn't getting any easier.

Back in the apartment Phoenix served tea and some of Suzy's favourite cookies. He brought out some of their old photo albums. It was still hard to believe she was never coming back. Donald said he was pleased Dale was settled in his new job and looked forward to hearing more. Phoenix deliberately chose not to mention his friendship with their Argentinian neighbour, worrying they would be hurt thinking Suzy was being replaced, but he couldn't deny he had feelings for this new woman.

* * *

Dale acknowledged his brief relationship with Rachel was a one off. It had been a moment they would both remember, but should not be repeated. Eventually girlfriends came and went, but Dale never gave up hoping that one day Rachel and he would get together. The company went through a period of stagnant growth and just keeping their heads above water was a challenge.

Worryingly, a new competitor appeared on the scene and the guy who ran it was Rachel's ex-partner, William. Dale was right: they hadn't seen the back of him.

Trading became difficult with tighter margins and adjustments had to be made to their company's product range. It would appear that William's company had embraced online ordering thus being able to reduce the number of staff employed. They had linked in with a company in New Jersey that manufactured the carcasses and delivered direct to his clients.

* * *

On a frosty New York morning, Rachel arrived to unlock the premises and was shocked to see the front of the building had been defaced with red paint. This time, not graffiti, but a message that read – *Closing down, last few days.* It wasn't long before Dale arrived and joined her to stare at the three-foot-high lettering.

Dale was first to speak, or rather shout, not caring if people arriving for work in other units heard him. 'I'll kill the bastard. William has gone too far this time. I'm going to sort him out once and for all.'

'How can you be sure it's him? I don't want you doing anything you'll later regret.'

'Don't play dumb, of course it was him.'

Out of breath and leaning on the brickwork for support, Dale looked unwell and Rachel was concerned. She pleaded with him not to get so worked up.

'Don't tell me to calm down. I have a measure of this guy and understand his game plan. He will go to any lengths to run us out of town. I told you last week our best client said William was running us down saying we were struggling to keep our doors open. It's got to be him.'

They were suddenly aware of someone shouting. They gazed up to the opened window and spotted Diana from accounts.

'It's your father on the line Dale. He says he wasn't sure if you meant him to collect the groceries from the store. He insists on talking to you.'

'Dale swore quietly before replying, 'Thanks, just tell him I'll ring him back.'

As Diana began to close the window she said, 'It's the second time he's rung this morning.'

'Okay, keep him on the line and I'll come up there.'

Rachel mentioned that when the warehouse guys arrived, she'd send them out for paint to remove the damning lettering. She also added that Phoenix was becoming a nuisance and Dale needed to stop him calling.

Dale's recent visit to the doctor had confirmed his blood pressure was riding sky high. Medication was helping, although this morning his face was a shocking bright red and he was out of breath.

Rachel grasped his arm. 'I'm worried about your health and all this anxiety over William can't be helping. The last thing I want is for you to get ill.'

Rachel drew him to her and he knew this was the turning point. It was a long time before she let go and when she did, they both were smiling. She then kissed him. It was a real kiss on the lips and Dale knew this meant the warmth had returned to their relationship.

'Oh Rachel, you must know I love you. I've waited for this moment for so long.'

She stroked his face and said, 'Me, too.'

'Just wait here. My dad must still be hanging on to speak to me.'

'Forget your old man and come here.'

* * *

With Rachel sorting out the repainting of the wall, Dale glanced at his face in the washroom mirror. He was still fairly young, but the stress of the last few years had been monumental. Shortness of breath was taking its toll and worry lines creased his forehead. Rachel was right; he had to be careful and decided to contact the doctor again. His father had been worried about him too, but he had maintained he was okay.

Things were tough, but they would get through. He was determined to sort out William as the guy had gone too far this time.

* * *

That night Dale and Rachel made love for the first time. In her cluttered first floor apartment off West Side, he felt like heaven was where they were laying. With previous girlfriends it had mostly been a hurried affair with a feeling of being left wanting. But now, she was holding him and sharing her love with him. She took him to heights he'd never believed possible and in return he took the time to excite her. Kissing her soft lips and feeling the eager tongue searching for his was bliss. After their lovemaking, they lay in bed for hours talking about their lives and planning the future.

The next morning over breakfast they agreed to go into work separately to avoid speculation. Dale wanted to shout out their news from the rooftops, but Rachel insisted he reserved his excitement for the bedroom. He also promised to make the appointment with the doctor although, at this particular moment, his rejuvenated-self felt strong again.

* * *

Choosing the right moment to tell his father about their relationship, he summed up with, 'I love her and all the current problems with work seem irrelevant.'

Phoenix raised his eyes to the ceiling and quickly back to his son.

'Irrelevant, I can't spell that son, but I get the meaning. I'm over the moon about you guys, but don't take your foot off the gas at work. You've got a lot of dough tied up in that place. Take it from a guy who knows, love and business are great but there has to be a balance.'

'I take your point and we plan to keep our evenings free of any talk about business. I may spend more time over at Rachel's apartment. I just thought I'd let you know.'

Dale observed the worried face and knew he must be concerned he'd soon be on his own. 'I don't want you fretting. My share of rent for this place will still be there. And another thing, I'll spend as many evenings with you as possible.'

Phoenix looked happier and switched the conversation to, 'How did your meeting with the doctor go?

'Oh no sweat there, she increased the medication for my blood pressure. I'm going to take care of my health. More importantly, how are you and Paulina getting on?'

'I've told you before I'm in a purely platonic relationship with this lady at present. There's no funny business going on there. What I can't deny is I'm attracted to her and I'm not saying never; let's see how things pan out. My fascination is to learn more about the good work she does for the charity group. I was apprehensive about helping, but now feel ready.'

'That's a really good thing you are considering; go at your own speed though.'

Mentioning the word speed, Dale's mind returned to his feelings for Rachel and the importance of not rushing her. The last thing he wanted was to scare her away.

* * *

Taking all things into consideration, life was panning out well for Phoenix who was still enjoying his work on the building site. There wasn't a day that passed that Suzy didn't come into his mind. He was convinced she would have wanted him to be happy and continue the friendship with Paulina.

The night that Paulina finally persuaded him to accompany her on a visit to see the homeless was a real eye opener. It shocked him to learn that there were reported to be record counts of homeless people. Many turned to the New York municipal shelter system, but there wasn't room for everyone. The highest numbers of homeless women and children were recently verified since the Great Depression of the 1930s.

Assisting Paulina was a strange experience as Phoenix, who recalled previously walking through the city on his own at night, had only ever noticed a few rough sleepers.

His friend explained that you just had to open your eyes to see the multitudes of unfortunate people, each with a story that would bring tears to the eyes. The shelters had full occupancy and alarmingly left many to fend for themselves relying on the goodwill of charities and passers-by. It was hard to comprehend the extent of the problem or predict when things would ever improve.

Walking with Paulina, a whole new world came into sight. People were everywhere living in the squalor of the dark streets. Damp doorways and alleyways revealed a cardboard city with drunks and so many homeless people who'd slipped off life's precarious ladder. Prostitution and drug dealing were rife, similar to most cities around the world.

One woman was lying flat out on the cold sidewalk. Phoenix nervously stepped to one side fearing she may be dead. The drunken woman suddenly moved and threw up close to his shoes. Paulina attended to her before calling her mentor, Danny, back at base in the church room for help.

Later in the evening they came across two roughly dressed girls who were clearly unhappy. This was their second week out in the open leaving them shocked and dispirited. Phoenix gauged their ages to be early twenties and it was impossible to imagine how they'd fallen on such bad luck.

Their anxious voices vying to be heard made it hard to work through each of their problems. Paulina's experience impressed Phoenix as she calmly gave advice about their damp bedding. They were not aware of the Mission room and kitchen or the support they could expect. A hot bowl of soup and bread were free of charge with a chance to warm up before returning to the streets.

The counselling and information available on shelters would be of assistance to them.

Helping to carry the girls' belongings, they walked past dirty Gothic-looking buildings that didn't look any better by day. Phoenix and Paulina led the way back to the warm and welcoming centre. He listened to their stories of vulnerability to thieves and gangs that ran rife in the city. One of the girls informed him that she had woken to find a man dragging her sleeping bag from underneath her. Her screams woke other rough sleepers who came to her assistance. The crazy individual ran off with her bag. Phoenix's heart went out to these unfortunate young ladies. He kept asking himself what had changed in their lives to bring them to this point.

He acknowledged where poverty existed, danger also ruled. There was always someone taking advantage of the needy. Gangs patrolling the areas regularly extracted money through the sale of drugs or protection. Thank God there were people like Paulina to pick up the pieces.

On arriving at the soup kitchen, the women were given food and Paulina took Phoenix into a utility room off the kitchen. She quietly whispered that many sleepers refuse to be helped. It was not uncommon for people to pass away on the streets of this so-called great city. He was particularly upset to learn that large numbers of people who end up on the sidewalks suffer with mental health problems. Phoenix admitted that he had experienced depression, but was fortunate to live in a warm apartment and have a wonderful son to support him.

When it was time for the girls to leave, they promised to register with the shelter the next morning. Phoenix thrust his hand into his pocket to extract a twenty-dollar bill and handed it to the older of the girls.

Danny, the guy who ran the centre, noticed this and took him to one side.

'That was an inordinately good thing you did back there, only it's not something we encourage our volunteers to do.'

'But I was only trying to help.'

The well-spoken young man, with the neatly combed hair and blue glasses, paused before replying. 'We have to stay neutral and not offer money. Some will simply use it to buy liquor or drugs and that won't help. What we do here is patch people up and encourage them to use the shelters. Saying that Phoenix, you did really well tonight. Will we see you next Thursday?'

Phoenix nodded. He didn't agree with the ruling, not that he had money to give to everyone he met, but he could see their point.

At the close of the evening he asked Paulina how she had come to help at the Mission. With sadness in her voice, she explained her mother as a young woman had lived rough on the streets of Buenos Aires. A wonderful city, a tourist haunt, yet a place in those days where danger lurked around every corner. Many of the vulnerable homeless just disappeared. Some were killed; others lived a life of unthinkable deprivation. She added that her mother had a lucky break when a man from a charity took pity on her and let her stay in his apartment for the whole of the winter. She never returned to live on the *avenidas* of the city and eventually her mother married the kind man who became Paulina's father.

Chapter 20

The market sector that Dale and Rachel operated in was taking a hammering, this time it was not down to William's intervention. Two huge competitors were hoovering up the sales and almost overnight there was little room for the middleman selling kitchen carcasses. Direct delivery from the manufacturer for bulk buys and online ordering was the way forward. Profits for their company were dwindling and however many new clients Dale brought in, they seemed to take two steps back. There were many anxious moments, which included reducing the staff levels and buying less stock. The value of their now outdated and unwanted products could soon force the issue of closing the business.

The two partners worked every hour possible trying to think of new niche products that would kick-start the ailing company, but to no avail. It was obvious they were running out of time and cash. The only saving grace was they had each other and, while weathering the storms, not once did they fall out. They were just so frustrated at the prospect of losing the business after all their hard work. Letting go of dreams was never easy.

It was also hard accepting that William had already moved his product range away from kitchens to retail and was growing a highly successful mirror and lighting business. Mirrors had been Rachel's baby and the guy had stolen her idea. In this relatively short time, people came from all over the city to buy from his industrial unit that had been transformed into a showroom and warehouse, while they were stuck in limbo waiting for the bank to pull the plug.

* * *

One weekday evening, Dale was stopping over at Rachel's apartment and it was his turn to cook. The incredible smell of spicy Mexican food filled the kitchen and all they wanted to do was eat and curl up in front of the TV to stream a movie.

The shrill of the intercom startled and annoyed Dale as he wondered who was calling at this hour. Holding the receiver to his chest he whispered, 'It's William. He says it's urgent he speaks with us.'

Rachel snapped, 'He probably wants to buy the lease of our place to open his next outlet.'

When William entered the apartment, they were taken aback to see him looking so poorly. Dressed in jeans with a white, open necked-shirt, the guy was shaking badly. He held onto one of his wrists to lessen the movement.

'Jesus, what's happened to you?' asked Rachel.

Dale offered him a seat in the lounge. This was the man he had learned to hate and yet at this particular moment his heart went out to him.

'I've got Parkinson's disease and it's scaring the shit out of me. The doc says it is relatively early days, but I've read up on the net otherwise. I could be facing total neuro-degeneration both mentally and physically.'

Dale was trying to think of something to say and only came out with not believing everything you read on the internet.

'Just look at me, I can hardly hold a pen with all this shaking. I've already given up driving and now take rides in taxis.'

Rachel edged along the couch to be near him. 'Oh William, I'm so sorry. Are you getting the best medical attention?'

'I've got all that covered with the health policy and a friend is looking out for me. Regarding the business, I know what I'm going to do with it.'

Dale bit his lip and dryly said, 'Yeah, wipe out ours to make yours stronger.'

'Behave, won't you,' came back the stern reply.

Rachel frowned. 'Well you've built that up into a profitable enterprise. Not like us, too slow in moving forward and now balancing on the edge.'

William sighed. 'That's why I came here tonight to make amends. I'm really happy you two are together. Deep down I always knew you would make it as an item. Now me, I've done well, but I'm alone and have my regrets.' He quickly added, 'My time's running out.'

It took a few moments before he spoke again. 'That business of painting on your walls was unforgiveable. I was a bitter old man and when one of my sales guys came up with the idea, I let him do it. I want to apologise.'

Rachel responded, 'And to rub salt into the wound, you nicked my mirrors idea and got yourself a winner. I was really disappointed in you, but seeing you like this today, the least we can do is accept your apology.'

'Tell me Rachel, what are you going to do if you are forced to sell?'

'Oh, don't worry about us; there are no creditors breaking down the doors. It's just losing everything that hurts. I suppose we will both look for work.'

William briefly smiled. 'You are survivors and I'm only sorry you guys are having a bad time.'

Dale responded, 'You didn't help, but that's all history. Tell us more about what you are going to do with your company?'

William got the shakes again and kept trying to settle his arm on the side of the couch. He was a broken man and it saddened Dale to see him like this.

'I've remained the sole owner and the mirrors and lighting is a busy retail market to be in. It's a seven-day week though and the online side is mental. The problem is I won't be able to work much longer. I don't think I can cope with this illness, but I have got someone to take it over.'

Rachel touched his shoulder. 'That's great. We just hope that the hospital care you will get will carry you through. There are so many incredible breakthroughs in medicine these days; aren't there Dale?'

Nodding, Dale tried to convey all the right things but deep down he knew William was on the bumpy road out of town. They would have to look out for him but couldn't worry about his company as they had enough on their plates.

He stood up to leave and for a moment William looked a little brighter, 'I gotta go now and before I forget.'

He pulled out his wallet to hand over an envelope and passed it to Rachel.

'Oh my God, there must be at least five hundred dollars here.'

'It's what I owe you both for painting on your walls. That action has haunted me for so long. I can't believe I sank so low. You see, you are the good guys and well I'm ...'

Both Dale and Rachel hung their heads low.

Rachel looked up and said, 'No, we can't take this. Anyway, it didn't cost that amount to clean up. What you did coming here tonight must have been a hard thing to do. Just remember you are one of the good guys as well.'

William insisted they keep the money and the conversation wavered between work matters and how cheated he felt with his crippling illness.

Dale accompanied William down to the street to hail a taxi and the two men shook hands. Before climbing in for the ride, he reiterated how wretched he felt about bringing them so much grief. Dale told him the air had been cleared and he should look after himself.

William forced a smile. 'Don't you go worrying about me. You get yourself back to Rachel; you make a wonderful couple. Thanks Dale, this evening has meant so much to me. I won't forget your kindness.'

* * *

Two weeks to the day, William was found hanging in his Seaport apartment. A note close to his body indicated that he couldn't go on any longer with the illness that would eventually take his life. Six days prior to his death, he visited his lawyer to draw up an amended will stating the entirety of the business was to be gifted to Dale and Rachel.

* * *

It was a terrible shock learning that William had ended his life in such an awful way. He could have left his thriving retail business to his ex-wife and not to Rachel and Dale. The guy was offering them a chance. It was his way of making amends.

It took a number of months for the lawyers to finalise the transfer of the business and in that time, Dale managed to dispose of the lease on their property. Selling off old stock was tricky as competitors were already purchasing the latest models. Eventually they sold to a company who were installing kitchens in tower blocks close to the Brooklyn Bridge. One of the last things Dale managed to pull off before closing their firm was to sell his drawings and rights for the pop-up carcass to Bud Phillips in Pittsburgh. Maybe in years to come, his invention would revolutionise the kitchen furniture market.

Chapter 21

As the seasons changed from cold to warm and back again, helping Paulina with her charity work became paramount for Phoenix as he gradually picked up his life. At long last, a feeling of self-worth was returning to this broken man. By assisting others, life was no longer just about himself. There were people out there who were suffering and he was determined to step up to the mark. When he awoke in the mornings, there was a desire to enjoy the rest of his life. Deep down he knew Suzy would want him to be happy and would be pleased that he'd met Paulina. This woman was special as she made him feel good with the fun she brought into his life. He was aware that Paulina had feelings for him, however, the memories of making love with Suzy were still too raw. The idea of getting closer to another woman was not out of the question, but not just yet.

* * *

On one particular cold night, the Mission decided to take out soup and bread to the homeless. The temperature was minus one with a warning for heavy frost. It was a moonless night and, as the wind whistled fiercely through the tall buildings, eerie noises competed with the heavy traffic that thundered close by. It was imperative the volunteers reached as many of the unfortunate street dwellers as possible who couldn't make it to the drop-in centre. Statistics recently reported in the press indicated suicides and premature deaths on the sidewalks were rising. Lives were being wiped out as the punishing New York weather hit harder and harder. If only there were more shelters and caring individuals like Paulina and

Phoenix out there, more people would have been helped.

As the two friends searched the backstreets, the weight of the hand truck with the hot drinks and refreshments became heavier with every step they took. They started to become uneasy about entering an alleyway where some youngsters were hanging about, but further up that route there were their regulars who would be cold and hungry and they had to reach them.

'Just ignore the troublemakers; keep walking and we'll double back later,' Paulina insisted.

Phoenix shone his torch directly at the derelict warehouses and the beam caught a group of young men who were clearly giving a lady a hard time. A robbery was in progress. The poor woman's blankets were strewn over the area as the troublemakers exposed the few possessions and any money she had hidden away.

Letting go of the trolley he told Paulina not to follow him. In a desperate voice she screamed, 'Come back, we aren't supposed to interfere – they may have knives or a gun.'

Ignoring the training he'd been given on not tackling offenders, he ran towards the gang of three. His loud voice and threats to sort them out had the desired effect. Turning on their heels, they dropped the woman's bag and fled into the darkest part of the city the tourists are never shown.

When Paulina reached Phoenix, he was comforting the lady who said her name was Debbie. Holding hands to their noses to attempt to shut out the dreadful smell of urine, they crouched down to help. Under a dimly lit streetlight they stared at the ragged clothes that surely must have been the ones the thrift shop threw out. The woman in her forties looked ill and her hacking cough echoed through the alleyway like a caged dog. The thinning hair was filthy and plastered to her scalp and her breath was unpleasant due to badly decayed teeth.

Empty beer bottles were strewn around her sleeping area along with pieces of used toilet tissue. Phoenix caught the expression on Paulina's face as she pointed to a condom that lay at the foot of a wall. He stood up and with the edge of his boot kicked the offending item behind a small bush that was growing out of a storm drain. Annoyance set in on discovering his footwear was now caked in dark brown excrement he stamped his feet in a frenzy to remove the mess.

Hovering above the buildings, the noisy clacking sound of a police helicopter made it impossible to speak. When the noise lessened, they helped the woman collect up her damp bedding. Concerned that she had been living on the streets for the last three years, they asked why she hadn't used the shelters. The reply stung hard – she didn't want to bother anyone or accept charity. She accepted the soup and snacks and promised to take care. It saddened them that she didn't feel she could move to a safer street because she would get moved on or possibly endure more attacks. Leaving her in that alleyway was a hard thing to do.

Glancing back for one final time at the unfortunate woman, Paulina said, 'I hope she takes our advice. The smell of pee on her clothes was overpowering. I'm used to it, but this was the worst I've experienced.'

'Yeah, it wasn't just the urine, something else I suspect. Poor lady.'

Under a street light he stopped to stare at his icy blue fingers and wished he'd remembered to bring gloves. His mind switched to the woman who had climbed back into the damp bedding and was probably coughing again. He hoped they had brought her some comfort, but guessed it would never be enough. Phoenix instinctively knew he would always want to help others and, as they returned to the Mission, he smiled to himself. Something wonderful was happening in his life and it was all down to the incredible woman by his side.

* * *

The following evening Paulina cooked dinner for Phoenix and she reminded him how dangerous it could be to tackle troublemakers. He shuddered as she related how, last fall, one of the Mission's helpers had been attacked and suffered a stab wound to the neck.

Paulina's quivery voice resonated with Phoenix as she said, 'It's so easy to lose your life. What you did back there was nothing short of courageous, but I couldn't stand anything happening to the man I love.'

Phoenix's back arched as his mind processed the implications of this woman's feelings for him. 'Now hold on there, romance is not on the cards for me just yet, so don't say things like that. I lost my wife and however much the years fly by, I still hold her dear to my heart. You gotta step off the gas on expecting more from me. For the time being I'm happy with things the way they are.'

The Argentinian woman, with long silver-grey hair and round John Lennon glasses looked disappointed. 'I'll wait as long as it takes. We have a great friendship and if the future includes a bit of fun together, I say bring it on. I never thought I'd get over losing my husband, but there came a day when I realised I hadn't thought about him quite so much.'

So many things were churning in Phoenix's head as he also recalled not talking to Suzy as often as he used to. So much time had gone by since her passing and, if he was honest, he missed the closeness of a woman. Whether Paulina was the right woman to take up with was not the issue; it was just bad timing. Why did she have to say she loved him now and spoil everything?

He gazed at the high-spirited woman who was close to his own age and his eyes traced her wonderfully slim body. For just one moment he pictured her naked and immediately regretted thinking such a thing. Here was this warm person willing to share her happiness with him and possibly more and yet he was hanging back. She had given him confidence and brought the spark back into his life. Where was the danger in showing a bit of warmth to another like-minded person for whom he felt great affection?

Paulina moved close to him and it felt like a thousand volts had hit his body as she caressed his fingers. He pulled away. Without thinking, and as a nervous reflex, he spoke cruelly to her, 'Stop hitting on me. Don't rock the boat; let's just go along the friendship line.'

Paulina hid her face from him. He was aware she was crying and so wanted to reach out to comfort her, but held back. Between her sobs, he heard her mutter, 'Whatever you say.'

Chapter 22

When Dale and Rachel closed the office door for the last time, the realisation thundered in their heads that a new chapter was about to begin. Just how many fresh starts had there been? The future now lay in the business William had left them.

Their skill had been in remaining in credit although, on finalising all costs for their old company, they would only realise fifteen thousand dollars each. Dale's share of the money would have to be put towards his first year's salary. Even with William's excellent profit record there was no projection for two directors' salaries. If they failed to keep the sales turning, Dale would have to seek extra work elsewhere.

William's enterprise *Stars Interiors,* proved to be a whole new challenge. Neither had worked in retail before but it didn't take rocket science to comprehend that you had to sell considerable amounts of retail products to match their previous company's net profit. Mirrors and lights generally sold at lower prices than kitchen furniture.

It was to be a steep learning curve for Dale and Rachel adjusting to this new market. Both worked in the showroom and, along with their staff, took turns on the rota at weekends. Trading hours were until nineteen hundred hours six days a week and Sundays until mid-day. Staffing was capped at seven to cover warehouse, showroom and the office.

Fortunately, William had employed a good office manager who had a keen eye for spotting products with potential for becoming best sellers. Sally was a youngish woman, with a toothy expression, straggly long hair dyed purple and heart of gold. A colourful serpent ran down her neck into her low-cut top that exposed far too much flesh for Rachel's liking. Sally had engaging eyes and was forever asking questions which, at times, proved to be exhausting for those around her.

All the staff were very welcoming, including two warehouse guys who kept a tidy ship and took turns to help out in the showroom. Ben and York both had Harley Davidson motorbikes that were kept on the premises. Going home time was always a noisy experience as the powerful motors thudded away before making the big exit.

The rest of the workers were older women with whom Rachel worked closely. They encouraged her to get to know the customers as they relied on them to recommend the store. The place seemed to be buzzing. What a kind thing William had done leaving them this thriving business.

* * *

Dale was being pulled between the showroom and warehouse when he answered a call from his father. Phoenix was having difficulty getting into the apartment and was struggling to contact a locksmith. He sounded stressed. Having agreed to help out, he went in to see Rachel to say he was off home for a short time. Entering her office, to his delight, she was staring at the diamond engagement ring on her finger. She looked so beautiful and happy. He thanked God for bringing her into his life.

She looked up and smiled, 'It's gorgeous, just like you Dale. I love you so much.'

'And I love you. Won't be long until our big day.'

She nodded. 'What have you got your coat on for?'

'No prizes for guessing, my dad called, yet

another adventure. He can't open the front door and wants me to try. I think he's embarrassed to call out anyone in case he's using the wrong key. I worry about his lack of confidence; I won't be long.'

* * *

Dale parked his red, five-year old BMW Mini outside the apartment block and took the elevator to the second level. There was no sign of Phoenix and, thinking he'd already managed to gain entry, he let himself in.

'Hello, it's me. So, you got in okay.'

There was no reply, only the slow-ticking sound of Suzy's clock in the lounge. He had a quick look around and tutted at the state of the apartment. The place was a mess with clothes scattered on Phoenix's bedroom floor. Three of the closet doors were fully open and it looked like he'd been searching for something. The remnants of chicken curry in an oven dish still lay on the kitchen work surface accompanied by stray rice that had missed his plate. The smell of masala sauce and onions was unpleasant and reminded him of the Indian restaurant two blocks down that he really didn't rate. The dishwasher was crammed full of dirty crockery heavily coated with food.

Dale's eye was drawn to the pile of unwashed dishes in the kitchen sink and a half-finished cup of coffee the colour of coal. It was a mystery why he hadn't used and emptied the dishwasher. A black plastic bag, that could only be garbage, was partly open and the smell of rotting vegetables made Dale cover his mouth. He spied the mostly unopened mail that lay on the dining table and it was obvious some were bills that needed paying. Since he left to live with Rachel, his father had taken his eye off the housework.

It was evident he had gone off somewhere forgetting his earlier call for help. Another false alarm. Dale drew out his cell phone and swiped the screen.

'Dad, where are you exactly?'

'Waiting for you, right outside our door.'

Dale drew breath. 'I bet you are on the wrong floor as I'm inside our place.'

There was a momentary silence followed by laughter. 'Oh, sod, you are right. I must be on level three. I didn't look at the number on the door as I thought it was ours. I still think I need you here as I have a problem.'

Dale took the stairs wondering what possibly could still be wrong. Reaching his father, he observed the lock on the door.

'Oh my God, what have you done now?'

'I kept trying the key and must have turned it too hard. It broke in the lock. Do you think we can get it out before grumpy Mr Davies finds out?'

It was obvious that, without the services of a locksmith to drill out the key, there was nothing Dale could do and he shrugged his shoulders. 'You don't do things by halves, do you?'

Phoenix was now poking at the key stub with the arm of his glasses.

'Don't do that, you'll break them.'

It was at this point they heard the elevator door open and both men jumped back. It was the apartment's tenant who was surprisingly welcoming thinking that they had come to see him. Normally he was so rude. He told them he had to get inside the apartment as he'd left a stew in the slow cooker.

As he drew out his key his eyes were drawn to the

lock and the scratches on the paintwork. He turned and, judging by the look on his face, was far from happy.

Phoenix stood well back leaving his son to explain.

Embarrassed and feeling awkward, Dale thrust both hands in his coat pockets and sighed.

'I'm afraid we may have a slight problem here, sir. You said the stew was in a slow cooker pot? Just how slow do you think the cooking can be in one of those things?'

Chapter 23

Running the new company had its moments when Sally, the office manager, was off sick leaving the owners to purchase stock. Rachel followed the guidelines for product replenishment before placing the orders online. One of the slower moving items was a large desk light and shade. They were expensive to buy and hardly sold, but they still needed a few to display and sell.

A week later, a large delivery arrived and Ben in the warehouse was struggling to find space to store the goods. 'I have a problem down here, Rachel. I just took in a hundred units of the Classic 406 and wondered if you have presold this item.'

Rachel immediately knew something was amiss.

'Am I reading you right, that's the one we only sell a few of. I only ordered ten for stock.'

Ben laughed, 'Oh, I see. It sounds like Sally has gone tits up on her orders. We'll never sell this lot.'

Rachel quickly put him right. 'No, the mistake was all mine. Store them and I'll see about organising a return.'

Examining the delivery note she called the supplier only to be left frustrated with their unhelpful response. She went into Dale's office to discuss the matter. He was on the phone so gestured for her to sit down and held his hand over the receiver. 'It's my Dad. I won't be long.'

He turned his attention back to his father. 'Are you still at work and how bad is the cut? Oh, thank God you are okay. I told you to be careful, didn't I? You get home and I'll see you later.'

On finishing the call Rachel leant forward and anxiously asked, 'What's happened, do you want to go and see him now?'

'No, he's seen a first aider and had treatment for a cut to his hand. He was unloading some material and got it wedged against the wall. There's no emergency or broken bones. Now what can I do for you, partner? Give me some good news.'

Rachel frowned. 'You know the 406 desk light?'

Dale smiled. 'Yes, our worst seller. You were going to try to get the supplier to sell you just a few.'

'They wouldn't budge, so I agreed to the minimum ten-unit order. I must have inputted another nought on the online order form and now they tell me there's a fifty percent return fee.'

Dale drew breath, 'You are saying we have a hundred of those monsters. He gave her one of his reassuring smiles. 'These things happen. Look at some of my close scrapes in our old company. I took risks to get us business, but I did get to sleep with the boss.'

Rachel's face turned to one of worry. 'What shall we do with all that stock?'

'We'll put them on special offer at cost plus three percent or I'll flog them to a wholesaler.'

In a triumphant voice he said, 'Now, do you want the really good news? I just got the figures for our first-year trading and we are up seven percent on our net profit. On top of William's incredible figures, we are really moving forward. It is mostly down to the increase on those online sales. I want to talk to you about giving the staff a bonus.'

Rachel crossed over and kissed the side of his face. 'That's awesome and yes, let's reward everyone. Your father will have a bit of a return on his investment.'

As Rachel turned to leave, he called her back. 'You don't want to buy a desk light or ninety-nine, do you?'

*　*　*

That night, Dale left his overnight bag in the hallway and went through to the lounge where his father was sitting quietly in the fireside chair. His face was expressionless and he barely acknowledged his son. His left hand was bandaged and he cradled it against his blood-stained sweater.

'Dad, what have you done this time? How bad is it?'

'It hurts and I'm not sure I will be able to accompany Paulina to the soup kitchen tonight. I gotta give her a call.'

'Don't worry about that now as I need to know about your accident. I wish you'd taken my advice about not working on a site again.'

'I wasn't paying attention as I tried to help unload the reach truck, only the guy hadn't finished straightening it up. My hand got trapped against a wall. It was my fault. It's not a deep cut but it's swelled up and hurts with this tight bandage. I want you to loosen it off for me.'

Dale undid the dressing and stared at the badly swollen wound. He took care to rebandage the hand, but this time a little looser.

'Shouldn't you have gone to hospital in case it's broken?'

'It's just a scratch. Look, I can move my fingers.'

Excitedly, Dale moved the conversation onto his work. 'One bit of news to cheer you up is we are paying a bonus and you'll get a return on the money you invested in me. It won't be much, but it's a start.'

'That's awesome. It was the best thing I've done in a long time and I'm proud of you son.'

Dale waved a finger at his father. 'Coming back to you, promise me you will take more care in future. I keep telling you how dangerous sites are. I don't know how you work so high up?' Phoenix shrugged his shoulders. 'If you must know, I didn't have my eye on the ball. I was thinking about Elizabeth. I realised I hadn't been in touch with her for two months. What sort of friend am I not checking on her?'

Dale was suddenly alarmed as he acknowledged the contact with their wonderful friend had broken down.

'Dad you must ring her in the morning. I'm sure she's fine, but we shouldn't have left it this long. Changing the subject, I've had a word with Rachel and we agree I ought to spend more time with you. I'm going to stay two nights here during the week for a while.'

'I could do with the company, but don't curtail your life for me.'

'I'm fine, but I am going to insist you leave the building trade.'

Phoenix pulled a face. 'Yeah, yeah, cut me some slack – I'll decide where I work. Do you want to know what else is really bothering me?'

Wondering what new drama was about to unfold, Dale waited patiently for him to speak.

'I haven't even thought about Cody for ages. What's wrong with me? Cody is where this whole story started.'

* * *

On contacting Elizabeth, it was apparent she was equally embarrassed about not keeping in touch and over lunch at the weekend she revealed her plans. She was returning to live in Ohio and had already given notice on her apartment. Phoenix was shocked and hurt to hear she was moving away. He cautiously mentioned Cody's name and her not being able to visit the grave. Her answer surprised him saying that Cody was everywhere she went and not just in that cold field.

Phoenix was clearly upset as he thought of Suzy lying in the cemetery with the long grass that kept trying to creep over the plot. He would never stop visiting his late wife or, for that matter, Cody.

Elizabeth told him that she belonged in Ohio and longed to live in the countryside again. She reminded him of the first time she and Cody had met him and Suzy. She painted the picture so well of those wonderful woods and the little brook they bathed their feet in.

Phoenix's mind skipped back to that special weekend away in the motel on the outskirts of the town. The glorious views of the countryside and quaint towns bathed in the warm sunshine had made them feel so happy.

On loading their car to go sightseeing, the motor had refused to start. It soon became clear that Phoenix was struggling to fix it. It was Cody and his wife who came to the rescue. A loose battery terminal was soon tightened and the foursome walked the short distance to take a coffee in the town. They were soon chatting like long lost friends. Both men were in construction and the girls had much in common. The friendship was sealed and they regularly met up. Shortly after Cody moved to New York to work on the scrapers, Phoenix and Suzy followed.

And now, after all these years, Suzy and Cody were gone and Elizabeth was moving away too. That just left Dale, and even he was picking up his life again. Soon he'd be left on his own.

* * *

It had been three years since Rachel and Dale took over William's business and their sales were motoring. They worked hard increasing market share with the mirrors still proving to be the mainstay of their company's income. Linking into reproduction Italian mirrors and lamps, the interest from New York customers was phenomenal. Online sales rocketed as their products sold all over America.

Working seven days a week took its toll on the couple and, with Rachel now in her late-fifties, it was agreed she should reduce her work down to two days a week. A general manager was hired along with extra staff. They moved out of Rachel's cramped apartment to a larger home two blocks down from where Phoenix lived. They were so much in love and were almost ready to make their wedding arrangements.

Phoenix was ecstatic with their news and revealed that he too had reached a turning point in his life where things were looking up. He enjoyed his friendship with Paulina and the charity work that was so important to them both. There was a purpose in his life again and he was convinced nothing could upset him again so badly.

Paulina was special to Phoenix and although he refused to admit it, his feelings for this woman were growing. He often stared at her beautiful trim body and the outline of her breasts though her shirt; she never wore a bra. With her South American habit of waving her hands about when talking, this left little to the imagination. She had made it clear enough that she wanted their relationship to move to the next stage and the thought of being that bit closer thrilled him. But, not just yet; he still wasn't ready. There was no denying he was falling in love with Paulina. The memory of Suzy held him back although, deep down, he had needs and his wife wasn't coming back.

Chapter 24

On the sixth anniversary of Suzy's death, Phoenix visited a local barber's shop in Queens to have his head shaved bare. The ponytail was finally gone and, with his now much slimmer body, he looked smart for a man of his age.

In spirit, Phoenix was a calmer person, yet there still remained regrets, things he knew he could never make up for. In essence, he was on a mission to redeem himself and look for the best in people that he came into contact with. Nowadays, he hung onto their every word and offered his friendship. He managed not to be so judgemental and stopped offering advice, something he'd done in the past. Looking out for others brought about a kinder person in Phoenix who now focused on the future.

Helping out at the Mission certainly coloured Phoenix's outlook on life. There were the drunks and mentally ill who all needed checking on and it could be scary witnessing their tempers and strange ways. It appeared everyone had a story to tell, a multitude of reasons existed for being homeless and his heart went out to these unfortunate people. He also took a great deal of satisfaction when the team improved someone's life. A move to a shelter or a return to normal life was always a wonderful thing to have brought about.

When Phoenix's mentor and friend, Paulina, walked the streets in her long red coat, people came out from their dark corners to talk with her. She was always careful not to promise something she couldn't fulfil. Her empathy with the homeless impressed Phoenix. For many, her friendly face and words of encouragement helped them through a bad patch.

Paulina insisted that the key to remaining safe was by working in groups of two and always to be on guard. There were times when people became violent or tried to persuade helpers to part with money. You had to accept in some instances there was a limit to what could be achieved in keeping people safe. Sometimes a helping hand along the way was all that was required.

On one occasion, a woman threw an empty glass bottle at Phoenix. She went on to chase him along the sidewalk shouting obscenities. This sort of behaviour went with the territory. Fortunately, most people were amenable and welcomed a visit.

* * *

With only a month away from Thanksgiving, one particular evening was really testing for Phoenix and his fellow volunteers. The place was fit to bursting with people all anxious for a warm meal and shelter from the cold. It was a mystery where everyone had come from. Phoenix took his turn to serve the food. With an apron wrapped around his waist he helped dish up the meals with the ingredients gifted by local stores and charitable organisations. It soon became evident, due to the demand, that they were about to run out of food and there was still a queue of hungry people waiting to be fed.

Paulina and Phoenix quickly left the centre in search of a supermarket to buy bread and cheese. Late at night wasn't the ideal time to find stores open, leaving the only option to buy some pizzas that could be divided up. They would worry about the cost later. The manager of the store, a young man wearing the regulation hat with an image of an orange looking pizza, was keen to hear about their charity work. To their delight he kindly offered a discount of fifty percent as a gesture of goodwill. Phoenix thanked him saying tonight was an emergency.

'No probs, sir. Let's just call it a two-for-one offer. Now let me chase up that last Margarita.'

He turned to the kitchen and yelled, 'Gray, where's the balance of sixty-seven?'

Eventually, the chef appeared and dropped the boxed pizza onto the counter and frowned. His name badge was pinned at an angle on the green shirt and read Gray Wakeman.

Phoenix stared at the large black man with the rugged face and tattoo of an evil-looking crow on his neck – something was familiar about this guy. And that's when the penny dropped; the last segment of the puzzle was finally revealed. He'd seen this man before, only this was the first time he remembered the name.

Phoenix's mind was racing as he acknowledged Gray was the guy responsible for putting him in that coma. Also, he could not stop thinking that if Suzy hadn't been travelling to the hospital that evening, she'd still be alive. It had been a long time since he had allowed himself to hate anyone, but now he was seething with anger.

Paulina was showing signs of wanting to leave. Phoenix glanced out of the window and spotted a taxi pulling up outside the store. He quickly ushered her out onto the sidewalk urging her to take the ride back without him. His hurried explanation was he had some unfinished business.

Astounded by his remark and harsh voice, she stood her ground. 'Don't take that line with me and there's no need to shout. There are people back at the Mission who are waiting.'

'I said I needed some time and surely you can carry six pizzas.'

Paulina, with an emotionally charged voice, pleaded with him. 'What's more important than returning with me?'

'Just get in the sodding taxi!'

* * *

Phoenix hung around the entrance of the pizza place and gazed at the opening times sticker on the door. Twenty minutes remained until they closed and he estimated that the staff would have further time cleaning up before being allowed home. Pulling on the collar of his coat for some protection from the wind, he let his mind wander.

His thoughts rested on the past years and once again the sadness of losing Suzy. The events that led to her death could have been avoided if only that crazy man on the building site hadn't attacked him. All the time he'd been in the hospital must have been so stressful for his wife. She was working to pay the bills, visiting him and holding down a busy job. If Gray hadn't entered their lives, the future would have panned out very differently and his son wouldn't have had to upturn his life to look after him.

Standing by the side entrance, he watched the staff gradually file out. Gray was one of the last to leave. The obese man shuffled along the sidewalk puffing away on a cigarette and loudly broke wind. He took a left at the next block and Phoenix followed like a wild cat stalking its prey. A new chapter was unrolling for Phoenix and gone were the kind feelings for his fellow man. With the click of a switch the lights were going out in his life. He was once again out of control. All he could think about was ripping the guy's head off.

Shadowing the man, he increased his pace and after taking another left turn, found himself standing behind Gray on a crossing. The wait for the illuminated *Don't Walk* sign to change seemed endless and eventually the two men walked across the busy road. Gray hesitated outside a shabby looking apartment block to search for his keys and ended up dropping them on the sidewalk. Phoenix moved forward and under a dimly lit street lamp bent down to retrieve them.

In a calm voice he said, 'Let me help, sir, you seem to have dropped your keys.'

Startled by the stranger standing so close, Gray stood back from the large guy with the bald head before thanking him. Phoenix stood perfectly still, blocking the man from moving on.

Gray grunted, 'Do you have problem – I'm only going to ask you once. Get out of my way!'

'You don't recognise me, do you?'

Gray pulled out his cell phone and activated the flashlight. Holding it up to Phoenix's face his reply came back as a snarl, 'Yeah, I remember you. You were the guy who ordered the six twelve-inch Margaritas. What's your problem, not enough oregano on top?'

'You still don't recall me. Try harder.'

'Get the shit out of my way mister or I'll beat you into strawberry jam.'

It was on hearing him say this that Phoenix's hate for the man overwhelmed him. These were the exact words that he had used that morning on the scraper before he carried out his attack. Gray pushed a finger into Phoenix's face narrowly missing his eye. 'Move piss head, you are doing my head in.'

This time, Phoenix stood back. Every muscle in his body was tense as he prepared to fight with the man. He screamed, 'Me, with a ponytail and you and me welding. Now do you remember?'

'Oh my God, you are Phoenix, the guy from the Clancy site. I didn't recognise you without the girly hair in the clip and you've lost so much weight. You're the guy who pushed his mate off the edge.'

'No, I didn't, it was a disagreement between friends – no more.'

Phoenix took a swing at Gray and missed, hitting his fist into a brick wall. Ignoring the horrendous pain and the warm sensation of blood, he shouted, 'I never pushed him and the police believed me. You were the one charged for causing bodily harm.'

'Yeah, and it was worth every moment landing one on you.'

Gray put two fingers up to Phoenix who then lashed out landing a blow to the shoulder.

The two men wrestled each other to the ground with Phoenix managing to pin him down. Their faces were practically touching and the vile smell of onion on the man's breath sickened Phoenix. With his free arm he kept punching hard into the huge man's stomach ignoring the screams for him to stop. The pain from his damaged hand didn't curb his strength as he continued to thump Gray.

The pair were disturbed by a car drawing up and two policemen dragged them apart. Both men calmed down and in unison said they had fallen out and were sorry. A verbal warning took place and the officers waited for them to go their separate ways before driving off.

Phoenix kept repeating the street name where this man lived. It was a good job the police had intervened or he may have been facing a murder charge. Sometime soon, he was going to beat the living daylights out of the guy, but he wasn't going to kill him. Phoenix had changed; his calm thought processes were long gone. The madness had returned and all he now wanted was revenge. It was payback time.

* * *

After a bad night's sleep, Phoenix showered and put on his dressing gown with the food stains on the front. He was annoyed to hear the sound of the doorbell.

'Who is it?' he shouted through the door.

'It's me Paulina, let me in.'

Screwing up his face and wishing she'd go away, he replied, 'I'm busy.'

'Please, just open the door.'

Reluctantly he allowed her in and as they stood in the hallway, he hid his damaged hand behind his back.

'What are you hiding?'

On seeing the reddened skin and nasty purple bruise, she demanded an explanation.

'It's only a nick; I slipped in the street last night and scraped it on a wall. I really haven't got time for this. I just want you to give me some space and leave.'

Paulina looked distressed, her brow was creased and he noticed she wasn't wearing any makeup. Gone were the glasses she always wore; it was the first time he'd seen her without them and she looked so much older. Her hair needed a good comb and there were signs of tiredness in her eyes.

'No, not until you tell me what happened last night. One minute you were your old self and the next it was like you didn't want to know me. I was cross you left me to return on my own.'

With a vacant look on his face he shocked her with his response. 'I've been doing some thinking about you and me. Well, I think we ought to take a break from seeing each other.'

She ran her fingers through her tangled hair. 'What do you mean by that? Just lately we have been getting on fine. We cuddle up now and again and you are always holding my hand. What about the time we went that bit further? We almost made love.'

'That meant nothing,' Phoenix lied.

Paulina looked heart broken. 'Well it meant something to me. You even said you had feelings for me. What's changed? You know I love you.'

Phoenix looked anywhere but into Paulina's sad eyes. 'That's just it, with you having feelings for me, I'm not comfortable.'

Paulina's lip quivered. 'I promise I'll back off, only please don't sever our friendship.'

Disregarding her plea to remain friends, he looked over to the dining table to the discarded identity badge he wore on the Mission evenings, and his voice went up a tone.

'And another thing, I'm no longer going to help out. After last night something changed in me. I'm not a good person to be around. I want you to leave now.'

She started to cry, and as much as Phoenix fought against wanting to comfort her, his inner voice kept repeating that she would be better off without him.

He opened the door for her to leave and, whilst his hand was painful, he pulled off the dress ring from his finger and passed it to her. It was the gift she had given him for being the most wonderful and caring person in her life. It was at that moment he had known he loved her but, with his track record, he didn't feel he deserved her. He was finally paying the price for his wrongdoings. In essence, he was turning into a nasty individual who was set for a fall. Only one thing mattered at this precise moment, and that was getting even with a certain person.

Impatient for her to leave, he waved his hand in a dismissive way in the direction of the already opened apartment door. He heard her sobbing as she made her way to the elevator and he closed the door. He was left alone in the apartment. All was quiet, even Suzy's clock had stopped.

For one brief moment he cursed himself for treating his lady friend so badly, but it had to be done. The silence was unbearable and turning the radio to full volume, he sat with his head in his hands. His cell phone started to ring and he glanced at the call screen to see Dale's name. He wasn't going to be nasty to him and would pretend to be okay. He put the phone on speaker mode.

Trying to sound upbeat he said, 'Hi son, it's good to hear your voice. How's Rachel? Oh, you want to come over this weekend. I'm sorry, I'm busy. Let's diary in the following one. We will catch up big time. Bye, son.'

Chapter 25

Seated in the pizza restaurant, Phoenix was one of the first customers to be served lunch. He was working on the theory that Gray would be working his shift, if not he'd come back in the evening. It was a cat and mouse game and there was to be only one winner.

When the waitress took his order, he went for the same type of pizza that Paulina and he had purchased the previous night – a twelve-inch Margarita. He enquired if Gray was the chef for the lunch period; the answer that came back pleased him. All the time he was waiting for his meal, his eyes never left the front desk or the opening to the kitchen. His plan was to unsettle Gray. He had every intention of keeping up the pressure to wear him down. Stalking this horrible beast of a man would bring him great pleasure. It wouldn't bring back Suzy, but the guy was going to suffer.

When his food arrived, he thanked the young girl with the frizzy, black hair and blue glasses. He hurriedly ate one mouthful and folded his arms. He waited to get the waitress's attention and was annoyed she was on her cell phone rather than looking out for customers. When she finally came over, she stared at the unfinished meal and enquired if there was a problem.

'No, on the contrary, can you tell chef Gray that the pizza he just cooked for Phoenix was exceptional?'

Off she went and within a minute the pizza chef was standing in the kitchen entrance. With a worried look on his face, Gray homed in on Phoenix who smiled back.

He must have been wondering if the crazy man would be waiting for him after his shift and whether another argument would kick off.

* * *

The next morning, Phoenix was up bright and early and positioned himself on the sidewalk next to Gray's apartment block that looked even more dilapidated by daylight. He walked over to the old, rusty fire escape on the front of the building to stand by rubbish that had piled up around the base. Condoms glistened in the bright sunlight alongside syringes and needles scattered on the ground. The putrid smell of rotting food was awful and Phoenix stepped back onto the sidewalk and swore loudly.

Eventually Gray appeared, dressed in his work clothes and carrying a coat. He failed to spot Phoenix lurking by a service entrance. He was clearly in a hurry but came to a stop on hearing him cough loudly.

Discovering Phoenix outside his apartment elicited an angry reaction. Trying to control his shaking, he shouted, 'Hey, you are doing my head in. I'm warning you to back off or you are going to regret ever being born. I'll wipe you out.'

Phoenix took pleasure in seeing the heavy man increase his pace and drop his coat on the wet sidewalk. On retrieving it, he turned his head in the direction of Phoenix, who was doing a slow handclap that turned to a thumbs up.

Off Gray dashed, regularly looking back to check if he was being followed. Phoenix had other plans. He was standing by the apartment block entrance looking up at the windows trying to work out which one was this man's bolthole. He then retreated to a local diner to treat himself to a huge breakfast.

* * *

Monday morning saw Phoenix ring his work to say he was sick and wouldn't be in for the rest of the week. Perpetuating the action between himself and Gray was his goal and when the time was right, he'd have one last swing at him. He felt no fear of the consequences that would undoubtedly result in him being arrested.

His mind, bubbling with hatred, was on autopilot taking him along this route. He was like a kettle that was boiling and refusing to click off. His reason for living had diminished leaving only regrets and depression to cope with. Suzy was gone, so what was the point of carrying on.

* * *

With the pizza place in view, Phoenix phoned to speak with Gray. He held on for a while and the expected reply was that he was not available.

On cue, ten minutes later, he spotted Gray hurrying away from the store. Phoenix gingerly stepped out into the street and began to follow him. Only this time the man wasn't dressed in his work clothes. He was clutching what looked like an overnight bag, which suggested he was going away for a few days to avoid further confrontation.

Moving faster than usual, Gray turned into the main drag in Queens and hailed a taxi. At that point Phoenix sped up and, on reaching the vehicle, surprised him with, 'Fancy seeing you here.'

'Oh my God, leave me alone. What do you want from me?'

He climbed into the taxi, but Phoenix prevented him from closing the door.

'We have some unfinished business. Tell the kind man behind the wheel you changed your mind about the ride.'

The driver, a tall man in his mid-forties with a commanding voice, slung open his door and was brandishing a baseball bat. 'You guys do your fighting elsewhere or you'll regret coming anywhere near me.'

By now Gray had shuffled across the back seat. Phoenix rushed round to the other door encouraging him to step out and return to the sidewalk. Nudging him to move he said, 'Do be careful with the traffic. I would hate you to fall under one of those cars.'

As Gray climbed out, he forgot about his travel bag and left it behind the driver's seat.

Facing the angry driver, Phoenix let out a chuckle and said the first thing that came into his head. 'Oh, that's my brother for you.'

Phoenix insisted Gray keep walking with him. For the moment the man was obeying his every command.

It was a windy day with dirty, dark clouds racing across the sky. The rain was already spitting with a heavier downpour threatening to soak the two men.

'Where are we going?'

'To the park. To a beautiful place where the birds sing sweetly. Suzy and I used to love it there.'

'Let's call a halt to all this.'

Phoenix shook his head and prodded him in the back. 'If only it were that easy.'

On reaching Astoria Park they continued to walk along the paths and, even with the gloomy weather, the views of the East River were spectacular. Gray must have been wondering why he was being brought there, but kept on walking.

With the rain now wetting their faces, Phoenix was relieved there was no-one around. This was the first time he'd been back to the park since Suzy died and this would be his last. He was going to have his final fight and wanted the guy to understand the misery he'd unleashed.

'Isn't this a wonderful place? The sort of place you could bring someone special to enjoy a stroll and take in all this beauty?'

Gray, breathing heavily, remained silent.

'Have the courtesy to answer me,' screamed Phoenix.

The man, who was clearly terrified of his captor, mumbled a weak acknowledgement.

'LOUDER, I want to hear you.'

'I... I... err, I'm sorry. Is this where you brought your daughter?'

There was no reply. Gray ran off down the path. Phoenix looked around to see if anyone was watching and sprinted after him.

Catching up, he grabbed him from behind and placed one of his arms around the man's enormous neck and increased the pressure.

'You're choking me, let go! I'll do whatever you want. I'm sorry, real sorry.'

Phoenix kept smashing the side of his hand against the distressed man's head and listened as two voices inside his own head competed: *Just squeeze a bit harder, that's all it will take.* The other was screaming, *Stop, you are going to kill him.*

He could hear wheezing sounds as Gray struggled for breath. Phoenix released his grip and stood back.

The man fell heavily to the ground and it was a while before he had the strength to raise his head and speak. 'I said sorry, what more do you want of me?'

Phoenix gazed over the parkland and then yanked him up onto his feet.

'As I was saying, the park is a great place to bring someone special and it wasn't where I brought my daughter – I have no daughter. It's where I brought my wife, Suzy. If you hadn't hit me and put me in that coma, she wouldn't have been on her way to visit me in hospital and would not been killed on that road. I'm done hurting you. You just keep out of my life.'

Gray stumbled and fell sideways onto the wet grass. Once again, he was gasping for breath. Phoenix's face changed to utter desperation as he realised the game had got out of control. There would be no more fighting but there must be closure.

Gray suddenly grasped his arm, then chest and screamed out in pain. Phoenix instinctively knew he was having a heart attack. He ripped off his coat and encouraged Gray to lie still telling him he would be okay. He was already on his cell phone calling the emergency services and answering their questions.

The wait seemed endless and all the time he comforted Gray. To Phoenix's relief, a young couple came to their assistance. They took off their scarves and placed them under the man's head. Phoenix panicked when he noticed the girl shaking her head.

Phoenix kept repeating the same words, 'Please God, don't let him die on me.'

On arrival, the paramedics took the vitals, administered oxygen and set up a drip. Moments later they unfolded the blue padded stretcher to carry him to the ambulance.

Phoenix was able to give Gray's name and the street he lived in. He bit his lip as he told them he was a friend and agreed to go with them to the hospital. Bumping along the park paths and grass there was now only one voice in Phoenix's head talking to him. It had a kinder tone telling him things were going to work out.

Hospitals always unnerved Phoenix but he waited patiently in the visitors' lounge praying for good news. Sitting alone in the stark room without any windows, he wondered if he should leave, but thought better of it. As much as it pained him, it was time to look out for Gray. Revenge was no longer on the cards.

A short while later a medic confirmed that Gray had suffered a mild heart attack and, although stable, was to be admitted for a few days' observation. An office administrator tackled Phoenix on the patient's lack of medical insurance. Without any hesitation he offered to pay the amount stated.

When Phoenix was eventually allowed to visit, the doctor asked him about the marks on their patient's throat. He coughed nervously saying he had no idea.

Propped up in bed, Gray was surprised when Phoenix walked in.

'I thought my time was up. You saved my life; you could have let me die. Accusing you of your mate's death was wrong. And, believe me, I didn't know your wife had died.'

Phoenix momentarily closed his eyes on hearing the reference to Suzy, and bravely replied, 'That's our slate wiped clean. Things got out of hand and now the line gets drawn.'

'They told me you paid my bill and I'll pay you back, I promise.'

'Behave, you just get better.'

Phoenix left the hospital with his head still in a muddle. That was to be the last time he would ever see Gray.

* * *

On his way home, Phoenix rested in the back of a taxi and ignored the driver who enquired if he'd had a good day. Good day! He'd attacked a man and his mind was spinning with the shame of sinking so low. Suzy would turn in her grave if she knew half of the things that had been going on. He'd sunk to the bottom of the heap and just now wasn't sure he wanted to go on living. Perhaps he should crawl into a hole because the world would be a better place without him. He cared little if he lived or died.

It was early evening when he arrived at the apartment and the first thing he did was reserve a seat on a plane and print off the boarding pass. The flight to Cleveland was for the next morning. Ohio was where he met Suzy and experienced so much happiness. Staying in New York was not an option now; he had to escape. He wasn't ready to face up to Dale just yet. Telling his son the truth was never going to be easy. With regard to informing his work he wouldn't be back, well he just couldn't be bothered to contact his supervisor or, sadly, Ethan for that matter.

He went online and transferred the balance of his inheritance from Suzy to Paulina's bank account. Having helped her out with a loan in the past, he already had her account details. The following morning, he packed a bag and placed his ID in the inside pocket of his long black coat. Out in the street he made his way to a courier company's office that Dale often used. He handed over a letter addressed to Paulina and his specific instructions that it must be delivered in three days' time, and not before. The documentation was completed with the date highlighted.

The message read: *Paulina, my dearest of friends and the person I love. However many days there are left in my life, I would still feel the need to keep saying sorry to you. The memory of treating you so badly will always haunt me and I hope one day you will find it in your heart to forgive me. Just to let you know that I have moved over to your account a sum of money that I would like you to donate to the Mission — Love Phoenix.*

Chapter 26

The courier company failed to read the despatch date correctly and delivered the letter a day earlier than requested. On reading the message alarm bells started to ring in Paulina's head, as she instinctively knew Phoenix must be in trouble. There had been no response to the messages she left him or to her ringing his apartment bell. In a state of panic, she frantically searched for the name of the site where he worked and put through a call. The supervisor explained that their employee was off sick.

She left it until late afternoon, just in case Phoenix had gone out and had now returned, but he was still not picking up. He normally had his cell phone on him and answered messages from her, but not this time.

* * *

Paulina made the short walk to Dale's company. On entering the magnificent lighting and mirror showroom, Phoenix's son was surprised to see her without his father. He quickly ended his discussion with his sales assistant to usher her into a side office.

'What are you doing here? There's nothing wrong with my dad, is there?'

Her words tumbled out, 'I don't want to worry you, and there may be a perfectly good explanation, but I can't get hold of him.'

'Don't worry, he may have gone into town with Ethan for a beer.'

'No, I tried his work and they said he was off sick.'

'Off sick, I didn't know he was poorly.'

Paulina was struggling to control her shaking. 'Neither did I. Odder still, he had this letter delivered to me when he could have popped it through my door. That's a really strange thing going to all that trouble and expense.'

Dale's voice rose to one of alarm. 'What did he put in the letter?'

'It was an apology, but I could tell he was disturbed by something. The most amazing thing was he transferred a huge sum of money to my account for our charity. I'm not sure I should do anything with it until I speak with him. I'm really worried something has happened to him.'

Dale raised a reassuring hand and touched her shoulder. 'You say he's given you a lot of money; I think I'd like to check that out.'

Paulina nodded.

'My father's idiosyncratic behaviour is always a worry to me.'

Her words gushed out, 'I spoke with Ethan who hasn't been in touch with him since last week, so now I've worried him.'

Dale was frantically trying to think of a logical answer and came up with, 'So he's not been well and not been at home. That explains why he put off seeing me this weekend, only he sounded fine. Possibly he's out walking or even gone to the doctor. I'm sure if we ring, he'll be back home or on his way somewhere.'

The worried expression on Paulina's face was unsettling Dale.

'Is there anything else I should know?'

'Only that over the last few days, I've left so many messages on his cell phone and he doesn't reply. We'd had a fall out and I could tell he wasn't in a good place.'

'You fell out. Was it serious and did you guys make up?'

'No, he broke off our friendship. Have you got your keys for the apartment with you?'

* * *

When Dale and Paulina arrived at the apartment, they were shocked at what they saw. The place looked like a bomb had hit it with books on the floor and discarded clothes on the hallway carpet. In the kitchen, worryingly, one of the electric rings on the cooker was glowing bright red, and a saucepan close by had the congealed remnants of an unappetising curry. It was evident that no washing up had been done for a while. Dale moved to his father's bedroom and searched through the drawers before returning to the kitchen. Paulina was in the lounge and pointed to the couch where Phoenix had been sleeping.

'Was the bedroom in just as much of a mess as the rest of the place?' she enquired.

'Yeah, like he was in a hurry to leave. What is worrying me is he has taken his ID and the small photo frame by the bedside. The one of Suzy that goes everywhere with him.'

Paulina sighed. 'Oh, God, do you think he's taken a flight somewhere?'

'Possibly as he's taken his passport. I suggest we tidy up here and you come home for a bite with Rachel and me.'

During their search they came across a piece of paper Phoenix had written on – Gray Wakeman was underlined a number of times. Dale never forgot a name and on seeing it, he was alarmed.

'I wonder if Dad's gone after that guy.'

'Who are you talking about?'

Weighing up scenarios Dale quickly replied, 'He's the animal who attacked him and you know all the rest that followed with him being in a coma.'

* * *

When they told Rachel, she was alarmed to hear their news and made suggestions about what to do next. Dale kept trying his father's cell phone and landline but to no avail. He spoke to Ethan who made Dale promise to update him. He said he would make a search around some of the bars they frequented.

'We can't contact the police just yet as it has to be at least twenty-four hours to report a missing person,' said Paulina.

Paulina helped Rachel prepare the meal, a simple ready-made fish pie that smelt good even though none of them felt that hungry.

Seated around the kitchen table, Rachel served up as Dale said, 'What I can't understand is the last six months he's been doing really well and we thought after all these years he was coming to terms with losing Suzy. I think it was the enjoyment of assisting at the Mission that really helped.' He turned to Paulina and muttered, 'And, the two of you were getting on so well.'

Paulina took off her glasses and laid them on the table. She grabbed a handful of her hair and started to twist it into a tight knot around her slim fingers. Her eyes travelled up to the ceiling. It looked like she was going to break down in tears.

'Hey, it's going to be okay, we'll find him.'

Paulina shook her head. 'It's like he's gone right off me. Last week we had a shortage of food at the

Mission. Your dad and I went to a pizza place to pick up some meals. It was there that Phoenix changed from being caring to horrible. He left me to carry the food back to the kitchen on my own.'

Anxious to learn more Dale muttered, 'Oh, that's terrible. I don't know what he was playing at. Tell me, did anything else happen?'

'Yeah, the next day I called at his apartment and he said he wanted a break from me. I said I loved him and he went sort of mental. It scared me when he said he was not a good guy to be around. Phoenix had definitely changed.'

Dale was gradually piecing the jigsaw together. 'I'm sure he's really fond of you. We just have to remember he's not well.'

'Do you think he's safe?'

'Not sure, and that's why we need to find him as quickly as possible. I can tell you he hasn't taken his medication with him. I think it's highly likely he has gone off travelling. I wonder if he's gone back home to Ohio?'

Rachel chipped in with, 'We could ring Elizabeth and Suzy's parents.'

Dale nodded. 'If I'm not mistaken, the note we found with Gray's name on it is a vital clue to all of this. I wonder if some time that night at the pizza joint, he had a go at him. Were you together the whole evening?'

She thought hard, 'Yes, right up to collecting the order.'

'And there we have it. He was either a customer or worked there. There's only one way to find out – what was the name of the place?'

Dale Googled the number and asked to speak with Gray. The girl's voice at the other end was far from helpful. There followed much probing as Dale lied that he was his brother and urgently needed a word. This time it provoked a response: their employee had left without working his notice and hadn't been seen since.

Dale rang Elizabeth who, to his utter joy, said how good it had been seeing his father the previous afternoon. He had turned up unannounced and stayed to lunch before returning to Cleveland.

He asked what state of mind his father was in. Her reply was worrying. He was terribly vague about a lot of things.

Elizabeth stressed he was casually dressed and the biggest shock for her was seeing his shaved head without the ponytail. Phoenix mentioned he would be moving on in a few days' time. She was devastated to hear that he was missing and offered her help.

Before Dale ended the call, he asked if he could stay a night or two as he was flying out to Ohio the next morning. He also suggested she contact old acquaintances who may have seen his father. He then called Donald and Marlene who were also concerned for Phoenix's safety. It was agreed Dale would contact them once he arrived in Ohio.

* * *

Over the next few days, Dale's search for Phoenix in Ohio drew a blank. It was bitterly cold with weather forecasts for snow in the coming days. He had a meeting with the Police and there were no reports of any new rough sleepers who fitted the description. He toured hotels, as well as homeless shelters in Cleveland, with a photo of his father but there were no leads. He was beginning to believe he'd moved on already, possibly taken another flight or a bus.

270

Elizabeth put him up for four days and showed him around. All the time they were popping into stores in the local towns handing out pictures in the hope that someone might recognise Phoenix.

One liquor store manager, to Dale and Elizabeth's delight, immediately reacted to their enquiries saying he had definitely spoken with Phoenix. Dale's heart was pounding as the man related his story.

Dale stared hard at the large man with flabby cheeks who wore an earring and an enormous green wristwatch.

'I remember him coming in for some wine late yesterday afternoon. He looked a mess and I wondered if he was an alcoholic. He spent ages selecting a bottle before eventually coming up to pay me. He handed over a twenty-dollar bill. I gave change and was surprised when he tried to pay again and wouldn't listen to my explanation that he'd already settled his bill.'

'What happened then?'

'It was really odd; he put the liquor back on the rack saying he wouldn't take something he hadn't paid for. I tried to return his money only he got funny with me and that's when I thought there was going to be trouble. I was relieved when he left and I still have his money here, which you are welcome to.'

'No thanks you keep it. My dad's a sick man and he's been missing for just under a week. We are desperate to find him. Do you know where he went?

'Sorry, no I don't. I wish you luck with finding him.'

They left the store with mixed feelings. It was good news that there had been a sighting, but where was he now? There was one satisfying thought that Phoenix wouldn't have been relying on liquor as he'd handed back his purchase.

The local supermarkets were unable to help as thousands of customers pass through these outlets making it difficult to recall individual shoppers. There was always the possibility he had already left town and they were chasing their tails.

During his stay, Dale hired a car and visited Donald and Marlene. It had been a long time since he'd seen them. They looked much older and, from the worried expressions on their faces, they were clearly upset to hear his news. They must have been wondering if this dark chapter of the family was ever going to end. Apart from the sighting in town by the liquor store manager, there was little to tell them.

Exhausted by his search, Dale returned home to New York. He was convinced Phoenix was on the move again. He was downhearted and just wished there was a glimmer of hope, but there wasn't.

Chapter 27

For eleven long days and nights, Phoenix moved from one area to another sleeping in alleyways and even in the basement of a derelict house. He had enough funds to stay in hotels but chose not to. Instead he hid in the daytime. His mood was low as he desperately tried to make sense of the incident with Gray. He regretted his actions and was worrying about this man's health.

He agonised over the anguish he must be bringing to Dale and Rachel as well as his lovely friend, Paulina, but he wasn't ready to speak to anyone. Suicidal thoughts still ran through his mind. The voices in his head urged him to end his life. They echoed his faults and the disgrace he'd brought on his family. Desperate, and not knowing which way to turn, his life was now all about waiting for the green lights to change to constant red.

Unshaven and in need of a shower, he was taking on the appearance of a tramp.

Since leaving New York his cell phone had been switched off and one rainy afternoon he chose to power the device up. He swiped the screen to discover thirty-two unread messages. The low battery indicator flashed up. Even if he'd brought his charger, where would he plug it in?

His home was now an outhouse to the rear of a derelict store. On the plus side he was dry and the sleeping bag he'd purchased was warm. Outside of the brick-built building there was some rough ground, which served as his toilet.

He was hardly eating anything and had been surviving on sandwiches bought from a store close by. More recently, the proprietor had told him not to come back. A vending machine that dispensed potato chips and bottled water became the source for his meals.

Healthwise, apart from deliberately eating less, he was in reasonable shape. However, mentally, that was a different matter. Without his medication he was swinging between sanity and madness all the time with bad thoughts that refused to go away. His haggard look and annoyance with everything resulted in people giving him a wide berth.

But not everyone was disgusted or scared of Phoenix. Two young men who helped out at a local charity for the homeless had been informed there was a new rough sleeper in town. Their supervisor warned them the man may be dangerous and they were to take care. Only gentle probing on his needs was on the agenda for their first contact.

It was mid-afternoon and raining steadily when they cautiously knocked on the broken door of the outhouse. They were shocked to see Phoenix lying motionless on some cardboard. His head was tilted to one side on the cold concrete floor. They focused on the sleeping bag draped over a chair. With all the cold weather, they must have wondered why he hadn't covered himself to keep warm. The crunch of broken glass underfoot was alarming as both men wore trainers. The closer they got to Phoenix, the putrid smell of urine hit their nostrils prompting them to hold a hand to their noses.

The younger of the two men, Kurt, was a big guy with a mop of curly black hair and shabbily dressed. He anxiously addressed his fellow volunteer worker. 'Oh, no, Lord, please don't let this guy be dead.'

His colleague whispered, 'I don't think we should touch him. Things look bad in here and the smell is unreal. I say we call our supervisor for assistance.'

Kurt, annoyed with the older man, snapped, 'He could be dying and you want to wait for backup. I'm going over to check if he's all right.'

Both men were startled by a sudden movement from Phoenix, who gave an enormous grunt as he began to wake from his sleep. They stepped back and stood in the doorway.

Phoenix was disturbed to see them and sat up. Anger rattled in his throat. 'I've got no money, so get out.'

Both men were terrified of the big man with the menacing face and took a step back to the safety of the yard. They were getting soaked by the rain that was now hammering down.

Kurt popped his head around the corner and said, 'Sorry to disturb you, sir, I'm Kurt.'

'What do you want?' roared Phoenix.

'We are from the charity Helping Hands based ten blocks up towards town.'

Phoenix laughed, 'Sounds like a kids' club.'

'No, sir, we are a soup kitchen.'

'I don't need any charity.'

'Just checking to see you were all right, sir. It's cold and wet out there and we wondered if you needed any supplies.'

Phoenix pulled a face at him but said nothing.

The older of the two men whispered something along the lines of their boss being right about being careful with this one. Phoenix heard every word and smiled. These were two raw recruits that needed guidance. How many times had he assisted Paulina with new helpers to ease them into the work?

The two charity workers made their apologies for waking him. They were about to leave when, to their amazement, they were called back.

Phoenix produced a wad of notes and counted out two twenty-dollar bills which he handed to the young man with the torn jeans. They were stunned to see this homeless man with so much money. Most rough sleepers live day-to-day on handouts and this guy... well... he seemed to be rolling in it. He was living in the most awful of places. Who exactly was he?

'What's this for, sir?'

Phoenix pointed to Kurt's jeans. 'To buy you some decent pants, son. You look a mess with those tears in the knees; and as you said, it's cold out there.'

'That's really kind of you, sir, but I bought them like this. It's the fashion nowadays. You should hear what my mom says about them.'

He handed back the money. Phoenix refused to take it and chuckled to himself. It had been a long time since he'd seen the humour in anything.

Warming to Phoenix, they asked his name.

Wondering if it was unwise to reveal his identity, he hesitated. He thought of Suzy's favourite bird in her parent's garden and said, 'Jay, my name's Jay.'

'Well, Jay, it's a pleasure to meet you. As we said, we are from a church shelter group and back at our place we serve up hot food and offer bathroom facilities. We can also give details about finding a shelter. Do you fancy coming along for a warm up to meet some friendly faces? Do you mind telling us when you last had a good meal?'

Phoenix told them that recently he hadn't been hungry. He felt ashamed of his appearance and ran a hand over his stubbly chin.

Kurt produced a card with details of where to find the drop-in and passed it over. 'Well Jay, we'll leave you in peace. Hope to see you again, possibly at our place.'

Phoenix, momentarily confused by the false name he'd given them, said, 'I might do that one day. I'll pop in to see how you are looking after the homeless and maybe give you a few pointers.'

Both men looked at each other. Judging by the look on their faces, they were surprised by his remark. They bid him farewell, leaving the stale smell of the storeroom for the walk back in the appalling weather.

Phoenix's mind was spinning. He was intrigued to know that there were groups in Ohio that looked out for people who had fallen on hard times. He was reminded of the charity he helped with in New York. Only this time there were people looking out for him. A tear started to run down his dirty face as he acknowledged just how low he'd sunk. It would appear now that someone was caring enough to pick him up. His emotions took over as he pulled out the small, framed picture of Suzy and wept uncontrollably.

The light was fading and although Phoenix was hungry, he couldn't be bothered to seek out a store or machine for food. He chose to turn in for the night. With the sleeping bag pulled up high he could hear the busy traffic thundering along the main drag that led into town. Loud voices were coming from a house to the side of where he was hiding out. It was impossible to sleep. His mind kept going over the fact that so much of his misery had been self-inflicted. Living like an animal in the backyard of an empty building was crazy. With the money he had in his wallet and on his credit card, he could move to a hotel, or could he while he looked like this? He was the down and out that nobody wanted in their establishment. The individual with a past so grim, even he was ashamed of himself.

This wasn't the Ohio he loved and remembered. Being holed up in this vile place was too much to endure. To all intents and purposes, he could have been four miles east of nowhere. He could even die here and nobody would know or care.

He was wrong. There were many people back home who were going out of their minds with worry. And not that far away was Elizabeth, who had been his wife's best friend, she was very concerned for his safety.

* * *

The following evening, Phoenix packed up his belongings and left the outhouse vowing never to return. He'd find somewhere else to sleep. He clutched the dog-eared card with the address of the soup kitchen and questioned where this next chapter of his life was taking him.

After a short walk he reached the building that served as a drop-in. It was a dark, uninviting warehouse that was possibly classed as derelict, hence its availability for this charity. A simple, oblong, yellow sign with the wording *Helping Hands* hung at an angle above the main entrance. It was hard to ignore the constant sound of water cascading from an overflow pipe or the strident wailing of an ambulance's siren as it raced along the freeway just a few blocks away.

The decay and neglect to this site suggested this was an area that would eventually be redeveloped for housing. Phoenix's eyes scanned the shabby structure with so many of the windows boarded up. Poorly painted murals depicting dinosaurs with faded graffiti did little to enhance the sorry-looking exterior. Areas of damp brickwork with broken window frames made Phoenix question if this was a safe environment for the homeless. He spied garbage on the concrete loading bay and the much-rusted remains of an old reach lift truck. He was convinced that the area had rats. Still, he'd come this far and he was going to check out what they were offering. He thanked God that Paulina's New York charity building bore no resemblance to this dreadful place.

There was a queue of men and women, many clutching belongings and gazing at the open door as they waited to be admitted.

Phoenix patiently stood in line. Once inside, with the noisy chatter of about forty plus people all keen to be fed, he joined others at the front desk to register. Inside the broad oblong room with the high ceiling, a large skylight had been patched up with green, plastic sheeting to keep out the rain. He glanced up at some rusty looking chains that held the lights over the kitchen area. A number of the bulbs were missing and temporary lighting had been secured to the walls. He was concerned to spot only six people helping out in the centre. How different to back home where the numbers had been greater.

Phoenix gauged the seating area would accommodate about sixty people. The chairs and tables had seen better days; some had broken backs and torn fabric. He observed the poorly painted cream walls and cobwebs on picture frames. Clearly, this was a charity that struggled to attract not only volunteers, but also funds.

His eyes were drawn to the counter where meals were being served. The smell of the soup and the snack was appetizing. Judging by those tucking into the meal they served good hearty food. He was greeted by an elderly woman with dark hair who kept apologising for the delay. She was about to ask Phoenix's name when someone interrupted her.

Phoenix was pleased to see Kurt who'd been so kind to him the previous day.

'Barbara, this is Jay, it's his first time here. I'll take his details.'

Phoenix dropped his things on the wooden floor and touched Kurt on the arm.

'Actually, young man… it's Phoenix. The mix up of my name was a bit of a misunderstanding on my part.'

'No problem, sir. Now, if you don't mind, I'll take the briefest of details and show you around. Would you like to freshen up before having something to eat?'

'I think the bathroom has to come first. Where can I leave my gear?'

'Best to always take it with you. I have to help with serving up the meal. We have vegetable soup and a pizza slice with bread. Just join the queue when you are ready.'

Phoenix's mind was doing somersaults as he recalled the pizza episode a few weeks back and the way he had treated Gray.

He quickly dismissed these thoughts and said, 'I'll give the pizza a miss and settle for the soup. And another thing, I'll pay my way.'

Kurt shook his head and proceeded to show him the way to the washroom. Phoenix kept asking questions about the soup kitchen's funding arrangements, also staff rotas. The young volunteer must have been deliberating on Phoenix's background and questioned how he had become homeless. He returned to join his colleague at the counter. Kurt pulled on his apron and spoke directly into the man's ears. 'Our mystery man from the other day is here. Jay is not his name, it's Phoenix.'

Slicing the pizza, the response was accompanied with a smile. 'Oh, I see. I've been thinking it was a bit odd him having all that dough. You don't think he stole it from someone, do you?'

Kurt was offended by the remark. 'No, I don't. He looks like someone who has gone through a lot and needs a helping hand.'

Phoenix eventually appeared looking refreshed. He thanked Kurt for the soup and bread and searched for a table. He proceeded to sit on one of the long benches where an old woman, with spidery hairs on her chin and long straggly dark hair, pointed her fork at him.

'You not trying the pizza mister?'

'No, it doesn't agree with me.'

Leaning towards Phoenix she eyed up his plate and the bread. 'Can I have that?'

Before he had a chance to reply she scooped up one half of his bread.

To his amusement, she pocketed it into her dirty blue cardigan and stared hard at him. 'You new here?'

Phoenix was aware of how bad she smelled and stared at her blue veined hands covered with scars. He told her that he was just passing through and was hoping to get advice on registering with a shelter. He wasn't sure she'd heard his reply as she was busy picking up her dish and various bags to move to another table. Over a period of fifteen minutes, the time it took to finish his soup and bread, he observed her move another three times to talk to someone new.

Looking around, whilst the surroundings were different to his charity centre back home, it was uncanny how the homeless people shared a similar appearance and mannerisms. There was someone who looked just like 'noisy Burt' with a voice that matched. There was even a kind Sarah who helped take up the dishes to the counter. On the whole, most people were considerate and appreciated the help from the charity.

On clearing away his plastic dish and plate, Phoenix approached Kurt to offer his help. The young man, who looked tired, explained there would be a further sitting and welcomed his assistance to tidy up. He said he was pleased to hear Phoenix had moved away from the outhouse and gave him advice and literature on the closest shelter accommodation.

Thanking Kurt, Phoenix acknowledged that this compassionate person must surely be an asset to the organisation.

Sweeping the floor whilst people still remained in the hall was difficult, but Phoenix was determined to be of help. He carried the dishes to the kitchen then wiped the tables down. The volunteers were impressed and joked that he should become a helper.

As Kurt bid Phoenix goodnight, his eyes fixed on the older man. 'I guess you have had a real hard time but I'm convinced your luck is going to change. Any assistance you need, I am your man.'

Phoenix was taken back and shook Kurt's hand gratefully before leaving the building.

Out on the sidewalk Phoenix was surprised to see the young man appear again with some candy for him. He joked he had better brush his teeth before retiring for the night. Cleanliness and hygiene had featured low on his list of priorities for a long time.

Unbeknown to Phoenix, Kurt was a Quaker, and his stance on life focused on befriending fellow human beings without being judgmental. He was no Bible pusher. Kurt had every intention, if given the chance, of showing Phoenix some kindness, just like someone had done for him when he reached rock bottom.

Chapter 28

It was too late to try for a bed and Phoenix looked for a shop front with enough covering to shield him from the weather. It may have been a cold night but, tucked up in his sleeping bag, he was warm and felt contented. His gaze remained on the starlit sky as he recalled how young Kurt had shown him so much kindness. Linking up with a like-minded individual who cared about people had calmed his nerves, controlled the temper that needed to be reeled in. He looked forward to going back to the drop-in and hopefully to seeing Kurt again.

* * *

Bright and early the next morning, Phoenix joined a large number of people all waiting outside to register with the shelter Kurt had suggested he try. Criteria for admittance was on a first come, first served basis and there were rules that related to conduct and respect for the staff.

It took over thirty minutes to enter the main hall of the establishment that was known as the Square Building. The title amused Phoenix who observed the mostly rounded appearance of the property. Similar to the drop-in the previous evening, this building had seen better days. There were signs of repair going on with some guys plastering the wall behind the front desk. The kitchen area looked in need of some refurbishment with an old electric stove and battered pans. A strong smell of disinfectant was present in the air. Phoenix noticed a young woman with a bucket and mop leaving the men's bathroom. She smiled kindly at him then carried on with her work.

He received a wonderful greeting from an elderly man, who introduced himself as Henry, and took his details, also mentioning the location of a food bank close to the shelter.

'Thanks for that. Can I stay here for a while?'

'I'm afraid you'll have to register each day, that way everyone gets a chance. You will not be able to remain here during the day though, only night-time. Nine am is checking out time.'

'Got that.'

'Now, Phoenix, if you would care to follow me, I'll show you around. You are on the third floor tonight.'

He handed over an oblong, plastic card that needed to be presented on entering the building later that evening. However basic room 211 turned out to be, it would be like heaven compared to sleeping in that outhouse.

'You are lucky to have a room on your own. All we ask is no drugs, liquor or visitors. If you break the rules, you will be barred from coming back.'

As they walked along the poorly lit corridor, Phoenix couldn't help notice volunteer Henry was badly out of breath. His face was bright red and he reached out an arm to steady himself.

'Do you want to stop for a moment, Henry? I'm concerned you don't look well. You can rest for a while and I'll go and get you some water.'

He grabbed the older man's arms and made sure he was steady on his feet before letting go. 'Perhaps you should sit on the floor.'

Henry coughed and in a gravelly voice replied, 'I'm fine thanks, I just need to get my breath back. We are supposed to be helping you guys and I'm grateful for your concern for me. You sound like a decent guy,

Phoenix. What brought you to this point that you need a helping hand?'

Phoenix briefly explained how low he had sunk and his desire to get back to being the person he used to be.

'It sounds like you've had a bad time. I've been helping out here for thirty years and I've seen a lot of people come and go. You know, I just have this feeling you are going to get back on track.'

'How can you be so sure?'

'Well, for a start, it's obvious you care about others. The way you looked out for me was awesome.'

Both men walked the length of the building and after seeing the bathrooms and main communal hall, Henry showed Phoenix to the front door to say goodbye. He was emotional and hung onto the kind man's hand for a long time before letting go.

Outside in the street there were still people waiting to see if they could get a room for the night and Phoenix's heart went out to them. Just how many more desperate souls were there crying out for help? He was determined to start thinking about others again and not just himself. He couldn't change the past but the future was another matter.

* * *

Phoenix once again visited the drop-in for sustenance and was disappointed not to see Kurt. He made an enquiry to be told the young man was off for a few days.

That night in the shelter Phoenix lay awake listening to the noise coming from the room next to his. A woman's voice rang out. She sounded distressed and was calling out the name Peter, followed by heart-rending sobbing. It brought home the fact that so many people have a story to tell. He deliberated on whether she'd lost someone. Possibly liquor or drugs had become her demon. Whatever her situation, no-one deserved to feel so alone. The walls between the bedrooms were really thin and Phoenix tried to communicate with her but got no response.

He fell asleep dreaming of Suzy, when they were happily married with plans for their future. Then on cue, the heartache rolled in again with Phoenix struggling to reach her. She was locked in an inaccessible place bringing home the reality, for the thousandth time, that she was dead.

Chapter 29

In New York the tension was building, as there had still been no news on Phoenix. Dale's relentless searching, contacting authorities and travel companies for any clues to his father's whereabouts drew a blank. He was convinced his father had moved on from Ohio. It was like he'd dropped off the edge of the world.

With Rachel's love keeping him going, he concentrated on his work. The business was doing incredibly well with profits exceeding their expectations. A competitor had made an offer to buy them out. Dale and Rachel were seeing their lawyer to go through the fine print of the contract. They would soon be wealthy and Phoenix was due his share, only they first had to find him. Dale wasn't giving up; he was convinced that eventually his father was going to make contact.

* * *

Four hundred plus miles from New York, Phoenix eventually caught up with Kurt. He'd been absent for three days and was recovering from a bad cold. He was pleased to see him again and listened to his news about staying in the shelter.

Kurt produced from his torn, designer jeans a voucher for a diner and showed it to Phoenix.

'It's a two for the price of one on mains. Tomorrow lunchtime I'm not working, so how about you and I dine out at this place off the Boulevard? We can eat at three o'clock and a few hours later I have to work. And I've checked there are alternatives to pizza on the menu.'

Phoenix laughed and held his hand up to high five Kurt. 'Good man, yes I'd love to come and this time I will have the pizza. Just one thing, you make sure you change those pants with the tears – you look a mess.'

* * *

Kurt made sure Phoenix had a good time at the diner. The manageress had to have a quiet word with them to keep their voices down. Phoenix felt like a heavy burden had been lifted from his shoulders as he briefly discussed the events of the last few weeks. Kurt was definitely the catalyst for bringing the spark back into his life with a desire for change on the horizon.

The odd thing was, over their meal, neither person revealed too much about their lives and yet they were talking like old friends meeting up after a ball game.

After thanking the young man for a wonderful time, Phoenix told him he wouldn't be coming back to the drop-in again. He was going home to his son, only first he had some unfinished business in Ohio.

The two men shook hands and went their separate ways. Phoenix was to hang around town and later head for the shelter, whilst Kurt hurried off to start his shift.

As Kurt walked the sidewalk, he threw up a fist in the air and whispered, 'Yes... ten out of ten. Who says miracles don't happen in Ohio?'

* * *

It was a long journey involving two bus rides and a walk to where Suzy had spent most of her childhood and teenage years. Phoenix was back on the Old Blossom

Road that had once been a track. He was saddened to see that it was now much wider with the tangle of woodland no longer present. There were construction trucks parked up with piles of timber waiting to be unloaded.

Long gone were all the wonderful hackberry and sycamore trees that screened the fields from the view of the busy town. The glimpse of the Ohio River in the distance brought back memories of their courting and the wonderful summer evenings they spent together. A massive housing estate was now emerging wiping out the beautiful countryside. A whole new town was being built on the land that included Suzy's old home. He was puzzled why Donald and Marlene hadn't mentioned the desecration of this once magical place.

Phoenix struggled to locate where Suzy's two-storey white clapboard house had once stood. Eventually he worked out that an area of concrete that hadn't been broken up must have been part of the foundations.

He remembered with such clarity all those years ago walking down the narrow Blossom Road and spotting Suzy on the veranda. She looked truly beautiful with the last of the afternoon sun lighting up her face. She rose from her grandmother's rocking chair and waited for him to mount the wooden steps. He kissed her warm forehead, and only when they pulled away, did he say that he loved her and produced a ring. There was no hesitation in her accepting his proposal of marriage. And now, all these years later, not only had he lost his gorgeous wife, her parents' magnificent property had been destroyed.

With a cold November breeze that seemed to be calling Phoenix's name, he sat down on the dusty base and looked around at the finished houses and ones still under construction.

There to his delight, close by, perched on some timber was a blue jay. He was pleased to see that even in this changed environment nature continued to thrive. They had been blessed with so many varieties of birds adorning Suzy's garden. She'd have been thrilled he'd seen her favourite blue jay there.

This brought back memories of all those years ago when she told him that in her next life she would come back as a bird, a brilliantly blue crested jay, and would definitely make contact.

Phoenix pulled out from his bag a half-eaten sandwich and threw pieces of bread a short distance onto some concrete. The jay immediately came down and pecked away at the discarded food. The bird kept coming back and he placed an apple core close to where he was sitting. Again, it pecked at the apple; Phoenix was convinced the jay was trying to communicate with him.

He played with the possibility that his new friend was indeed his former wife. She was sending out a message that now was the time for him to be strong and carry on. He spoke softly, 'Suzy, I know it's you. This time I won't let you down.'

On his feet, he checked his much-battered watch and went to leave. Only first he waved at the bird and said goodbye to Suzy for the last time. He walked away from the Old Blossom Road with his head held high.

* * *

Elizabeth's excited voice thrilled Dale. He put the phone on speaker mode and Rachel clung to his arm.

'I have Phoenix here and he's safe.'

Tears streamed down Dale's face waiting for his father to speak.

As Phoenix grasped Elizabeth's iPhone, he stared at his sorry looking image in the hallway mirror. His face was a mess and badly in need of a shave. He looked like a tramp and didn't smell that good.

'Dale, I'm so sorry.'

His son practically screamed down the line. 'Thank God you are okay. Where did you go? We've been searching for you.'

'I've been in Ohio all this time.'

'Ohio, we went looking for you there. We've been so worried about you.'

'I hid away feeling ashamed. I got so low and at times, although I was in a big city, I felt like I was lost forever. Now I'm thinking straight. I'll take up Elizabeth's kind offer to stay a few days. I need to get cleaned up and sleep and see a doctor to get my medication; my head has been in a mess. I still have my bank card, so I'll arrange a flight and let you know when I'll be home.'

'No, I'll get the first flight out and bring you back.'

'Definitely not, I have to do this myself and then the rest of my life can begin. And one other thing is I don't want you meeting me at the airport. I'll take a ride to the apartment and then ring for you to come over.'

'Okay Dad. We can't wait to see you. Call me on my cell if there are changes to the flight.'

'Stop worrying about me. Please let Ethan know I've finally got my feet on solid ground.'

Dale said, 'I'll tell Paulina as she's been out of her mind with worry. Do try and ring her.'

'Tell Paulina, I've been thinking of her a lot. Send her all my love, and I mean all my love. Say I'm looking forward to seeing her.'

* * *

Two showers later and dressed in clean clothes Elizabeth had borrowed from her neighbours, he reflected on the chaos and worry he'd brought to those who loved him. The nightmare was over and the final journey had already begun. At times there had seemed little hope and now the gloomy fog had dissipated into a memory best fit for the trash can. He could hear Suzy's voice, this time more distant than ever before, telling him to move on and snap up any chance of happiness. The *Phoenix and the Blue Jay* chapter was finally complete. He knew instinctively that the path was clear to be with Paulina. The feeling of wanting to hold her close was so strong and he longed to reveal his true feelings. He trembled at the prospect of sharing his love with her for the rest of his days and picked up his cell phone to call her.

* * *

Phoenix stayed for just over two days with Elizabeth. He went into town with her to buy new clothes and paid a visit to the drugstore for his medication. A much smarter man emerged who was ready to go home to his family. Twice a day he called Dale and Paulina, the two most important people in his life. On his last day in Ohio, Donald and Marlene dropped in to see him. He told them that at long last he had found himself. There were tears, followed by much happiness and laughter. One final hug and Phoenix said goodbye to Suzy's kind-hearted parents promising to keep in touch.

Chapter 30

On the morning of Phoenix's flight, Elizabeth kissed him on both cheeks then watched him enter the busy airport building. He cleared security and made his way through to the departure lounge. Glancing up every so often to the information screen for an update on boarding details, he was finally ready to go home.

There was a delay to his flight due to a technical fault and a substitute smaller capacity aircraft had been allocated. Boarding was delayed by forty minutes. With fewer seats being available on this aircraft, Phoenix wondered how many of the passengers would get seats.

People became anxious and he overheard snatches of conversations from business travellers, many with deadlines. There were also families all keen to beat the rush by flying in early to New York.

He joined the noisy crowd, some of whom were jostling for a closer position to the desk as the staff now had details of the seat allocations. It would appear they were calling for twenty passengers to take the next flight and asked for volunteers.

Phoenix was determined to be heard, 'Miss, I'll take the next one.'

The staff on the desk looked relieved that someone had started the ball rolling.

'Thank you, sir, and if you would move to the next desk my colleague will make all the arrangements.'

More people agreed to the changes. Phoenix was pleased he'd decided to wait for the next flight as there were families and older people who could get home quicker.

* * *

As Phoenix boarded the plane, he realised he hadn't rung Dale or Paulina to advise the later flight details. It was a good job he wasn't meeting them at the airport. The journey time was short and he'd soon be home, so there was no need to worry anyone with the changes.

Window seat 11A was over the starboard wing and Phoenix looked out as the plane was being refuelled and the last of the baggage stowed. The cabin was noisy with the slamming of overhead lockers and passengers locating their seats.

As the pilot made his announcement, Phoenix pulled on his belt and adjusted the air control above his head to maximum. He listened to the flight attendants as they carried out the safety checks. There was a jolt as the plane was pushed back, the overhead lights flickered, and then the heavy sound of the enormous engines coming to life.

He observed the young couple in the seats next to him. They looked happy and were holding hands and smiled over to him. The jolt of the pushback pleased Phoenix who now longed to see Dale and Paulina. The announcement for 'crew to seats' took place and the plane moved forward making its way along the tarmac to join a queue of about ten aircraft waiting for take-off. The safety video was played and he noted where the exits were located. It seemed an age with the stop-start procedure as Phoenix watched the planes climb into the wonderful blue sky.

The aircraft turned on the circle and, with the massive increase in engine thrust, it thundered along the runway. Phoenix tugged on his belt. This was his favourite part of flying. The take-off was always thrilling.

Glancing out of the window at the airport and fields. He leant forward to get a better view as the plane gathered speed and the terminal building shot by.

Unbeknown to the passengers of flight XZFN963, inside the cockpit there was a moment of panic as the crew wrestled with an imbalance of thrust between the two engines. With catastrophic failure to one of the engines, it had to be shut down. An attempt to abort the take-off was made. A yawing motion followed with the plane at speed moving away from the middle of the runway markers.

Phoenix felt the back of his seat being pulled as the man behind started to scream. He acknowledged the plane was slowing down, but out there on the wing, to his horror, he could see a line of smoke coming out of the back of the powerful engine.

The aircraft shuddered with lockers falling open and passengers being thrown forward in their seats. Shouts and screams came from people frightened for their lives.

The plane was definitely losing power as the pilots struggled to take back control, but out there on the wing a ferocious fire was building.

The noise of the remaining engine being put through the reverse thrust process was deafening. The plane juddered and an enormous bang came from the underneath. It was then that the smell of aviation fuel filled the cabin. Passengers' screams increased and the flight attendants' pleas to observe the safety instructions were mostly ignored.

All of this was happening in the space of about thirty seconds and the stricken plane had almost come to a stop when there were two further loud bangs and the fuselage creaked violently. Phoenix looked out to the wing and was terrified to see it totally engulfed in fire. Furious orange flames licked the fuselage and he could feel the immense heat.

Then with a jolt the plane veered off the runway onto the grass and collided with a concrete barrier. The noise from the impact was like a bomb going off. Many of the passengers were trying desperately to release seat belts. Immediately everyone started to clamber from their seats to join others jostling in the hellishly full aisle. The doors were opened with the emergency evacuation slides activated.

The brief draught of fresh air was soon replaced with the distinct smell of aircraft fuel. Smoke was now entering the plane. The couple next to Phoenix were trying to climb over the seat in front in an effort to reach the emergency doors just seven rows up.

Phoenix, who'd been unable to move, hesitated on realising the anxious sea of passengers wedged in the aisle would probably prevent his escape. You could see they were scared they wouldn't reach the doors. The heat was now overwhelming. He was aware of the sound of sirens, which he took to be the airport emergency vehicles approaching.

Phoenix put his sleeve over his nose and mouth as he was beginning to experience breathing problems. Now the crush of people in the aisle had decreased, he spotted several elderly people who were struggling to vacate their seats. There was no way he was going first while there were others at risk. He just had to help those guys. It would be wrong to say he wasn't frightened, because he was.

He stopped to help a woman and shouted that she was going to be all right. Pushing and shoving her, she managed to hang onto seats and reach the exit.

By now the interior of the plane was immersed in smoke and a red glow was coming from further ahead suggesting the fire was spreading. Phoenix feared that many of the passengers would die. He prayed the emergency crews would reach them in time. His breathing was now so affected that he fell sideways onto one of the seats but he still got up. His eyes cloudy, he could barely see the next row ahead of him.

He could have saved himself, but hung back for the last two people to escape, encouraging them forward to the door. It was too late for Phoenix as he collapsed onto the floor.

They say your whole life flashes through your mind as you are about to die, well it certainly did for Phoenix. All the happy moments and sadness cushioned together. His thoughts shot back to Suzy and how he missed her and Paulina, who he would never see again.

And now with his own life coming to an end, he reflected not on the terrible events of the last years, but on the calmer and worthwhile things he'd put in place.

He was happy he'd managed to make a bank transfer of Suzy's money to Paulina's charity. Dale was now settled with Rachel and a wedding was on the horizon. And today, he was proud of himself for helping others.

His last thoughts were of the strikingly beautiful blue jay he'd seen on the site that used to be Suzy's home. He said a last goodbye to her and his mind went blank.

Chapter 31

Dale was having coffee with Rachel in the kitchen and turned on the TV news to hear the horrendous report that a plane at Cleveland airport, flight XZF963 for New York, had failed to take off due to a catastrophic engine failure that led to a fire. The plane came off the runway and crashed. Unconfirmed reports were that two people had died. There was an emergency number to ring.

He let out a scream and reached for his cell phone to check the e-mail from his father on his flight times. Relieved he called out to Rachel. 'His was an earlier flight and not the one on the news. He should be back in New York by now. I'm going to ring him.'

One hour after Phoenix's flight was scheduled to land, Dale became more worried as there was no reply to the many texts and calls he'd made to his father. They rang his apartment and still he wasn't picking up. Then they spoke to Paulina and Ethan, who also hadn't heard a thing from him.

Rachel remained calm and said, 'What we don't know is if your dad went for a beer at the airport and missed the plane or if he is back and gone for a drink on his own in town. You know what he's like; we've been through these scares before.'

With panic in his voice Dale muttered, 'I say we ring the emergency number.'

Rachel agreed with him. 'They can check the passenger lists, but I'm sure he's okay.'

Dale rang the number on his iPhone. With the speaker enabled they listened to the recorded message and waited to be put through. It felt like his heart was going to burst out of his chest as the minutes slowly passed. Not dad, he prayed. Hadn't they all been through enough?

Twenty long minutes later he finally got through and answered the security questions. He panicked as the man at the other end of the phone delayed in responding to his questions.

'My father, Phoenix Harrison, was booked on the earlier flight which arrived in New York nearly two hours ago and I can't get hold of him. I need you to check the passenger list for this morning's accident.'

The man was dismissive. 'With all respect Mr Harrison, if he was on another flight, I am unable to assist.'

Dale shot back with, 'Now, hold on there. My father's an ill man and how am I to know he didn't switch flights. He may have been on standby and taken a later plane. You are there to help, so please help me.'

'I'm doing my best Mr Harrison, but would you mind lowering your voice. You have to understand this emergency is still going on and we are working through the passenger list, but details are still being collected.'

Dale grasped Rachel's hand and whispered to her, 'God, he's dead, I just know my dad's dead.'

'Are you still there, Mr Harrison?'

'Yes – have you any news for me. Was my dad on that flight?'

The voice still without any emotion worried Dale.

'I've checked the passenger list and I can confirm him being on the flight in question and one of our officials will be ringing you back shortly. There are procedures to follow and we should know more…'

'No, tell me, is he alive?'

There was a long pause.

'I can only confirm we are still processing passenger information. Please give us another hour and we should have an update. Where can I reach you?'

'Call me back on my cell. Have you got the number?'

'Yes, we have you on our system. Please Mr Harrison, believe me we are doing our best to get the information out. We will be calling you as soon as we have more news.'

Dale disconnected the call and dropped the phone on the kitchen table. Rachel was already on the computer looking up the next available plane to Ohio. His heart sank on learning that all flights were cancelled due to the incident.

Ninety long agonising minutes passed and they both jumped out of their skin when Dale's cell phone vibrated and then let out a shrill.

Dale panicked as he swiped the call screen, 'Here we go; this will be them.'

'Hello is that Mr Harrison? We spoke earlier and there is someone here who needs to speak to you. Please hold the line while I put you through to a different extension and they will be able to help.'

The wait seemed intolerable and eventually the call connected but there was only the sound of bleeping.

'Hello, is there anyone there, hello?'

Still nothing. This went on for some time with Dale shouting down the line for someone to answer. Then the line went dead.

Dale hit the kitchen worktop hard with his hand and looked helplessly at the phone screen that displayed the call ended message.

Within seconds his phone rang. It was Paulina calling.

'I still haven't heard anything, is there any news?'

'Dale unable to contain his outburst screamed, 'You'll have to get off the line.'

As soon as he disconnected the call, it rang again.

'I'm sorry we got cut off. I'm going to have another go at putting you through.'

Dale was relieved to be speaking to the same person again but raised his voice. 'No, don't transfer me! That's what happened last time and I lost the call.'

It was exactly as before with bleeping followed by silence. He persevered for a few moments and was just about to hang up when he heard a faint voice.

'Hello, who's there?'

'It's me son.'

Dale almost dropped the phone with his sudden excitement. 'Dad, is it really you?'

The croaky voice gasped, 'It was a close thing. I'm in hospital and struggling with breathing. I want you to know I love you. They said I only survived because I was on the floor of the aisle. The smoke didn't finish me off.'

Dale held the phone tight to his lips and, with tears streaming down his cheeks, whispered, 'Thank God you are safe and, yes, I love you too. This time I'm coming out there to fetch you and I'm not going to take no for an answer.'

***

Back in Ohio, on the site of the Old Blossom Road, the happiest blue jay in all the world was flying above Suzy's old home. It came down to perch on an upturned hackberry tree, the very one that had grown on her parents' large circular lawn. The much-loved garden was where she first played with her dolls and later walked with the man of her dreams. Today, although the area was changing, the sky was just as blue as in days gone by and the birds still swooped over the banks of the Ohio River. The beautiful blue jay flew around what remained of the base of the house for the last time, then over towards the water meadows and out of sight.

www.blossomspringpublishing.com